MRS ALI'S ROAD
TO HAPPINESS

MRS ALI'S ROAD
TO HAPPINESS

Farahad Zama

ABACUS

First published in Great Britain as a paperback original in 2012 by Abacus

ISBN 978-0-349-12270-0

Typeset in Bembo by M Rules
Printed and bound in Great Britain by
Clays Ltd, St Ives plc

Papers used by Abacus are from well-managed forests
and other responsible sources.

MIX
Paper from
responsible sources
FSC
www.fsc.org FSC® C104740

Abacus
An imprint of
Little, Brown Book Group
100 Victoria Embankment
London EC4Y 0DY

An Hachette UK Company
www.hachette.co.uk

www.littlebrown.co.uk

To London, where my head lives,
and Vizag, where my heart abides.

CHAPTER ONE

A woman's work is never done. And it will not be done while the woman is lying in bed counting rice grains, thought Mrs Ali. However, she lay there for a few more moments before getting up. She didn't need as much sleep as she had when she was younger, but her body didn't have the energy that had enabled her to get up at five in the morning, day after day after day, grind the lentil batter for dosas and idlis in a heavy stone mortar, and make sure that her husband and son never left home on an empty stomach.

The black-granite floor felt cool under her feet. At the door of the bedroom, she glanced back at her sleeping husband. He looked so peaceful – he wouldn't be getting up for almost another hour. Once again, she envied her husband's ability to sleep whenever and wherever he wanted – like a baby, as they said. Though, of course, any mother would testify babies didn't actually sleep that well.

In the distance, the azaa'n could be heard, calling the faithful to the mosque for prayer. As she listened to the familiar, haunting sound, some nightmare that had dogged her during the early hours faded away, leaving just an impression of disquiet, like the high water mark on walls after a flood has retreated.

Hayya 'ala salat,	Make haste towards worship,
Hayya 'ala l-falah,	Hasten towards the true success,
Al-salatu khayru min an-nawm.	Prayer is better than sleep ...

There was no danger of the muezzin's call disturbing her husband's slumber. It would take an earthquake, or a demolition crew, to wake him up.

It was a full two hours before Mrs Ali had her first moment of respite. By then drinking water had been collected from the pump and the overhead tank filled for the day; breakfast had been made and eaten; vegetables cut up for lunch; soiled clothes soaked for an afternoon wash, water heated, baths taken; the maid seen off after cleaning the dishes and sweeping the house. Mrs Ali went to the verandah in front of the house, sat down in a wicker chair and picked up the newspaper. Her husband, shaved, fed and bathed, had already skimmed through the paper and was sitting at the table of his 'office', the self-same verandah.

'Three cheques came in the post today,' he said.

She nodded and glanced at the headlines in the paper – something about elections for the municipal corporation and the state legislature and, below that, the photograph of a famous actress holding an award.

'Three! That's pretty good, actually,' he said.

She glanced up. Oh, dear, he seemed peeved. 'Yes, that's

great,' she said. Her eyes were dragged back towards the paper, but she resisted. 'Normally you get none or one, right?'

Her husband still looked disgruntled.

'Where are they from?' she said, to keep the peace.

He held up a light-green cheque. 'This is from Hyderabad ...'

Luckily for her, the front gate beyond the small courtyard rattled before he could pick up the second one. Aruna walked in, a sleek white car disappearing behind her, taken away by her family's driver. The young woman looked healthy – her hair bouncy, cheeks glowing and stomach showing a small bump. She must be, what, about four months gone ...

Mrs Ali wondered whether Aruna was expecting a girl. In her experience, mothers expecting boys didn't look as good. They were more tired, their hair limp, their complexion darker – as if the male spirit of the baby was trying to dominate the mother. Not always, of course, which was what made the whole 'is it a boy', 'is it a girl' question so interesting.

'Morning, madam,' Aruna said, her face breaking into a smile. She turned towards the table. 'Morning, sir.'

Mrs Ali got up: time to make her exit. Their house was long and narrow, with all the rooms laid out single file like carriages on a train: first the verandah, then the living room which also had a bed for their son Rehman, the bedroom itself, the dining room, the kitchen and then the backyard. She was still in the living room when she heard her husband saying to Aruna, 'We got three cheques in the post today.'

'That's great! Was one of them from the Bopatla family?'

When she heard the enthusiasm in Aruna's voice, she felt guilty at her own lack of interest.

The verandah was the office of the Marriage Bureau for Rich People, run by her husband with the assistance of Aruna. Mrs Ali liked the human side of the enterprise – the clients and their requirements, the desperation of some and the pernickety nature of others. But the financial side of it held little interest for her.

The marriage bureau charged fees from clients and spent the money on advertising, postage, stationery, Aruna's salary and a myriad other things. As far as Mrs Ali was concerned, they were doing well as long as more money came in than went out – she didn't care whether the two differed by one rupee or by a thousand. Her husband had retired after a lifetime's service as a government clerk and they had his pension, modest though it was, to live on. He got caught up in the thrill of getting new members and making money. Just like a man, she thought, to start a task and forget why he was doing it in the first place.

After retirement, her husband had for the first time started spending all his time at home, interfering with her set routines – *why don't you have a specific day of the week to wash my clothes, instead of asking me whether I am running out of shirts?* – and they had fought more often in those initial few months than in all the previous decades. She had enlisted the help of her brother Azhar, and the three of them had come up with the idea of a marriage bureau to keep her husband busy. Of course it was gratifying that it had become so successful, but that hadn't been the primary intention of setting it up.

She remembered that she needed to get the medicines that the doctor had prescribed for her knees. She changed, picked up the prescription chit and her handbag, and made her way back to the verandah.

'I am going out for half an hour to pick up vegetables and medicines.'

Aruna smiled at her. Mr Ali nodded absent-mindedly. Mrs Ali wondered what her husband would have said if she had declared, 'I am going away and never returning. Do your own cooking from now on.'

He would probably nod in exactly the same way, not paying any attention. Not that she would ever do such a thing, of course. Long ago, a neighbour had done just that. One day, *she* had stepped out of the house and vanished. The family had been distraught and in their distress had not thought to keep the matter secret. The woman's husband and teenage sons had searched high and low for her, following rumours of dead bodies in public morgues and crazed amnesiac women in nearby market towns. It wasn't as if the woman was particularly pretty or flighty – she had been an ordinary housewife, with a pleasant enough face but overweight, living a seemingly normal life, cooking for her family, making pickles and buying saris. Ten days later, the woman had returned, looking as if milk khova wouldn't melt in her mouth, and taken up her place in the household, refusing to answer all questions. The woman had never said anything to Mrs Ali either, but for years and years afterwards every time Mrs Ali looked at her, she had wanted to ask, 'Where did you go? What did you do in those ten days? Whom did you meet? Why did you go?' And, just as important, 'Why did you come back?' It was as if the whole lifetime of activities of the woman – school, marriage, motherhood, innumerable visits to saints' tombs – were all nothing compared to those ten days of absence.

It was too late to find out now. The woman had died a couple of years ago, taking her mysteries to the grave. Would *her* husband have taken her back if Mrs Ali had walked away like that? Some things in a marriage just should not be tested, she thought.

At the front gate she came face to face with a young man in khaki shirt and trousers carrying a stainless-steel torch and a notebook. His skin was dark and a saffron-coloured string circled his wrist – a talisman from some temple.

'Namaste, amma,' he said, bobbing his head and smiling at her. His mouth was as wide as the Bay of Bengal.

Her nose twitched – a sure sign that something was wrong. 'Who are you?' she asked.

'Meter reader, amma,' he said, showing her an ID card issued by the electricity board.

She stared at it suspiciously for a moment and then felt guilty as everything appeared in order. She supposed he couldn't help having a wide mouth or obsequious manners.

'There are people inside to show you the meter,' she said and left the house.

Aruna slit open the next envelope and extracted its contents. 'Another member, sir,' she said, turning to Mr Ali with a smile. 'It's a festival of cheques today!'

Apart from her salary, she got a commission for every person who joined the marriage bureau. So not only was she happy for the business, she had a personal stake too. Her husband's family was very wealthy and money wasn't a problem for her any more, but her parents were poor, relying on what she gave them to run the house and keep her younger sister Vani in college, her father's pension lasting barely half a month. She would not – *could* not – use her husband's money to support her parents and sister, which was why she had continued working after marriage. And she was running out of time. The bump in her stomach was growing by the day and she would have to stop working soon. If only . . . no! She thought. The baby was hers and Ram's; it was not a problem. The baby was an accident, it was true, but no less loved for that. The rest of the world would just have to manage somehow.

The door rattled and she glanced up, startled out of her thoughts. A man was standing there, smiling and exposing his teeth. His mouth seemed wide enough to fit in a minister dosa – a six-foot-long pancake reputedly eaten by rich politicians – broadside, without tearing it into pieces.

'Namaste, saar, amma,' said the man, bobbing his head. 'I am the meter reader.'

Mr Ali looked at him blankly for a moment before calling out, 'Wife . . . '

'Madam has gone out, sir,' said Aruna. She turned to the stranger and said, 'The meter is here.' She stood up and pointed to a wooden cabinet on the wall behind her.

The man flicked his torch on and flashed it into the gloom of the cabinet, then wrote down some numbers in his notebook. 'Do you want to verify the reading?' he asked.

Mr Ali shook his head. 'That's all right,' he said. 'We trust you.'

The man closed his notebook and the cupboard. 'What

good people you are!' he said. 'I can tell you that there is very little trust in the world. I read hundreds of meters and you are the first people who didn't want to make sure that I've written it down correctly.'

His eye was caught by the letters and the forms on the table, and Aruna got the feeling that he had heard their earlier comments about the cheque.

'What do you do here, sir? That's a lot of letters you've got. Your business must be doing very well.'

Mr Ali smiled proudly. 'Yes, we are quite successful,' he said. 'We are a marriage bureau.' He saw the man's puzzled look and continued, 'When parents want to arrange the marriage of their son or daughter, they come to us. We take their details and match them to the kind of people they are looking for – same caste, similar economic backgrounds and so on.'

'Oh, like a wedding panthulu!' said the man.

Mr Ali's face took on a pained expression. Traditionally, marriage brokers went from house to house carrying lists and horoscopes of eligible boys and girls. The panthulu, as they were called, had a bad reputation for pushing unsuitable matches because they were paid only when a marriage was settled.

'Our business is not at all like a panthulu,' said Mr Ali. 'We don't go chasing after our clients. They come to us. And we get paid for our efforts, whether or not the wedding is fixed.'

'I am not married, sir. Can you help me find a bride?' The man's smile grew even broader, though Aruna wondered how that was possible.

'What is your name?' asked Mr Ali.

'Shyam.'

Mr Ali shook his head and said, 'Don't take offence, Shyam. Our organisation is only for rich people. You must be a college graduate and earn a minimum of ten thousand rupees a month.'

'I am not a graduate,' Shyam replied. 'Do you have a lot of members?'

'Of course,' said Mr Ali. 'We have Hindu, Muslim and Christian members. We are the most popular marriage bureau in all the coastal Andhra districts – probably in the whole state. People come to see us from faraway places like Hyderabad or Bangalore. The other day, a family from New Jersey in America sat on that sofa and became members.'

'Very good, sir!' said Shyam, looking at the sofa that had been lucky enough to be sat on by somebody from America. 'Is there another meter that I need to read?'

'No,' said Mr Ali. 'That's the only meter in the house.'

'Namaste, saar. Namaste, madam,' Shyam said, taking his leave. Aruna had the feeling that he went out just a little more jauntily than he had come in.

Mrs Ali walked up the road back towards her house, reaching the culvert where the road narrowed. The traffic was horrendously bad here – four lanes merging into two, with cars, buses, three-wheeled auto-rickshaws and two-wheelers all spewing smoke and creating a din with their honks. Meanwhile, the steady stream of pedestrians was squeezed to the margins of the road among the roadside stalls and carts selling vegetables, plastic goods and sweets. The culvert was hemmed in by a Muslim graveyard on one side and a mosque on the other.

Across the road from her, hard by the mosque, stood a row of whitewashed shops. Mrs Ali stared with disquiet at the fresh sign that had been hung in front of one of them – Rao's Marriage Bureau.

'Aapa,' said a familiar voice and she turned, temporarily forgetting about marriage bureaus and competition.

'Azhar, how are you?' Her younger brother had obviously come from the mosque, which puzzled her. 'What are you doing in the mosque at this hour?' she asked. 'It's not yet time for the afternoon prayers.'

Azhar shrugged. 'Even godly places need worldly maintenance. The mosque committee asked me to oversee the repairs to the rear wall.'

His hair and neatly trimmed beard contained equal amounts of black and white. Azhar was shorter and a bit stockier than her husband, and fitter than most men his age. His skin had darkened after a lifetime of exposure to the sun, but his face held few lines, except around his eyes and mouth.

'There are many men who want to be on the committee,' she said. 'But there's a shortage of those willing to stand in the sun, supervising workers.'

He laughed and asked, 'What did you buy?'

'Oh, just some vegetables. Have you seen how expensive onions have become? I told the man that I wanted just a kilo of onions, not his whole cart.'

'It is not only here. I went to the Poorna Market yesterday and it was the same there.'

'Well, the government will have to do something. You can make a ridged-gourd curry if cauliflower is expensive, but onions are used in both. How can we manage without them?'

Despite her disdain for the financial side of her husband's business, Mrs Ali would have to take more interest in it if costs continued going up like this.

'I am sure they will do something,' said Azhar. 'There is an election coming soon.'

'Hmm—' said Mrs Ali. 'I will ask any candidate who comes canvassing for my vote what his plans are for reducing these famine-inducing prices. If people like us are finding it difficult, how can the poor manage?'

They walked away from the mosque and the culvert. The road widened and the traffic eased up. 'Can you come to Faiz's house on Monday?' he asked.

Mrs Ali thought for a moment and nodded. Faiz was Azhar's granddaughter – the child of his oldest son and just ten years younger than his own daughter, in fact. Faiz had been married about eight months ago to a young man from Kothagudem village who worked in the Rural Electrification Board as a clerk, but his family owned several acres of fertile land in the village.

'It will be best to get the visit out of the way before Ramzaan starts,' she said. Fasting during the holy month meant that travelling was best avoided.

Azhar said, 'I am thinking of taking a microwave oven as a gift.'

'A microwave?' Mrs Ali said, doubtfully. She knew that these contraptions could be used to cook cakes and other 'modern' dishes, but was hazy on what the difference was between a microwave and a normal oven.

'It's her first big festival in her in-laws' house,' Azhar said. 'She wanted something that nobody else in the village had.'

At the next street, Azhar took his leave and turned left to his house. Mrs Ali continued straight down the main road, walking along the dusty edge, dodging hawkers, street dogs and parked vehicles. She reflected how her happiness in life was bound up along this one road. Her own house was further up; Azhar and his family, her husband's younger sister, Chhote Bhaabhi and her family, her many friends, the mosque that they all belonged to, the doctor who treated them and the graveyard where they would be buried when the doctor finally gave up: all lay along this stretch of tarmac.

She reached the medical shop that was her final destination and slid the chit of paper towards the young man behind the counter. On every wall, floor-to-ceiling glass-fronted cupboards were stacked with boxes and bottles.

'Where is the owner?' she said.

'I am the new owner. I bought the shop from the old man.'

'Oh!' said Mrs Ali. 'Where is he now? What is he doing? He wanted to give this pharmacy to his son.'

'The old man has retired and gone on a pilgrimage to Haridwar and Kashi. His son didn't fancy sitting behind a shop counter all day. He got himself a job as a medical rep pushing drugs to doctors.'

Mrs Ali remembered the previous owner. He wasn't that old – in fact, he was several years her junior. He had run the pharmacy for years and his fondest dream had been to hand it over to his son. 'I will continue to sit behind the counter even after my son takes over,' he had often told her. 'Until they lay me out feet first.'

He had made his son get a degree in pharmaceutical practice, so he could run the shop. 'This is the best way to earn a living, madam. You sit under a cool fan watching the world go by and people come to you for pills if they are unwell and tonics if they are not.'

His son had evidently disagreed and used his education to find a job more suited to his temperament. She hoped that the father had found peace on his pilgrimage. At least the son was using the education that his father had paid for by becoming a medical rep instead of going into something completely unconnected – like computers or insurance, for example.

The new owner glanced at the prescription, went to the second shelf on the right-hand wall and took out a box of tablets. How did these pharmacists know which medicine was where in the shop?

The owner's mother was sitting at the cash till and she looked at the vegetables that Mrs Ali was carrying. 'Have you seen the price of onions, amma?' she exclaimed. 'We will have to start weighing them with a goldsmith's balance at this rate.'

Mrs Ali smiled grimly. 'A government can get away with being corrupt and incompetent, but mess with the price of onions and the wrath of millions of housewives will descend on them. The Janata Party fell and Indira Gandhi came back to power in the seventies because of the price of onions,' said Mrs Ali. 'If the current trend continues, the current party will share the same fate as that government.'

The medicines were put in a packet made from recycled newspaper and pushed across the counter. As Mrs Ali was paying, the owner's mother said, 'By the way, amma, if you know anybody who is looking to rent, the upstairs portion of our house is empty.'

After some more discussion about rent, the escalating cost of everything and the difficulty of finding reliable tenants, Mrs Ali finally left, having obtained a ten per cent discount on her bill.

CHAPTER TWO

The mosque was unusually crowded for a normal Friday. Mr Ali would have been happy to sit at the back of the large, open hall, but, like a pet student, Azhar pointed to a tiny gap in the third row from the front. They made their way forward, stepping carefully between the rows of seated men. Mr Ali had hoped that the gap would be bigger than it had appeared, but, to his dismay, it was just as small up close as it had looked from a distance. With mumbled apologies and smiles directed towards their neighbours, the two men squeezed into the gap and sat down on the marble floor, wriggling and somehow making space for themselves. A young man finished adjusting the mike in the mihrab, the imam's alcove, and a black-bearded man stood up and started the azaa'n, the call to prayer.

The afternoon air felt like a warm pool, despite the best efforts of the fans dotted around the ceiling, and combined with the melodic azaa'n, exerted such a powerful soporific effect that Mr Ali struggled to keep his eyes open.

Earlier in the day, right after lunch, Azhar had turned up at

Mr Ali's house, dressed like a late Mughal-era dandy in a knee-length silk sherwani, sporting gold buttons with a mother-of-pearl inlay, and wearing a maroon-coloured fez with a black tassel. His greying beard was neatly trimmed and a perfume of attar of roses wafted from him.

'Are you going to a wedding?' Mr Ali had asked.

'Would anybody organise a wedding on a Friday afternoon after lunch, brother-in-law?' said Azhar, raising his eyebrows.

'No,' conceded Mr Ali.

Theoretically, all the men, and definitely the imam who would have to preside over the wedding, would be at the mosque for the weekly prayers while the women would be praying at home.

'But why are you dressed so grandly? It's not a festival.'

'A new imam is starting today. And I want you to come too.'

'Oh! What happened to Haji Saab?'

Mr Ali liked the old preacher, a gentle soul, given the honorific title Haji after he had completed the Hajj pilgrimage to Mecca about fifteen years ago. He came once a month to collect a subscription for the mosque and always sat down for a chat and a cup of tea with Mr and Mrs Ali.

'Nothing has happened to Haji Saab. But the mosque committee felt that he was getting old and that we needed new blood to invigorate the community.'

'What about Haji Saab's nephew, Nasrullah? He is a good man – knows the Qur'an by heart and has been groomed by his uncle to take over.'

Azhar shook his head. 'He doesn't have any formal qualifications. The committee wanted somebody stronger. The new imam has been to a Deobandi seminary and is a scholar of Hanafi's work on the Hadeeth and Islamic jurisprudence.'

Mr Ali didn't like the sound of this at all. If a man spent so much time studying religious matters and philosophy, how would he have any time left over to experience real life?

'You go ahead,' he said. 'I never attend the Friday prayers anyway. I have too much work to do.'

Azhar looked at his sister, prompting Mrs Ali to speak up. 'What kind of excuse is that? Too much work to say your prayers? You are talking as if you are some Lord Governor-General. It is not every day that the mosque gets a new imam. It will be good to show him your support on his first day and meet other members of the congregation as well, rather than burying your head in the marriage bureau all the time.'

It had taken some more persuasion, but Mr Ali had eventually conceded and got ready quickly, changing into fresh clothes and carrying out the ritual ablutions, washing his face, nose, hair, feet and arms up to his elbows three times.

'Where is Rehman?' said Azhar. 'He should come too.'

'Rehman is meeting some people from a water-management charity. He was saying that they might offer him a job,' said Mrs Ali.

Ah! I bet the salary will be measly, thought Mr Ali, knowing his son very well.

There was a stir at the back of the mosque, rousing Mr Ali from his catatonic state, and he twisted round to have a look. Several older people, members of the mosque committee, men whom Mr Ali had known for years, were picking their way through gaps in the seated crowd. Behind them came the new imam. He had a straggly beard and was clad in a one-piece Arabian robe from which two thin legs poked out. Mr Ali regarded Azhar in surprise.

'You didn't tell me he was a stripling—'

The muezzin's calls were extra-loud as the mosque committee took their places in the front row that had been reserved for them. Mr Ali noticed that Haji Saab, the previous imam, had been shunted off to one side and got a place to sit, at the far end of the front line, only with the help of his nephew and one-time heir, Nasrullah.

'In the name of Allah, the merciful, the beneficent . . . '

The usual formulaic Arabic phrases that few in the assembled jamaat fully understood were uttered before the new imam started the khutba. Mr Ali stared with interest as the new imam gave the sermon. He is not even as old as Rehman, thought Mr Ali. At some point in Mr Ali's life, imams, like policemen, had suddenly started to seem younger, but they had always been reasonably mature. Even Nasrullah was in his late thirties, which Mr Ali had thought rather young at that. The man in front of them giving the sermon was only in his twenties!

He looked very sincere though and, if he was nervous about addressing a new congregation for the first time, he hid it well.

'This jamaat, this congregation, is a microcosm of the great ummah, the global brother-and-sisterhood of Muslims. Young and old, rich and poor, healthy and unwell – we are all equal here before Allah. The only distinction that Allah makes between us is the strength of our ibaadat – our faith. The question He asks us is, what kind of Muslim are you? Are you a once-a-lifetime, once-a-year, once-a-week or once-a-day man?'

Mr Ali cautiously peered around at the congregation. The imam had the people's attention.

'The once-a-lifetime man is one who never attends the mosque for prayers. But when he finally dies, his friends and family bring his body in for the funeral prayers before burial. The once or twice a year man comes to the mosque only for the Eids, the festivals of Ramadaan and Bakrid.'

Mr Ali noticed that he pronounced Ramzaan with the hard 'da' of Arabic instead of the soft 'za' used by the Urdu speakers of the Indian subcontinent.

'The Qur'an prescribes that we pray five times a day. Look at the world around us: we have air to breathe, water to drink, food to eat, clothes to wear, shoes to soften the impact of the ground on our feet, flowers that smell nice, vehicles to aid us in our travels – the Lord God has given them all to us.' The imam bent forward and scanned the congregation, picking out individual men. 'And in return, brothers, He asks of us a small thing – a tiny task that is well within our capabilities. He has asked us to pray five times a day. Isn't that a truly small duty for the bounty he has provided?'

Mr Ali flushed. It sounded so reasonable. Of course, Mr Ali was in the twice-a-year camp – coming to the mosque for the festivals and rarely at any other time.

The imam was carrying on with his sermon. 'The ummah, the population of Muslims, is like a body and we should all be united. Just as the whole body suffers a fever if an arm or a leg is injured, we must feel the pain of our brothers and sisters wherever they happen to be in the world. We must fight for the rights of those killed in Gujarat or driven out of their homes in Palestine and Chechnya. We cannot remain indifferent to their suffering, burying ourselves in our secure surroundings.'

After the sermon came the namaaz, the formal prayers, with a recitation of two chapters from the Qur'an and prostration. As soon as the prayers ended, there was a rush to embrace the new imam and congratulate him. Mr Ali and Azhar joined the crowd.

Above the hubbub, a committee member announced, 'Brothers, we have started a new collection for finishing off the second floor. Please donate generously . . . '

Eventually, they made their way out into the courtyard of the mosque along with the rest of the congregation. Mr Ali greeted a man in his forties with a bulging belly that his cotton shirt strained to hold. 'Razzaq Mian, how's the seat-cover business?'

Razzaq smiled and bobbed his head. 'Alhamd'ulillah!' Praise be to the Lord. 'It's going well,' he said. 'Your idea of advertising in the newspaper worked well. We are getting several new customers.'

'Good!' said Mr Ali, pleased. Seeing a teenager standing behind Razzaq, he said to him, 'Don't hide like a bashful girl, young man. How's college?'

The teenager came forward with a shy grin and touched the fingers of his right hand to his forehead in a salute. 'Salaam, Chaacha. College is going well.'

Mr Ali's wife had told him that the teenager, Saajid, had been seen with other boys *and* girls in a cake shop and that his grades the previous year had been merely average. Mr Ali just smiled and said nothing as the boy's father looked proudly at his son.

Other men joined them. Razzaq said loudly, 'Today Allah created a wonder. He made the holy, fasting month of Ramzaan sneak past us without anyone noticing and made today the festival.'

The crowd eyed him questioningly. 'Do you mean the new imam?' asked one of the men.

Razzaq shook his head. 'Imams come and go,' he said and pointed dramatically towards Mr Ali. 'When have you known our friend turn up at the mosque when it was not Eid?'

Everybody laughed, including Mr Ali. Azhar said, 'I had to twist his arm to bring him here.'

Razzaq said, '*You* brought Ali Saab here? Now I understand why they say that the whole world standing on one side is not a match for the wife's brother standing on the other.'

There was more laughter. The men found their footwear and walked out of the mosque, chatting convivially.

'The new imam is really good, isn't he?' said Azhar.

Razzaq and Saajid nodded enthusiastically. Azhar turned to Mr Ali. 'You don't look convinced,' he said.

Mr Ali shook his head. 'Oh, nothing like that. He knows his stuff, but I cannot help wondering why we had to go far away to hire somebody when Haji Saab's nephew, Nasrullah, was right here.'

Azhar bridled. 'Are you still on about that? Nasrullah would have continued in the same vein as his uncle: don't rock the boat, concentrate on your personal behaviour – like a frog in a well. The world is changing and we should realise that we are part of the wider ummah and that's why the mosque committee chose somebody new.'

Mr Ali frowned. Many things will change, he thought.

But in a changing world, a mosque should represent continuity – not add to the welter of confusion outside.

The next morning, Mr Ali was standing in the front yard of his house, staring pensively at the plants, when Pari and Vasu walked in.

'Salaam, chaacha,' said Pari brightly.

At the sight of the young woman, Mr Ali's expression brightened. Her twenty-something skin was fair and glowing, her dark hair tumbled halfway to her waist, her lips curled in a happy smile. It was difficult to believe that she was a widow – except if you looked closely and noticed that she wore no jewellery except for a pair of antique-silver earrings, and her sari was dark maroon and plain with no zari, the interwoven gold thread that gave the edges of saris their shimmer. The boy with her was eight years old, thin and dark, and his hair stuck out in every direction. If he didn't resemble her, it was because he was adopted. He too had a wide smile, but in contrast to Pari's even teeth, Vasu's open mouth revealed a gap where one of his milk teeth had fallen out.

'What are you looking at?' the boy asked curiously.

Mr Ali pointed to a bright-red hibiscus flower. 'They missed that one,' he said.

Mr Ali had a running battle to protect his garden from marauding temple-goers. People in Vizag did not consider it stealing to pluck flowers from somebody else's garden, as long as the blooms were used for prayer. Mr Ali, like most garden-owners – Muslim or Hindu – didn't agree.

'It's because the flower is below the level of the wall and cannot be seen from outside,' said Vasu.

'You are right,' Mr Ali said. 'I have to tell the plant to bear its flowers so they cannot be seen.'

'Plants bring out flowers so they *can* be seen,' said Vasu. 'That's how they get pollinated. I learned all about it at school.'

Mr Ali acted as if he were impressed. 'Help me water the plants.'

Pari carried on into the house, to find Mrs Ali sitting with Aruna and a couple she did not recognise.

'This is Gita and that is Srinu,' said Aruna, indicating the newcomers.

'Oh! You are Gita and ... I have heard so much about you. Welcome to Vizag. Are you settled in?'

Srinu and Gita were good friends of Aruna. Having just moved from the village to town, they were busy with the many things that moving house entailed. Pari was able to chip in with her own tips because not long ago she had moved to Vizag from her father's village and, even more recently, into a two-bedroom flat next door to the Alis' house, from a cramped room opposite.

Finally, Aruna stood up. 'It's full-moon day and I want to go to the temple before the driver comes,' she said.

Gita said, 'We'll come with you. It's such an auspicious day.'

Most Hindus viewed the full-moon day as particularly blessed. Others regarded the tenth day of the lunar cycle as favourable too. Many considered Tuesdays and Fridays to be a good occasion to visit the temple, as were days on which any new task – like a job or an exam – was to be carried out. These auspicious days were, of course, in addition to all the other propitious festivals. All in all, Hindu temples in India tend to be busy most of the time.

Pari had a sudden idea. 'Can you take Vasu?' she said. She herself was a Muslim and had never gone to a Hindu temple.

By this time, Vasu was watching a Pokémon cartoon on television and was not happy to leave. 'I don't want to go,' he said.

Pari had adopted Vasu, a Hindu boy, when his grandfather had died. His extended family had refused to take him in because they believed he carried an ill omen and would bring bad fortune to his guardians. After all, Vasu's father had died in an accident, after which first his mother had committed suicide and then his grandfather had followed suit. As Vasu's great-uncle had asked, what were the odds of that happening purely by chance?

'*I* want you to go,' said Pari. 'The temple is just down the road and Aruna-Auntie will take you there and drop you back.' She turned to Aruna. 'Does he need to take anything with him?'

Aruna shook her head. 'There's no need,' she said. 'But if you want, you can give him some money to put in the hundi as an offering.'

Pari took out her purse and handed Vasu a two-rupee coin. 'Don't lose it,' she told him. 'Aruna-Auntie will show you where the collection box is and you must put it only in there.'

'I know what a hundi looks like,' he said. 'I've been to temples before.'

Pari felt instantly guilty. He hadn't visited a temple since he had started living with her. I should take more care, she thought, to make sure that Vasu does not forget the religion and customs of his birth parents.

They all walked into the front yard where Vasu put on his sandals. Mr Ali too came out from behind his desk and joined them.

'The flower's beautiful, isn't it?' he said.

'Very nice,' said Pari.

Beads of water glistened on its glossy petals like dew. Vasu reached out and, before anybody realised what he was doing, plucked it off the plant.

'Vasu!' shouted Pari, but it was too late.

Mr Ali's mouth opened and closed silently while his face turned a red that matched the colour of the flower in Vasu's hand.

'Why did you— That is stealing,' spluttered Mr Ali.

'No, it is not,' said Vasu. 'I am taking it to the temple. That's what everybody does in the village.'

'It's not stealing,' said Mrs Ali, after they had left. She couldn't help giggling when she saw her husband's angry expression. Pari struggled mightily to keep a straight face for a few seconds and then burst into laughter, which she had to turn into a cough when Mr Ali glared at her.

The imam was chairing his first meeting of the mosque committee, whose members sat on piled-up cotton rugs and reed mats on the flat roof of the mosque. It was cooler there and they could catch the occasional breeze.

'Why do we need to build another floor?' asked the imam. 'From what I have seen so far, the downstairs is more than enough for normal occasions and, on special Eid days, the people can just pray here on the open roof.'

Some of the committee members took that as a rebuke.

'We are sorry, imam-saab. This is a big congregation, but the people are not religious enough. That's one of the reasons why we have brought you here. We want to revive their sense of ibaadat and get them to attend the mosque more regularly. When people see that the mosque is growing in size, and we have repainted the walls and set up new lights and fans, they will be attracted here.'

Just then Azhar joined them. 'Is the back wall fully repaired?' one of the men asked him.

Azhar nodded. 'Insha'Allah, God willing, it will outlive all of us,' he said, then turned to the imam. 'Except you, of course, sir.'

The committee, all retired men of a certain age, laughed. 'Azhar miah, how much will the construction of the roof cost?'

The discussion became technical: the material cost of cement, bricks, sand, iron; the labour costs of construction, watering, the concrete ... Finally, they all fell silent. The only thing that was clear was that it would involve more money than the mosque accounts held – in a non-interest-bearing current account, of course, because the Qur'an specified that charging interest, or riba, was usury and a sin.

The imam stroked his straggly beard. These men were all much older than him, but his position gave him a gravitas that somebody his age would otherwise never have.

'The second-floor construction is a distraction,' he said finally. 'If people start coming in bigger numbers, Allah will fill our coffers to expand the mosque. He will not turn away one of His worshippers from His door. So let's talk about how to achieve that.'

The committee instantly agreed with the imam that this

was obviously the right way to approach the problem. The discussion moved no further over the next fifteen minutes, however, until one of the committee members turned to Azhar. 'What is your niece's name? The widow who lives next door to your sister?'

'Pari? What about her?'

'Yes, Pari. Doesn't she have a so-called son, the Hindu-born boy?'

'That's right,' said Azhar. 'Vasu's an orphan and she adopted him.'

'Looking after an orphan is a good deed,' said the imam. 'But I am troubled. Does his name mean that the boy is not being brought up as a Muslim?'

Vasu was another name for Vishnu, the Preserver-God in the Hindu Trinity. Brahma, the Creator, and Shiva, the Destroyer, being the other two.

'That's correct,' said Azhar. 'Unfortunately, the boy is not being brought up as a Muslim. I have spoken several times to her about it but she is a headstrong woman.'

The committee member who had raised the issue turned to the imam. 'That's the level of jahilya – ignorance – that abounds in our town. You will have your task cut out to make this town more religious.'

The imam said, 'There are no two ways about it. Evil follows evil. Such wilful flouting of our traditions must not only be dealt with, but this must also be seen to be done by everybody.' He turned to Azhar. 'I will need your help to find out more about this case. The boy cannot remain a Hindu. We will have to do what it takes to convert him to Islam.'

★

The temple was not particularly busy when Aruna and the others walked into its courtyard. Aruna was carrying a thin, blue polythene bag containing a string of white jasmine flowers and a bunch of bananas. They took off their shoes in the courtyard and made their way barefoot onto the tiled main area of the temple. Srinu rang the bell that hung from the ceiling. Vasu would have liked to ring it too, but it was too high for him and he didn't yet feel comfortable enough with this relative stranger to ask to be lifted.

In an alcove at one end of the covered hall stood a statue of Lord Rama, six feet tall with a bow over his shoulder, and accompanied by his wife and faithful brother. Two tall brass lamps were lit on either side of the idols, their edges black from the wicks. The smell of camphor and incense became stronger as they approached. A priest took the bag from Aruna and the hibiscus flower from Vasu, and then they all made an obeisance to the Lord. Vasu joined his palms in front of his chest, closed his eyes and lowered his chin. After a few seconds, he could not resist opening one eye slightly and peeking at his companions. Aruna and Gita's eyes were closed and their lips were moving in prayer. Srinu shot a glance at him and Vasu hastily closed his eyes again.

When they had finished, the priest gave Aruna a betel leaf with rice grains and red vermilion powder on it. She took it with her right hand and touched it to her forehead. Then they made their way to the exit, making sure not to show their backs to the idols. As they were putting on their shoes, a bearded man wearing saffron clothes stopped them.

'You cannot leave without praying to Shani,' he said and

led them to a small stone idol on the far side of the courtyard. Shani was the planet Saturn and heralded bad luck.

'We cannot afford misfortune, guru-gaaru,' said Srinu. 'We were kidnapped by Maoists from our village and that's why we've moved to the town. I now want to start a snack-food business.'

They propitiated the god of ill luck.

'I would like to help in the temple if I may,' said Gita.

The guru nodded. 'We always need volunteers,' he said. Patting Vasu on the head, he said to Aruna, 'Is this your boy?'

She shook her head. 'No, sir. He is the son of a friend.'

'Who are the boy's parents? Why haven't I seen them in the temple? Don't they live in this area?'

The temple official's questions set alarm bells ringing in Aruna's mind. Nothing good could come of revealing that Vasu was being brought up in a Muslim household. She looked at her watch. 'Oh no, is it already so late? My mother-in-law will be waiting. Let's go.'

She took Vasu by the arm and started walking away, glad that she had averted disaster by her quick thinking.

The saffron-robed man stared at their receding backs, his mouth half open in surprise. 'Of all the rude—' he began.

Vasu turned. 'I live with my mother,' he said loudly, his young voice cutting through the crowded courtyard like the peal of a newly cast bell. 'She doesn't come to Hindu temples because she is a Muslim.'

Meanwhile, Mrs Ali was in the kitchen with Pari. Mrs Ali took a fillet of kingfish that had already been coated with ginger, garlic and chilli powder and lowered it into a Teflon-coated pan with a little hot oil in it. The fish sizzled and steam rose from the pan, releasing an aroma of fish and spices.

'I am going to Kothagudem tomorrow,' said Mrs Ali.

Pari nodded. The visit to Faiz, Azhar-maama's grand-daughter, had been talked about for a while and only the date of travel was news.

'Azhar is taking an oven – one of those microwave things,' said Mrs Ali.

Pari's eyes widened. That was a gift she hadn't expected.

'Foolish, if you ask me.' Mrs Ali slid the edge of the wooden spatula – received free when she had purchased the non-stick pan – under the frying fillet. 'I am always amazed how the fish doesn't stick to this pan,' she said, changing topic like a car changing gears. 'You end up using so much less oil.' Mrs Ali quickly turned over the fish, bringing a fresh sizzle. 'What was I saying? Yes, a microwave ... Nobody in the village has seen one, that's why he is taking it. I can understand the girl thinking about ostentation and showing off – she is young, after all, but elders should have more sense than that, nai?'

Pari was embarrassed. This was the first time that Mrs Ali had criticised one of her family members in front of her and she didn't know how to react. Not that she particularly loved Azhar-maama. Soon after Pari had moved to Vizag following her father's death, Azhar-maama's much younger daughter – who was just ten years older than his granddaughter – had become pregnant. He had invited Mrs Ali to go with him and his wife to bring her home for the delivery but had not asked Pari to come along. Darling Rehman, Mrs Ali's son, in his usual bull-in-a-china-shop style, had brought the matter out

into the open and Azhar-maama had admitted that he
considered Pari, as a widow, to be an inauspicious presence on
the occasion of a much desired birth. Since then, Azhar-
maama kept dropping hints that she wasn't a good Muslim
because Vasu was still being raised as a Hindu and continued
to bear the name of a Hindu god. So, no . . . She couldn't say
that Azhar-maama was her favourite uncle.

As Mrs Ali popped the next fillet of fish into the frying
pan, she said, 'They live in a village and have a large household, with in-laws and servants and farm workers. Most of
their cooking is done on wood fires – they burn coconut
leaves and pine logs. I doubt if they even have reliable electricity, so how useful will a microwave be? It's a completely
useless gift.'

'Didn't you tell him?' asked Pari.

'It's pointless giving advice to people who will not listen. It
only reduces the value of your words.'

CHAPTER THREE

Aruna slit open another envelope. It was the day after her visit to the temple and she was alone in the office. The letter held a complaint from a man who claimed that he had joined the marriage bureau for his daughter the previous week and had not yet received the promised list of bridegrooms. You sent me the application form very fast, he had written. Has your interest in service dropped once I sent you the fees?

Aruna sighed. Mr Ali was insistent that all letters be answered within one day of being received. There was a slight – a very slight – bias towards first answering requests for information on the bureau and how to become a member, but they never left more than a couple of days before replying to any letter. She looked up the man's name on the computer and pulled out his details from the wooden wardrobe they used as a filing cabinet. As she had suspected, they had sent off the lists several days ago.

She now had a dilemma: had their reply just been delayed in the post and would it make its way to the client in the next day or two, or was it permanently lost? Mr Ali was out on an evening walk with his friends, so she couldn't ask him. Before she could decide, a young man walked in through the door. She was quite used to dealing with clients when Mr Ali was not there.

'Namaskaaram,' she said. 'Please take a seat.'

The young man's name was Raju and he was a Christian. 'Not just a Christian, but a converted Kapu,' he made a point of saying, keen to emphasise that he was not from one of the lower castes who made up the bulk of India's Christians.

Aruna nodded, thinking, you can take an Indian out of the caste system, but you cannot take the caste system out of an Indian.

He paid the fee of five hundred rupees and became a member. 'I don't mind whether the bride is Christian or Hindu, as long as they are from a higher caste.'

Aruna dutifully noted the details on his form. Soon after Raju left, Mrs Ali came out to sit in the verandah. The sun had gone down but it was still very hot. The rains had come and gone a couple of months ago, and the heat again had the country in its grip. Mrs Ali sat silently under the fan for a moment and then said, 'How are things at home?'

'Very good, madam,' said Aruna. 'My mother-in-law is so sweet. She does not let me even let me lift a mortar and pestle in the kitchen now. She says that because I am pregnant, I should let the servants do all the work.'

Mrs Ali smiled. 'That's nice.'

'The other day, I wanted a glass of water and as soon as I stood up to get it, she rushed to do it for me.'

'Well, a lot of daughters-in-law would love to be in your position,' said Mrs Ali. 'Enjoy it while it lasts.'

Aruna shook her head. 'It made me uncomfortable – letting an older person do my work for me.'

'That's because you are a well-brought-up girl,' said Mrs Ali, approvingly. 'Of course, you do realise that she is not doing the work so much for you as for her unborn grandchild.'

Aruna laughed. 'Of course,' she said. 'My mother-in-law said that I should take special care with the first grandchild of their house. I pointed out that her daughter Mani already has two grandsons, but she just dismissed them. They are not our family, she said. They belong to her husband's family.'

Mrs Ali shrugged. 'That's normal. Your child will be their first paternal grandchild, after all.'

Aruna said, 'I mean she is so loving when Mani's sons come to visit us. She plays with them, gives them sweets and then she just makes a statement like that . . . She went to the temple the other day to pray that my first-born will be a son.'

'I see.'

'Both of us told her that we don't care whether we have a son or daughter, but . . . '

The gate to the yard opened with a rattle and the conversation stopped. Four men in khaki came in, accompanied by a fifth in a smarter shirt and trousers. Aruna and Mrs Ali looked at each other, puzzled. Mrs Ali stood up and went to the verandah gate.

'We are from the electricity board, madam,' said the official-looking man, showing an identity card.

'Yes . . . ' said Mrs Ali cautiously.

'We have come to disconnect your supply,' he said, waving a cyclostyled form with her husband's name filled in.

'What? Why?'

'Is this number forty-five Abid Road?'

'Yes,' said Mrs Ali, 'but why are you disconnecting our supply? This is ridiculous. We are not in arrears. In fact, we paid the last bill only a week ago. Wait, I'll get the challan.' She turned to get the receipt of payment.

'No, madam. This has nothing to do with non-payment. We have determined that you are running a commercial enterprise on a domestic meter.'

'What? I don't believe—'

The official spoke to his men. 'Come on, boys. Do your job.' He turned to Mrs Ali. 'Please stand aside, madam.'

'My husband and son are not here. You can't just barge into a house when only the ladies are at home. Come back later.'

'Sorry, madam. We have the disconnection order signed by the executive engineer. We have full authority to disconnect the power supply, by entering your house if necessary.'

'But—'

Eventually, Mrs Ali stepped aside and the men walked in. Aruna quickly saved her work and shut down the computer. They both watched dumbstruck as one of the workers turned off the mains switch, plunging the house into darkness. The men had come prepared with torches and they pulled out the heavy porcelain fuses. A paper was pasted over the fuse box. Then with the aid of a smoking lamp red sealing wax was melted over the place where the paper overlapped the wooden board holding the electric equipment. A heavy seal was pressed into the wax while it was still soft. The wax dried to a hard crust that would break off in chunks if anybody tried to force it.

The official gave Mrs Ali a copy of the disconnection order

and said, 'It is a criminal offence to tear or remove that paper, madam.'

'What do we do? How do we get our power back?' Mrs Ali asked.

'You will need to apply to the executive engineer's office – at the big electricity office opposite Green Park Hotel. You will have to get a commercial meter for the property.'

'Commercial meter?' Mrs Ali was appalled. The sweet-shop owner down the road had been converted to a commercial meter and he said that his electricity bill had soared after that. 'That would ruin us,' she said.

The official shrugged and the men left, taking with them even the glimmer of light from their torches. Mrs Ali stood, too shocked by the suddenness of the event to say or do anything. Aruna suddenly remembered that they had a rechargeable emergency lamp and, feeling her way in the darkness around the table, managed to find it and switch it on. A pale fluorescent light illuminated the verandah.

Mrs Ali sat back heavily in the wicker chair. 'I don't know . . . What commercial enterprise? We are not running a shop here.'

'They mean the marriage bureau, madam,' said Aruna delicately.

'The marriage bureau? It's just you and sir sitting behind a table. How can that be called commercial?'

And the computer, thought Aruna. And the lights and the fan.

But, of course, she said nothing. She went back behind the desk and tidied it up with the help of the emergency lamp.

Mrs Ali looked up at her and said, 'Better call your driver.

There's no point wasting your time here.' After a few moments, she added, 'I don't understand how they knew about the marriage bureau.'

'Erm . . .'

Mrs Ali looked up sharply at Aruna's face. 'You know something,' she said. 'What is it?'

'Well, I am not sure, but the other day a new meter reader came to the house—'

Mrs Ali remembered the man with a wide mouth and obsequious manners. 'What about him?'

'Well, he was asking sir all sorts of questions about why we were receiving so many letters and so on.'

'I see,' said Mrs Ali. 'I shouldn't have left when I saw the man at the gate. I should know by now that sir is no good at dealing with anything outside his marriage bureau.'

Mrs Ali switched off the emergency lamp to conserve the battery, lit a candle and sat on the verandah. Power cuts were common, especially in summer, but this was different. Somehow, the fact that theirs was the only house without lights made it seem darker and gloomier than when the whole street was without power.

About half an hour later – Mrs Ali couldn't read the time on the wall clock – her husband walked in.

'Is there a power cut?' he asked, before looking out to the street again. 'Hey, all the other houses are lit. What happened? Has a fuse blown or something?'

'Or something,' said Mrs Ali. 'How many times have I told you not to go about boasting to strangers? But when do you ever listen to me?'

'What—'

'Pride comes before a fall, haven't you read that? This is where your pride has got us. We'll be ruined and it will be all because of you.'

'Arre, baba, tell me—'

'Ruined, do you hear? Commercial rates are four or five times higher than domestic rates. Don't think I don't know these things.'

'Will you stop wittering on and tell me what is going on?' he said, irritation evident in his voice.

'Wittering on, am I? That's all my talk is to you ...' began Mrs Ali, but then she took a deep breath and explained more calmly what had happened.

'But how did they know—'

'Did you or did you not tell that meter reader – may all food turn to ashes in his mouth – about the marriage bureau?'

'Yes, but—'

'But, nothing. Why did you have to tell him all these things? Who was he? Just a random daily-wage worker off the streets. Why did you have to boast to him? Tomorrow morning, I am going with Azhar to Faiz's house. I will come back late in the evening and by that time I want the power restored.'

'The office—'

'Forget your precious bureau. If you have to spend the whole day at the electrical engineer's office, that's what you will have to do.'

Mr Ali nodded, then glanced at his desk and remembered that he had created several ads on the PC that he had planned to print off after his walk. 'The computer! My ads—'

'You are worried about your computer? What about my fridge? I have milk and curds in there. I made bhindi-gosht, lamb with okra, and bean-fry for you to eat tomorrow when I am away and all the dishes are in the fridge. In this heat, they will be spoiled by morning. Such a waste! Serves you right that you will have to eat some junk in a restaurant instead of nice home-cooked food. If you get a stomach upset, it will teach you a lesson.'

She packed some of the curry in a tiffin box and sent it with Mr Ali to Pari. At least then it wouldn't be completely wasted.

Early the next morning, Azhar arrived with a taxi to collect Mrs Ali. There was not much traffic in town and they were soon travelling on the newly constructed highway. The driver seemed to regard anyone overtaking him as an insult to his manhood. Their fast progress was interrupted only by a herd of buffaloes, or by local villagers riding their carts and bicycles in the wrong direction down the carriageway to avoid going to the nearest break in the central reservation.

Azhar's phone rang and, after speaking for a few moments, he handed it to Mrs Ali. It was his granddaughter Faiz, whose house was their destination.

'Naani! I am glad you are coming too. You should have got Rehman-Chaacha to come as well.'

It was odd to hear Rehman being referred to as Uncle, but even though there was only a few years' difference between them, Faiz had always referred to Rehman by the proper term. As she spoke to Faiz, Mrs Ali couldn't help smiling. Faiz was a good girl – open and friendly and respectful of her elders.

Azhar's son Arif lived in Bangalore and worked for an American electronics company that designed computer chips. He had told them that he could not come home for the festival, as he was busy with some clients who were arriving from Germany. He had sent the money to buy the microwave and other gifts for his daughter, Faiz, and her husband's family. Hindus celebrated many festivals, but Muslims celebrated just two main ones – Eid-ul-Fitr and Eid-ul-Adha. Eid-ul-Fitr, commonly called Ramzaan, was now just over a month away and it would be the first festival for the recently married Faiz in her in-laws' house. After a long conversation, Mrs Ali handed the phone back to her brother.

Less than twenty years ago, they would have gone through Vizag in minutes and been speeding past green fields dotted with the occasional village. But now the town just seemed to go on and on, never quite ending, a chain of houses and markets that stretched for miles along the road, like a garland of marigolds.

'How many people there are in this world!' said Mrs Ali.

'Yes,' said Azhar. 'And then you go somewhere like Telangana, around Hyderabad, and the place is so empty – you can travel for ages without seeing a single soul.'

Mrs Ali thought of all the gifts in the boot of the car. Apart from the microwave, there were saris for the ladies of the household, cloth for shirts and trousers for the men and foodstuffs. There was also a jaanimaz – a prayer mat that had been brought all the way from Mecca by somebody from the mosque who had gone on the pilgrimage the year before, though Mrs Ali had noticed a 'Made in China' tag when she had rolled it up after admiring it. In fact, there were so many things in the boot that it had not been possible to close it fully and its half-open door had had to be tied to the bumper by a nylon rope. When the car went over a series of three pot-holes, shaking its passengers as if it were a camel, Mrs Ali hoped that nothing had fallen out of the boot.

Before settling down in Bangalore, Faiz's parents had trav-elled a lot in the early years of their marriage, leaving Faiz behind in Vizag with Azhar and his wife. By the time Faiz was in her teens, Arif's travels had dwindled and Faiz had gone back to live with her parents. Over the years, Faiz had grown very attached to her grandparents and there had been many tears when the time came to move away, but Faiz had seemed to find her feet well enough and had started going to college in Bangalore.

But maybe not that happily, thought Mrs Ali. One day, while Faiz was in her second year of college, Arif had turned up in Vizag and said that the moment had come to find his daughter a bridegroom. Everybody had been surprised. What was the hurry? It was not as if it had been a generation ago, when a girl had to be married off before she turned twenty or she would be considered an old maid. Moreover, they said that there must be many more suitable matches in Bangalore than in a smaller place like Vizag. Yet others claimed that it showed how grounded Arif was, despite his job as a vice-president in a multinational company and his extensive worldwide travel. Azhar himself had taken that attitude and had been immensely proud that Arif had come back home to find himself a son-in-law.

A groom had come to light fairly quickly – a software engineer with IBM, the grandson of a local car mechanic who also attended the same mosque as Azhar. However, Faiz did not want to get married until she had graduated with a college degree. There had been tears, sulks, threats and ultimatums, but her father was adamant. Finally, she had turned to her grandfather, who had taken her side. Faced with the combined opposition of his daughter and his parents, Arif had backed down on condition that she married whoever he selected once she had graduated.

A year later, the ink on her BA certificate was not quite dry before her name was being written on a marriage certificate. The boy chosen this time was good-looking, but he had a modest job in a village. Many people had expressed their astonishment at such an unsuitable match, but Arif had paid no attention whatsoever. Why had he been so keen to get his daughter married off so quickly?

Faiz must have had a boyfriend or, worse, a lover! The thought came to Mrs Ali just as the car stopped.

'Toll,' said the driver and Azhar took out a five-rupee coin.

Mrs Ali looked around with interest. They were finally out of the city, the road cutting through nothing but green rice fields, except for a single garage selling fuel. As the car sped up again, Mrs Ali went back to her thoughts. She didn't believe that Faiz had a lover. Mrs Ali had known the girl quite well from the time she had lived with Azhar; people changed, of course, especially when children became teenagers, but ... No, thought Mrs Ali, Faiz wouldn't do that. She might have been friendly with a boy but she wouldn't have taken that additional fatal step. But then, why?

Mrs Ali turned to Azhar. 'Why was Arif so eager to get Faiz married off?' she asked.

Azhar blinked in surprise. 'I don't know!' he said. 'It was as if a demon was riding on his shoulder. He wouldn't listen to any argument.' He looked out of the window for a moment and then shrugged. 'Anyway, we shouldn't talk about such matters now.'

Mrs Ali nodded. Any objections to a marriage must be raised before the wedding. Once it had been solemnised, everybody must forever hold their peace. No good could ever come from questioning a match once a couple were married.

The wedding had been a grand affair. Arif had spared no expense on his daughter's wedding and if Faiz didn't look ecstatic, she hadn't appeared unhappy either. The Beach Road marriage hall had been the venue for the oath-exchange or Nikah ceremony. More than twenty thousand rupees had been spent just on the lights and the sound system. Multicoloured fairy lights had been strung across the whole façade of the hall. Cooks and waiters had been hired from a well-known restaurant to serve tea and snacks to guests at any time they wanted over the three days of the ceremonies. A nearby house had been rented for the week and given over to the groom's side as a base during the ceremonies.

Of course, a bridegroom's party is never satisfied. Men and women who will happily walk a mile to catch a bus suddenly can't bear to cross the street to pick up a snack at a wedding if they are on the groom's side. They had complained that the single bathroom in the house was insufficient and had demanded bigger accommodation. Mrs Ali's husband had gone with Azhar to see what could be done. On his return, Mr Ali had told her that he had been surprised to find out that half the bridegroom's party were Mr Ali's relatives – cousins, nephews; boys he had played with when he was young. It turned out that the bridegroom's mother was Mr Ali's second cousin. Mr Ali said he had spent a couple of hours reminiscing about the old days, besides managing to pacify the gathering.

Haji Saab, the then-imam of the mosque, had conducted the marriage service, with Azhar and the bridegroom's grandfather as witnesses. As soon as the bride, groom and the witnesses had signed the marriage certificate, crystal sugar and almonds still in their shells had been thrown into the crowd, leading to a mad scramble by the children and not a few adults. Songs of romance and devotion were sung and the hall was reconfigured with long trestle tables for lunch. It had taken three sittings to feed everybody – the menu being the traditional lamb biryani, brinjal-and-gourd gravy, kachoombar raita and a choice of jalebi or gulab jamun for dessert.

Nadeem Bhai, Mrs Ali's older brother, had buttonholed her between food sittings two and three. 'The groom is just a clerk who lives in a village. Azhar has lost his senses, spending hundreds of thousands of rupees on this ceremony.'

'Azhar is not spending the money,' said Mrs Ali, defending one brother against another. 'Faiz is Arif's daughter. He is the one who is footing the bill for all of this.'

Nadeem waved his hand dismissively. 'Arif is just a foolish boy. Azhar should have more sense. Anyway, why did Azhar even agree to this match? He and Arif should have found an engineer or an executive in Bangalore.'

'It's too late for those kinds of remarks now. The Nikah is

over and you shouldn't speak like that any more. Have you eaten? How was the food?' Mrs Ali knew that one way to distract any Muslim at a wedding was to talk about the food.

'I ate in the first round. I got a bone in my biryani,' her brother complained.

'I haven't eaten yet and the third sitting is starting. I'd better go.' When Mrs Ali had extricated herself, Nadeem Bhai went to find somebody else to complain to.

One wedding leads to three as they say, and this was no exception. She had seen a couple of families eyeing prospective matches and sending out cautious feelers. She had even received an indication of interest from one of her husband's second cousins for a match between the cousin's daughter and Rehman. Mr Ali had flatly rejected the idea out of hand, surprising his wife with his vehemence. He had muttered something vague about the family not being suitable. There was obviously some history there. Even after so many years of marriage, there were still things she didn't know about her husband's life!

CHAPTER FOUR

Just before nine in the morning, Mr Ali got ready to go to the electricity board office. His wife had put in a plastic bag the documents he needed to take: the meter reading card, the ration card – just in case it was needed as proof of identity, the disconnection notice and the electricity book showing that they were up to date with payments.

'Be careful with the papers!' Mrs Ali had told him . . . several times.

'Of course I will look after them,' he had finally replied in irritation, on the sixth, or maybe the seventh, time that she had mentioned it. He knew how much work and running around would be necessary to replace these papers if he lost them. Not to mention the fact that he would never hear the end of it from his wife.

'The way you looked after Rehman at the fair?'

'What—' He shook his head. That had been twenty years ago when Rehman had been a little boy. They had found him fairly quickly, less than a hundred feet from where he had been lost – no, wandered away. 'Don't be silly,' he said. 'That was different, entirely different.'

He heard the sniff in his wife's voice.

He parked his scooter under a gulmohar tree – the black faux-leather seats absorbed too much heat if left out in the sun – and walked over to the office, which turned out to belong to the administrator whereas he needed the engineer. Several minutes later, after asking a few people, he located a small single-storey structure behind the main building. It was almost a cube, with cement walls and a flat, concrete roof. From a rusty water tank above it an ugly, red stain ran down one wall to the ground. A foot-high banyan tree had sprouted in a small crack where the roof and the wall joined. The glass window was small and so grimy nothing could be seen through it.

A painted sign on the door said, 'Executive engineer's office. Open: 9 a.m. to 5 p.m.'

He looked at his watch and smiled. He had timed it perfectly. He walked in to see a peon, the office factotum found in all Indian offices, sitting on a three-legged stool; only a couple of desks had clerks behind them; most were still unmanned. Behind the peon, a wooden partition clearly denoted the engineer's office.

'Excuse me,' Mr Ali said to the peon. 'Our power has been disconnected.'

'Didn't you pay your bill?' asked the peon.

'We are up to date with our payments. They said something about needing a commercial meter.'

'Oh! Commercial meters. People are running stores, offices and even welding shops on domestic meters. We have had orders from high up and the engineer-saab is very strict about it.'

'But we are not running a shop – welding or otherwise.'

'That's what they all say,' the peon said. 'Take a seat, sir, and I'll let you know when the engineer can see you.'

Mr Ali perched on a chair with a broken back and looked around the office. The two clerks didn't seem particularly busy, discussing a new movie that one of them had seen the previous evening. After a while the peon disappeared, at which point the clerks stopped reviewing the movie and started talking about a cricket match – something about IPL and Twenty-twenty that Mr Ali, who was not interested in cricket, didn't understand. Over the next hour, more clerks turned up and joined the discussion regarding the cricket match. Mr Ali tried to catch their attention to see whether one of them could help him, but they ignored him as expertly as a waiter in a restaurant ignores diners.

Finally, the peon came back and Mr Ali asked whether the engineer would see him now. 'Oh, the engineer isn't here yet.'

'What?' said Mr Ali and looked at his watch. It was almost half past ten. 'The sign says—'

'The engineer doesn't come in until eleven.'

'Why didn't you tell me earlier? I could have been doing something useful instead of sitting here listening to your men's cricket commentary.'

'You didn't ask me. And sometimes the engineer comes early.'

'You mean by half-past ten?' said Mr Ali.

'Even earlier sometimes. Last week on Thursday, the

engineer was here just before ten. Some of those clerks hadn't yet turned up and they were very embarrassed.'

'I can imagine,' said Mr Ali. 'How thoughtless of the engineer to turn up unexpectedly early and show up the clerks like that! Were you here?'

'I always come to the office on time,' said the peon. 'I live in a small one-room house with a wife and three daughters, and the only peace I get from women is here.'

The conversation lapsed and Mr Ali wondered what he should do. In the end, he decided to stay where he was.

Just before eleven, the sound of a jeep could be heard outside and the peon jumped up. The clerks moved to their individual desks and started untying the red tape that bound files of papers.

A middle-aged, overweight man, with short legs and a big belly, walked in. The peon moved forward and took his briefcase. The engineer glanced at the industrious clerks and went straight into his cabin. The peon followed him with the briefcase, then returned to take him a glass of water.

Another half an hour passed while the peon shuttled in and out. Mr Ali caught his eye a couple of times, but was just waved down. Although he was increasingly frustrated, there was nothing he could do.

At last the cabin door opened and the engineer walked out. Mr Ali stood up and said, 'Sir, our power has been disconnected—'

The official nodded. 'Later,' he said and strode out.

The peon came back, wiping his forehead. 'He won't be back until three,' he said. 'You might as well return then.'

The clerks had stopped working and were now gathered

round one of the desks, discussing where to go for lunch.

Mr Ali gave a deep sigh and trudged back to his scooter to find a big white bird dropping smeared across the black seat. He looked up into the tree, but the bird was long gone.

Meanwhile, Mrs Ali and Azhar were still en route. The car lurched into another pothole and they were thrown around like dried peas in a pod.

'Sorry, sir, madam,' said the driver. 'The recent rains have left the roads in bad shape.'

They had already lost half an hour when one of the tyres had been punctured. The driver was now going slowly to avoid another puncture. Finally the road became smoother and they picked up some speed, reaching the village just before noon.

'A microwave. Thank you, daada!' squealed Faiz and hugged her grandfather.

Her in-laws too were happy to see them and even happier as each of them had been given their personal gift. Mrs Ali could see Faiz's sisters-in-law surreptitiously comparing their saris, but as much thought had gone into selecting the saris as into any military campaign by Alexander the Great. Mrs Ali was sure that the ladies would not find any issues with the absolute or relative value of their gifts.

'What is this microwave?' asked Faiz's mother-in-law. 'What does it do?'

'It is an oven that cooks without fire,' said Faiz.

'This is all too advanced for a simple villager like me,' said Faiz's mother-in-law. Mrs Ali silently agreed.

They unpacked the gadget and found their first problem.

The only electrical point in the house was in the living room where it was already used for the TV. The TV was unplugged and the microwave was put in its place. The blinking clock elicited exclamations from the assembled ladies. With its clean, white, high-tech-gadget looks, it attracted the men as well, even though they normally did not have anything to do with cooking.

'Get a glass of water,' said Azhar.

One of the women ran into the kitchen and came back with a brass tumbler. Azhar shook his head. 'No, you cannot put metal in the microwave. Get something non-metallic.'

'Chinni?' asked the woman.

Azhar nodded. China was fine. The shopkeeper who had sold him the microwave had given him a quick lesson on how to use it. The lady came back with water in a teacup.

Everybody gathered round as the light came on in the microwave.

'It's going round!' said Faiz's mother-in-law.

A minute later, the microwave switched itself off with a ping and Azhar took out the now-warm cup and it passed from hand to hand.

'What strange things will people keep inventing?' said Faiz's mother-in-law.

Mrs Ali had been impressed as well but she kept a stiff upper lip in front of these rustic in-laws. She was a city woman after all and had to maintain her sophisticated image.

Just then, Faiz's husband, Sharif, came in. 'Hello,' he said. 'What's going on here?'

'Look!' said Faiz happily. 'Abba has sent us a microwave oven.'

Sharif gave his wife a tight smile, turned to Mrs Ali and Azhar, greeting them with polite salaams, and handed three eggs to his mother. 'I found out where the red hen is laying its eggs – by the side of the long hedge.'

Faiz's face fell, but only Mrs Ali seemed to notice.

'Oh, good!' said Sharif's mother. 'I wonder why the hen changed where it lays eggs.' She turned to one of her daughters-in-law. 'Boil them and add them to the khatta.'

Azhar said, 'Give me the eggs. The microwave should be able to boil them inside their shells.'

'Are you sure, Bhaijaan?' said Sharif's mother. 'It's no trouble at all to boil the eggs.'

'It'll take just a couple of minutes.'

The eggs were placed inside the microwave. 'Look,' said Azhar. 'They are turning round the opposite way from the water.'

Nothing happened for forty-five seconds. Then there was a loud explosion and the inside of the microwave disappeared in white shrapnel and a yellow, gooey mess. Azhar froze and the only part of him that moved was his mouth, opening and closing like a goldfish. There was another explosion and the glass front became even more smeared with mess-of-egg before Azhar reacted and jabbed at the door-release button. The door swung open just as the third egg exploded.

'Eeuw!' screamed the ladies as they were spattered by bits of yolk and white, but it was Azhar who caught the main force of the blast.

Two boys – Faiz's nephew and a neighbour's son – came running in and stopped in surprise at the sight of Azhar. 'What's happened to uncle?' the neighbour's son asked.

'Shhh . . . ' said one of the ladies.

'Egg,' said Faiz's nephew confidently. 'On face.'

Amid the clean-up, Mrs Ali's mind wandered. This was not the first time that gifts had caused a problem for Faiz with her in-laws.

Faiz's wedding day had started normally. The Nikah ceremony had been held in the morning. Oaths had been exchanged. Sharif and Faiz had been pronounced man and wife – in theory, sight unseen. A few hours after lunch, the Jalwa had been held, in which the bride and groom were shown to each other, officially, for the first time ever and the bride was formally placed in the care of her husband's family.

It was then time for Faiz, who had symbolically changed from her wedding sari into another provided by her in-laws, to depart with her new family. As the guests started leaving, the father-in-law had come to Arif, Faiz's father, to say that they needed help to take away the bridal gifts.

Apart from the dowry and two hundred and twenty grams of gold jewellery, the gifts included a wooden bed frame, a foam mattress, a steel wardrobe, three kilos of silver platters and tumblers, a full set of stainless-steel dishes, melamine crockery and other bits and bobs. The entire trousseau had been laid out in one corner of the hall for everyone to admire during the ceremonies.

Unfortunately, Mrs Ali's older brother, Nadeem Bhai, had overheard the request for help to take away the gifts. He had been complaining all day about the expense of the wedding and had taken offence at not being given the deference he considered his due as the oldest member of the family.

He butted into the conversation and addressed Faiz's father-in-law. 'As you are the bridegroom's father, it is your responsibility to take the gifts away.'

Mrs Ali silently agreed with her brother. That much was tradition. The bride's family's job was to deliver the bride and her trousseau to the wedding hall. Once the ceremonies were over, the bride and gifts belonged to the new family, to be taken away by them. But why make such an issue over a simple matter?

Arif tried to placate Nadeem Bhai, saying that as the bride-groom's family didn't know Vizag, he didn't mind arranging a truck for them. But Nadeem Bhai wouldn't be shushed.

'We have already spent far too much money on this wed-ding. And if you don't even have the capacity to take it all away, why did you demand so many gifts? Your son is just a clerk, after all.'

Mrs Ali was dumbstruck. An even more important tradi-tion than the bridegroom's family taking away the trosseau was that the bride's family be obsequiously polite to the groom's family.

The groom's father's face turned an interesting colour. 'My – son – is – a – diamond,' he said deliberately. 'He could have been an officer anywhere in the world and if he chose to remain in the village, it's because he is a well-brought-up boy who loves his family. My son doesn't need to work at all. My grandfather was a well-known barrister during the British times. We have fertile fields not only in our own Kothagudem but also in the village of Kattulapalem – the village of swords. The whole taluqa – sub-district – knows us wherever we go.'

By this time, he was shouting, which brought Azhar over. 'Sir, it's nothing. We'll sort out a truck—'

Nadeem Bhai interrupted his younger brother. 'Everybody knows that Kattulapalem isn't about swords. The name means the village of knives, and your family probably handle the blades because they are barbers. That'll explain why everybody knows them.'

Mrs Ali raised her hand to cover her open mouth.

The groom's maternal uncle immediately lost his temper and rushed at Nadeem Bhai, shouting, 'How dare you insult my family?' and landing a blow on Nadeem Bhai's head. When Nadeem Bhai shoved back, the man lost his footing and fell down. Some of the groom's young men rushed to support their elders and Faiz's cousins moved in; a free-for-all developed within seconds.

Mr Ali and a few other senior men managed to separate the groups.

'We are not taking the bride with us until your brother apologises,' said the groom's father to Azhar.

'Why should I say sorry?' said Nadeem Bhai. 'I haven't said anything that's not true.'

Mrs Ali realised that a major scandal would ensue if the bridegroom and his family left without Faiz. Nobody else would marry her and the young woman's life would be ruined. Mrs Ali tugged her older brother's hand and forcibly pulled him away, still protesting self-righteously. She led him into a small room, told him that she would get him a glass of water and locked him inside.

When she came back to the scene of the fight, her husband, her other siblings and many others on the bride's side were apologising profusely to their opposite numbers. Eventually, they were able to calm the groom's family.

No, thought Mrs Ali as she saw Azhar return, washed and wearing Faiz's father-in-law's kurta. Faiz didn't have much luck with her family's gifts to her in-laws.

Mr Ali spent the afternoon in the electricity office, waiting for the engineer to turn up. Finally, at four, he gave it up as a lost cause and returned to his scooter, which he had parked away from the trees after the morning's experience with the bird's droppings. As he took it off the stand, he wondered how his wife would react when she returned to a still-dark house. He plonked his seat on the scooter, then jumped up and down like a grasshopper, almost falling off. The black seat had absorbed hours of strong afternoon sun and was scorching hot.

Even though the sun had not yet set, the verandah was dark because it was shaded by the guava tree and the thin curtains behind the iron grille-work. Mr Ali had sent Aruna home early and sat by himself, drawing up his advertisements all over again. Thank God for paper records, he thought. Computers are very good, but only while they are working. Otherwise, they are no more use than a paperweight.

Somebody rattled the iron gate and Mr Ali looked up. A family was standing there – two parents and a young girl. 'Is this the marriage bureau?'

'Yes,' said Mr Ali. 'Please come in and take a seat.'

'We were not sure because it is so dark,' said the man, as he sat down.

'Sorry, we are having some issues with our electricity supply. Anyway . . .'

After the pleasantries, Mr Ali discovered that they had seen an ad for a bridegroom a couple of weeks previously and wanted to find out more details about the match.

'Which one is it?' he asked.

'The Kamma caste man working in the fishery business.'

Mr Ali remembered the ad. For some reason, he hadn't got a very good response for it.

'It's a very good match,' he said. 'They are traditional land-lords with fields elsewhere, but the bridegroom himself lives in Vizag. He is doing very well in his career and his salary is almost thirty thousand rupees a month. Why don't you become members? We can call them right now and have a word with them, so you can introduce yourself. We have other matches too that are just as good. Here's a form. Please fill it in.'

The man took the blank form and a pen and filled it in rapidly. Mr Ali felt that it was one of the easiest sales he had made in a while. The parents looked well off and it didn't appear as though the fees would be an issue for them. Over the last year or so that he had been running the marriage bureau, he had developed a sixth sense for who would become a member and who wouldn't. He was not one hundred per cent accurate, of course, but he could usually tell – and this family was a definite prospect.

The man passed the form back to Mr Ali and said, 'First, can you give me an idea of the kind of people among your members who would be interesting to us?'

'Of course,' said Mr Ali, and then realised that he could not do it without the computer. 'Sorry, sir. We don't have power at the moment, but as soon as I can get the computer running again, I will be able to pull out a special list for you.'

The man thought for a moment, looked at his wife and daughter, and then turned his gaze back to Mr Ali. 'OK, in that case, we'll come again another time.'

'If you become a member now, I can send the list to you by post as well, sir. Why trouble yourself to make an extra visit?'

The man shook his head. 'No, no. We'll come back another time.'

As they were walking out, Mr Ali heard them talk about visiting another marriage bureau that had opened recently by the culvert down the road.

This was really annoying. He was now losing business because of this power cut.

He switched on the emergency lamp, but it flickered and went off – it had been used too long already. Mr Ali sighed and hunted for a candle. His wife would have known exactly where it was, but he had to search for it and then for a match-box. How was he going to explain to his wife that there was still no power in the house when she came back?

The phone rang, its sudden shrill tone startling him. He picked up the receiver and said, 'Hello, hello . . .'

When the phone continued ringing, he realised that the cordless phone would not work in the absence of electricity. He rushed to reach the main instrument before the ringing stopped. It was his wife.

'What took you so long to answer the phone?' she said.

'Never mind that,' he said. 'How is it going?'

'It's OK. But we need to stay here overnight. Is that all right?'

Sudden hope gleamed in Mr Ali's heart. He had a day's reprieve. 'Humph,' he said, trying to disguise his relief. 'Why?'

Mrs Ali's voice dropped as if she didn't want the people round her to hear what she was saying. 'There are problems between Faiz and Sharif. I'll try to have a word with them before I leave.'

Mr Ali nodded. 'All right,' he said.

'I've spoken to Pari,' said Mrs Ali. 'She is making dinner for you. You can go and eat in her flat. But she will be busy in the morning, getting ready for work and school, so it is best if you get breakfast for yourself.'

Mr Ali said, 'That's all right. I can go to Sai Ram Parlour and get idli with coconut chutney.'

It was only after he put the phone down that Mr Ali remembered that he had not asked what the problem was between Faiz and Sharif. Oh well, his wife probably couldn't have spoken freely anyway.

Now, how was he going to sort out the electricity problem before his wife came home? And before his business started going down the drain?

CHAPTER FIVE

Mrs Ali walked slowly down the village path towards the tomb of the Sufi saint. Sharif kept pace with her, while Azhar and Faiz were a few paces ahead of them.

'I have heard that the urs – the anniversary – of the saint is celebrated quite grandly,' said Mrs Ali.

Sharif nodded. 'Yes, Maami. Both Hindus and Muslims come from all over the district to attend it. We have an all-night festival with qawwalis and big feasts.' Qawwalis are Muslim devotional songs sung at the tombs of Sufi saints.

'I'd love to see a qawwali performance. It has been a long time since I've attended one.'

'You've just missed this year's urs. It comes early in this month of Shaabaan. But you should definitely come next year, and bring Maama too. Last year we commissioned two different qawwals – one man and one woman – and it worked really well as they each tried to outdo the other. The singing went on well past midnight.'

'It will be good for your maama to lift his head out of the marriage bureau. Insha'Allah, we'll come next year.'

Unusually, Faiz called her naani – or grandmother, while Faiz's husband, Sharif, called her maami – or aunt, because they were related from both sides. Faiz, of course, was her brother's granddaughter while Sharif was the son of her husband's cousin. As they walked through the village, Mrs Ali thought back to her English lessons. English was such a strange language – expressive in so many ways, but so bland in others. It used the same word for maternal and paternal grandmother. And the word uncle was worse – it was used when referring to a maama, a mother's brother; a chaacha, a father's brother; or a phuppa, a father's sister's husband. And yet they had two words where one would do – gate and door, for example – as if the subtle difference between them was more important than the major distinctions in the family.

Mrs Ali's ruminations stopped when they reached the sun-drenched dargah with its whitewashed walls and onion dome, in the midst of a green lawn dotted with gravestones. A thin, old man was cutting the grass with a sickle and putting the clippings into a bamboo basket that he dragged behind him. Two ravens flew past with raucous caws. From the distance, beyond the dargah's compound, could be heard a cow's long moo.

Sharif and Azhar put on white lace skullcaps. Faiz and Mrs Ali draped the ends of their saris over their heads. All of them took off their footwear and walked gingerly over the hot flag-stones to the marble floor that was cool under the dome.

Word had been sent ahead that they were coming and a priest was waiting for them. Mrs Ali gave the imam a bunch of bananas, a packet of incense sticks and some jasmine flowers. The priest lit the incense sticks from an oil lamp and stuck them in one of the bananas to hold them upright. The perfumed smoke rose and filled the corridor in which they sat. In front of them, a tiled room with a low door held the saint's grave, covered by green cloth. The priest led the four of them in saying the dua, the prayers, and finished by touching their heads with a peacock-feather fan. Half the bananas were returned to them and they all stood up.

All of them, including the priest, left the tomb. Sharif asked him, 'When do you think the month of Ramzaan will start, sir?' Turning to Mrs Ali and Azhar, he added, 'This gentleman is also the imam of the village mosque.'

'When Allah wills that we see the crescent moon, then the holy month begins,' said the imam.

'Nowadays, they announce on television when they've sighted the moon in Delhi or Mecca, don't they?' said Faiz.

'I don't believe in all this new technology,' the imam said. 'God gave us eyes to see and a simple rule to follow. Sight the moon and start the fast. Sight the moon again to determine the end of the month and the end of the fast. Why do we need to complicate things?'

A phone rang and Azhar fumbled through his pockets, but it wasn't his phone. The imam took out a mobile phone from the pocket of his kurta and answered. 'Yes,' he said. 'I've finished here. Ask Abdul to stay there, don't let him go. I am coming.'

He took his leave. Faiz looked speculatively at the imam's receding back. 'Doesn't believe in new technology!' she said. Azhar frowned at his granddaughter, but the others laughed.

'Let's sit here for a moment,' said Mrs Ali to Sharif, indicating a cement platform around the trunk of a huge banyan tree. The platform was cracked but clean, except for a few twigs, and was shaded by the tree's overhanging aerial roots.

Sharif nodded and sat down beside her. Mrs Ali, who had sent Faiz and Azhar back home straight from the dargah, was enjoying the cool breeze in the shade of the tree, listening to the silence that only a village offers.

She said, 'Sharif, are you happy with Faiz?'

'Of course I am happy,' he said quickly. Too quickly.

Mrs Ali didn't say anything. After several seconds, Sharif cracked and said, 'But I get the feeling that Faiz is not entirely happy.'

'Why do you think that is?'

'I don't know, Maami. She gets moody and won't talk to me for days. She doesn't get involved in all the tasks around the house with my mother, my sister and my sisters-in-law. I think that if she has a child, it will help, but she says she is not yet ready to become a mother. I just don't know what to do.'

'Have you talked to anybody about it?'

'No. I don't want to talk to Ammi and Abba because they will blame Faiz and I don't want them to do that. If I say anything to anyone else in the family, word will get back to my parents, so I haven't done that either.'

'Faiz is a lucky girl,' murmured Mrs Ali.

'What—'

'Nothing.' Mrs Ali shook her head.

'I treat her well – no different from the way my father treats my mother or my brothers treat their wives. I don't know why she becomes so glum.'

'Everybody is different,' said Mrs Ali. 'Your mother and your sisters-in-law aren't educated beyond high school. They grew up in big families. Faiz lived with her grandparents and then as a single child in Bangalore. She is a college graduate.'

'I know that, Maami. She is really intelligent and I like that about her.'

'You've been married for, what? Six months?'

'Eight months, actually,' said Sharif.

'In those eight months, where have you taken her?'

'Taken her?'

'Yes, you know, movies, holidays, trips . . . '

Sharif's face reddened. 'Nowhere, really. I don't like movies and you have to go to the market town six miles away for the cinema. Wait, we came to the qawwali at the saint's anniversary and we went to the village fair by the river a couple of months ago.'

'Was it just the two of you who went to the fair?'

'Yes . . . no . . . At the last minute, my mother asked me to take my sister as well, so the three of us went.'

'Let me get this right. In eight months, you and Faiz have not gone out anywhere on your own.'

'Father says that one should not spoil women. Otherwise they will climb on your shoulders and dominate you.'

Mrs Ali smiled at Sharif. 'That's a really old-fashioned way of thinking. I don't want to criticise your father, but the world has changed. Once upon a time, the roles were clear. Women didn't care about what was going on outside as long as their menfolk brought home the money to run the household. Now women, especially educated women like Faiz, want to be partners with their husbands – to share in their men's triumphs and their troubles. I think that is better. In the long run, it will lead to greater happiness for the couple.'

'Yes, but—'

'No buts, Sharif. You care for Faiz, don't you?'

'Yes, of course.'

'The very fact that you have kept all this bottled up inside you, and not spoken of it to anybody for fear that they might think ill of Faiz, shows that you love her. But it is not enough to feel the emotion. You have to show it too.'

'What do you mean?'

'Tomorrow, when you come home, don't bring eggs for your mother. Get some flowers for Faiz.'

'But . . . but . . . my brothers will make fun of me.'

'But your sisters-in-law won't. And they will keep your brothers under control. Or you could start with a more discreet gift. But bring her something. If you do that, I can bet that your sisters-in-law will force your brothers to change too. Take your wife out. You may not like going to movies, but Faiz does.'

'But what about my sister?'

'I am not asking you to be totally selfish. If you go out sometimes on your own, Faiz will not mind if your sister accompanies you at other times. Faiz is a very good girl. Just like you, she too has not uttered a single word of complaint to her father or grandfather. Since marriage, your own life has carried on as normal, but think about her. She has moved from a big city to a small village and is living in a big family with people she doesn't know. She likes books and loves magazines. Where are they in your house?'

Sharif stayed silent for a long time, staring into the blue, cloudless sky.

'Let us go,' said Mrs Ali, touching him lightly on the arm. 'You and Faiz are now married. For good or ill, you have to stick together and make a life out of what God has given you. This time when you are newly married is very special, Sharif. It is a time when you have to bond together and create memories. Think of it as a bank account into which you are depositing not money, but emotions. There will be times in the future when you will need to withdraw from this account to see you through. But to do that, make sure it is well funded now.'

As they walked back towards Sharif's home to eat chicken curry, Mrs Ali wondered whether her talk would do any good. It's difficult to change people, she thought, and words are like ripples in water that agitate the surface for a bit and then disappear without a trace.

The following afternoon, Mr Ali woke up, feeling irritated because his nap had been disturbed. This was very unusual because he could usually fall asleep anywhere, at any time.

He had spent another morning at the electricity office. The peon in the engineer's office, taking pity on him, had escorted him on a round of the clerks, but they had each just passed him on to the next like a parcel at a children's party game. He was finally told to wait for the engineer.

'How long will that take?'

'No idea, sir. Elections are coming, so the engineer is very busy answering the politicians' questions. It might take some time.'

Meanwhile, Mr Ali's business was suffering. Worse still, the knowledge hung over him that his wife would be back later that day and would be unhappy at having to run a household without electricity.

He lay in bed, glaring grumpily at the fan, but it stayed stubbornly motionless. When a faint sound came from the front of the house, he realised that it wasn't the lack of breeze that had woken him up, but the rattle of the gate. He wondered why his wife was not answering it, before remembering that she was still in the village, thank God. Bleary-eyed, he stumbled to the verandah to find a dark man with a wide mouth, grinning at him. He looked vaguely familiar.

'Yes?' he said, then added, 'Madam is not here if you are selling something.'

'I am Shyam, sir. The electricity meter reader. May I come in?'

'Electricity, pah! Don't talk to me about it,' said Mr Ali but he went back into the house, got a key and unlocked the gate.

'The peon in the engineer's office told me that you had gone round there to get the power connected.'

'Yes. Fat lot of good it did me.'

'I am appalled, sir, that a senior citizen like you had to run around to the engineer's office. The electricity department staff show no consideration for age or status. They know that they have the citizens over a barrel and they take full advantage of it, secure in their permanent jobs.'

'Hm . . .'

'Yes, sir. Otherwise, a respected man like you would not be ignored while you sat outside the engineer's office for a whole day. Such a situation is just wrong morally. That's why I came straight here as soon as I heard, sir.'

'My business is sinking into the Bay of Bengal and my

wife will be back in the evening, asking how she is supposed to manage without the fridge or the grinder. We need the power back.'

'See, you admit that you are running a business here. You need to go on the commercial meter, sir. If you agree, I can arrange to have the power restored today and I will sort out the paperwork to change your tariff. For a small fee, of course.'

Mr Ali was about to agree when he remembered what his wife had said.

'We cannot run the whole household at commercial rates. It will bankrupt us. Our business is entirely run from this verandah.'

Shyam looked around speculatively, nodding to himself. 'You are right,' he said finally. 'It will cost a bit more. Three thousand rupees. We'll put a new meter in for this verandah and set that to commercial rates. The rest of the house can remain on the old meter at domestic rates. I will do all the work, including the meter installation and getting it signed off by the electricity department afterwards.'

'And I won't have to go to the electricity office again?'

'Oh no, sir! You just sit in that chair and I will sort everything out for you.'

'But I need the power now. I can't wait for the new meter.'

Shyam nodded. 'If you give me two hundred and fifty rupees, sir, I can organise that.'

Mr Ali almost went for his wallet before a lifetime's experience asserted itself. 'Get the power restored first,' he said.

Shyam shrugged. His fish was on the hook; it might

wriggle, but it was not going anywhere. 'All right, I'll be back in an hour with the lineman.'

By evening, Mr Ali was looking on proudly as Aruna typed into the computer the details of the people who had joined the bureau in the last couple of days. The fan was whirling round at full speed and the tube light cast a comforting white glow. A car stopped outside and Mrs Ali got out. The taxi sped away before he could go into the yard.

'You've managed to get the power back!' said Mrs Ali.

Mr Ali waved his hand dismissively. 'Of course,' he said. 'Not an issue at all. How was everybody in the village?'

'Everybody's fine. They all asked after you and said that you have to come over for the saint's urs next year.' She walked onto the verandah. 'Hello, Aruna. How are you?'

Aruna smiled and bobbed her head. 'Namaste, madam.'

By the time Mrs Ali came back onto the verandah, Aruna had finished typing and was going through their filing cupboard to weed out old lists. Soon after, she heard the sound of the outside gate opening. When no one came in for almost a minute after that, she peered out into the yard. Through the thin curtains, she saw a tall, old man walking painfully slowly, holding a walking stick in his left hand. He was being supported on the other side by a younger man. An expensive car stood at the roadside.

The two men finally came in and sank onto the wooden settee. The older man was probably in his seventies. But for his injured hip, Aruna would have said that he looked well for his age and quite fit. The younger man was in his late forties or early fifties and appeared to be some sort of retainer.

'Would you like water?' asked Mr Ali.

'No, I am all right. It's just that this broken hip of mine hasn't healed properly and is a nuisance to walk on.'

'How can we help you?'

The older man was obviously old-fashioned and didn't like to introduce himself. He nodded to the younger man, who started speaking for him.

'My uncle is Mr Koteshwar Reddy and, like his name, he is a millionaire.'

Koti, or crore, was the word for ten million. Mr Ali had once read that no other ancient civilisation had words for such large numbers. Maybe it was not a coincidence that the zero and the decimal number system had been invented in India. Indians, even today, had a surprising facility for figures.

The man continued to speak. 'Uncle was the regional director in MMTC, the Minerals and Mines Trading Corporation, but of course he is retired now. He has several houses in town. Do you know the Sukumar theatre?'

Aruna and Mr Ali nodded. It was one of the oldest cinemas in town, once grand but quite run-down now, like an elderly dowager's mansion. It occupied a prime spot of real estate that would be worth a substantial amount if redeveloped.

'The cinema belongs to us. Besides that, there are ancestral lands in three different districts. Uncle has one son, Sukumar.'

The old man waved his hand dismissively. The younger man inclined his head in slight acknowledgement and carried on. 'We have come here for Uncle's granddaughter – Sujatha.' He went through the bag he was holding and handed a photograph to Mr Ali. 'She is a graduate from St Joseph's College with a first-class degree. As you can see, she is pretty.'

Mr Ali nodded and handed the photo to Aruna. The girl in the picture was fair, with clear eyes, a lovely smile and even features, and wore her hair in a stylish fringe.

'Not only is Sujatha pretty, but she is a very natural, nice girl.' He glanced at the older man and added, 'The money and her grandfather's love have not spoiled her.'

'I see,' said Mr Ali. He took out an application form and handed it along with a pen to the younger man. 'Why don't you fill this out for us? It tells us the kind of details we need to know.'

Name, caste, date of birth, star (for horoscope), height, complexion, number of brothers and sisters, education, job (if any), salary, father's job, parents' wealth, dowry . . .

'What is your name?' Mr Ali asked the younger man.

'My name is Bobbili, sir. I am Uncle's sister's son. I've been with him since I was a little boy.'

Mr Koteshwar stirred. 'Bobbili is my right-hand man. He is more like my son than my own son. I don't know what I'd do without him.' He turned to Bobbili. 'While we are here, why don't we make Venkatesh a member too?'

Bobbili squirmed. 'This is a marriage bureau for rich people,' he said. 'Not for the likes of me and my son.'

A cloud passed over Mr Koteshwar's face. He turned to Mr Ali and explained, 'My sister was very unlucky. She became a widow soon after Bobbili was born and she was kicked out by her husband's family without a single paisa to her name. She lived with me until she died a few years ago.'

Mr Ali took the filled-in form and went through it. There were no surprises really. The girl was twenty-four years old and the only unexpected thing was that an attractive, rich girl like her from a good caste needed to come to a marriage bureau in the first place.

'Excuse me for asking,' said Mr Ali, 'but why are you here? I would have thought there would be a queue of suitors wanting to marry Sujatha. The only reason I am asking is because that's what the families of prospective matches will ask me and it is best if I have an answer for them. On the face of it, you should be beating off suitors from your door, not going out to look for them.'

'That is the mystery, sir,' said Bobbili. 'We've had several enquiries, but nothing seems to come of them.'

Mr Koteshwar shook his head. 'What is the point of sugar-coating the truth, Bobbili? Let us tell it like it is.' He turned to Mr Ali and Aruna. 'I named my son Sukumar – or good son. And the gods played a joke on me. He is a drunkard, a gambler, always dreaming about the next big scheme to earn money. I think he is driving potential matches away.'

Bobbili squirmed and looked pained. 'You shouldn't say—'

Mr Koteshwar made a chopping movement with his hand, silencing his nephew. 'Who feels the shame of a useless son more than I? But hiding the truth is not going to change it. The people who come to see my granddaughter will find out about my son sooner or later. They might as well know up front.'

Aruna spoke for the first time. 'But sir, do you think that her own father would put obstacles in the way of Sujatha getting married? Maybe you are mistaken.'

Mr Koteshwar smiled gently at her. 'You are a young girl and I don't think you've seen as much of the world as I have. You don't know the depths to which people will degrade themselves for money. Because of my son's character, I've made a trust and transferred all my money and property into it. After me, the trust and all its wealth will go to Sujatha. If my son wants any money, he will have to go to his daughter and beg from her like a dog for its scraps.' The old man's face had taken on a stern and forbidding look.

Aruna was about to say that she still found it difficult to believe that a father would jeopardise his daughter's chances of a wedding and then she remembered . . .

Before she had worked for the marriage bureau as an assistant to Mr Ali, her father had fallen ill and their savings had been wiped out. His pension had been cut because of an administrative blunder and they were forced to rely on the salary she brought in as a salesgirl in a department store. Shastry-uncle, her mother's brother, had found several matches for her but her father had refused them, saying that not only could they not afford to pay for a wedding, but they also needed her salary to survive. If she hadn't met Ram at the marriage bureau, she would probably still be unmarried. If her father, a morally upright man, a Sanskrit scholar who knew the holy books and could quote verbatim from the Vedas, was willing to hinder his daughter's marriage, then why not a weak man – an alcoholic and a gambler?

The old man must be right, she thought. The love of money can make people do anything.

CHAPTER SIX

It was six-thirty in the evening and the sun was about to set. Pari walked into the Alis' house while Vasu skipped in ahead of her.

'We have sighted the moon!' he shouted as soon as he saw Mrs Ali.

'Did you really? How clever of you? I couldn't see it from here.'

'We went to the terrace on top of our building.' He pointed north-east. 'It was in that direction. I was the first one to see it. Amma couldn't see the moon until I pointed it out to her.'

The newborn moon is a thin, silvery crescent that appears in the sky for a very short time and doesn't rise fully before it sets again. Clouds, haze, bright lights – anything at all can obscure it. Its sighting marks the beginning of a new month in the Muslim calendar and is especially important to the average Muslim twice a year, once, as now, when it signals the beginning of the holy month of Ramzaan. In this month, Muslims fast from the false dawn to sunset, and recite special evening prayers. The end of the holy month, twenty-nine or thirty days later, is marked by another new moon, the signal for people to stop fasting and to start feasting for the biggest festival, Eid-ul-Fitr.

Pari and Mrs Ali embraced and told each other, 'Roza Mubarak – Blessed Fasting!'

When Mr Ali came in, Pari turned to him. 'Ramzaan Mubarak, Chaacha. Are you going to fast too?'

Mrs Ali rolled her eyes. 'Your uncle, fast? You must be joking. I have to prepare breakfast and lunch for him while I am fasting. And he has passed on the same attitude to our son.'

Pari laughed. 'Where is Rehman? I haven't seen him in ages.'

'He has gone to a village called Mutyalapadu – something about a water project. He will be back in a few days. You know how Rehman is.'

Pari nodded. Mr Ali broke in, 'There is a saying in English: a rolling stone gathers no moss. I am afraid that applies precisely to our son. He has no stability.'

Mrs Ali said, 'He is an engineer and any time he wants, he can get a job. Don't always keep criticising him. He is doing good work.'

Pari raised her hands and laughed. 'Don't start the month of Ramzaan by arguing.' She said to Mr Ali, 'Chaachi is right. Don't worry about Rehman. Not everybody has to have a job and a flat, and worry about gas and electricity bills, you know. Allah has made a vast sky and all sorts of people can take shelter under it.'

Mrs Ali said, 'See, even a young woman has more wisdom

than you. Listen to what she is saying.' She turned to Pari. 'You tell him, Beti. He is willing to talk philosophy and ethics and all sorts of high ideals with his clients, but when it comes to his own son, he is blind.'

Mr Ali went back onto the verandah and Mrs Ali made for the kitchen. Pari shrugged and stayed where she was.

Mr Ali, as Rehman's father, of course had the right to criticise his son. But Pari didn't like anybody saying the smallest negative thing about Rehman – not even his own parents. She looked around her for a few minutes before she realised that there were no photos of Rehman anywhere. In fact, except for a photo of the Kaaba in Mecca, there were no pictures on the walls at all – not of Rehman, nor even of Mr and Mrs Ali. Strange that she hadn't noticed it before.

Now, she just wanted to plaster the walls with posters of Rehman ... It was his eyes, she thought, that are the most attractive part of him – dark, limpid pools that she could drown in. No, she decided, a moment later, his best feature was his slow, easy smile. Then she remembered his lean body that was deceptively muscular and her stomach performed a flip-flop. Warmth spread through her from head to toe and a million tiny drops of moisture appeared on her forehead – like dew on a mango leaf in winter.

The phone rang, interrupting her daydream. It was Piya, the wife of the dethroned heir to the post of the mosque's imam, calling to greet Mrs Ali on the start of the month of Ramzaan. The phone then didn't stop ringing as various friends and relatives called with news of the moon-sighting. Their local mosque and the Pension Line mosque both announced that the fasting would start the next day, but the Chengal Rao Pet mosque in the old town declared that, as far as they were concerned, they had not seen the moon and therefore the fasting would start the day after next.

Mrs Ali rang Faiz in her village to ask, 'Has the moon been sighted there?'

'No, Maami. The sky was cloudy and we couldn't see it. The men told our imam that the moon had been sighted in Vizag, but he said that doesn't count for him, so our fasting will start the day after tomorrow.'

'Every year, it is the same problem,' said Mrs Ali, laughing. 'If there are only two Muslims stuck in a desert, they'll still argue about when to start fasting.'

The alarm rang at four in the morning, and Mrs Ali got slowly out of bed. After brushing her hair and washing, she took out the dough she had kneaded the previous night and started rolling out the chapattis. Pari walked into the kitchen through the back door.

'Salaam A'laikum, Chaachi.'

'Wa'laikum Assalaam. Is Vasu sleeping?'

'Yes.' Pari and Vasu lived in a second-floor flat in the building next door.

'Chop the onions for the anda'khaaraz,' said Mrs Ali. Scrambled egg with onions and chillies were delicious, filling and, just as important, quick to make. They didn't have much time. 'That reminds me, something funny happened at Faiz's house.'

She recounted what had happened when the eggs had been cooked in the microwave.

'I hope it taught Azhar a lesson about being a show-off,' Mrs Ali said and laughed.

'Are they going to use the microwave?'

'I doubt it. They cleaned up the inside where all the eggs had made a mess – though the mess had penetrated through the mesh on one of the oven walls – and put it for display next to the television. I think it will just be shown off to any visitors who come to their house by warming cups of water.'

Between the two of them, the chapattis and the eggs were quickly prepared and they sat down to eat for the sahri – the pre-dawn meal that had to finish about one and a half hours before sunrise. After the meal, Mrs Ali took out the small card that Azhar had given her the previous night, showing the start and end times of the fast for each day of the month.

'Another five minutes to go,' she said. Pari poured them a glass of water each. Mrs Ali closed her eyes and said the neeyat. 'In the name of Allah, the merciful, the beneficent, I intend to keep fast this day of Ramzaan.' She picked up her glass and downed the contents. There would be no food nor drink, including water, until sunset. She thought about all those modern women who are always trying to lose weight. They should try the Ramzaan diet, she thought. Not only would they lose weight, but they would also get blessings – a double benefit.

Mrs Ali was lying in bed, relaxing in the cool, dark room with the curtains drawn and the door closed. It was only ten in the morning, but lunch had already been cooked for her husband and she was taking it easy. The first few days of fasting were the most difficult, until the body got used to it.

Her husband walked into the room and said, 'I am just going to the bank and the electricity man has come to install the new meter.'

She followed him to the verandah and sat in the wicker chair. Aruna saved her work, switched off the computer, shut the filing cabinet and moved to the end of the sofa closest to Mrs Ali. The meter reader switched off the electricity at the mains, then took out a long red screwdriver and a pair of cutting pliers covered with a rubber sleeve.

'Your name is Shyam, isn't it?' said Mrs Ali, after a couple of minutes.

'Yes, madam.' He bobbed his head and smiled with his really wide mouth.

'And this is what you do, is it? Go into people's homes and then report on them to the electricity board so you get the business of reconnecting them?'

'Me, madam? I—'

'If you are going to act in an underhanded way, at least don't lie about it. We are not fools, you know. You are lucky that it is Ramzaan and I don't want to speak harshly to anybody while I am fasting. But what you did was very sneaky.'

Shyam silently cut a metre-long length of electrical cable from a big blue roll.

'You saw a couple of pensioners in the house and you took advantage of them, didn't you?'

'No, madam.' Shyam cut a length from a red-coloured roll of cable to match the blue one. 'Power supplied to households is subsidised. The department loses a lot of money when people use electricity for commercial purposes.'

'So you are just helping the department out of the goodness

of your heart? Do I look like a priest with a flower tucked behind my right ear to believe everything I hear?' Her sarcasm was evident.

Shyam did not reply.

'How much are you charging us for putting in the meter?'

'Three thousand rupees, madam.'

'I am not going to pay more than two thousand rupees.'

'But Sir agreed—'

'You waited until he had spent a day and a half at the engineer's office and was desperate, didn't you? Don't you have a mother and father? Would you treat them as you have treated us? And I talked to the halwai, the sweet shop owner, on the ground floor of that building there,' she pointed across the road, 'and he said that he paid only two thousand rupees.'

'Prices have gone up, madam. I have to pay the linemen, the clerks and the engineers at the department. I also have to pay for all the material myself.'

'Two thousand rupees.'

'Madam, you are going back on your agreement. I even got the power restored within one hour. If I walk away from this job, you will not have electricity for days and days.'

'Elections are coming. People from different parties will be coming here asking for votes. I can talk to them and get you transferred away from this lucrative area to a faraway residential colony where you'll have none of these opportunities for extra income.'

'There is no need for such an aggressive attitude, madam. I am doing you a favour by sorting out your illegal connection. But two thousand rupees will put me out of pocket. Two thousand five hundred, madam.'

Mrs Ali shook her head. 'Two thousand.'

'You are not giving me a choice, madam. I have so many expenses. All right, two thousand two hundred, madam. Final offer.'

Mrs Ali sat silent for a moment and then nodded. 'All right, two thousand two hundred.'

Shyam went back to his work. Aruna smiled at Mrs Ali, discreetly pressing the tips of her right thumb and forefinger to show that she was impressed. Mrs Ali gave a small nod and looked out at the traffic on the road, satisfied with her morning's work.

A few minutes later, Shyam spoke again. 'My mother died of a snakebite when I was a small boy. And my father died when I was twelve. My older brother and sister-in-law brought me up. They looked after me like their own son, madam. I never lacked for anything. My older brother told me not to move to a city, madam. He said that people in the city are much more forceful than villagers.'

'What does your brother do?' asked Mrs Ali, turning her attention back to him.

'He is a lineman in Kotturu.'

'So electricity is your dynastic business,' said Mrs Ali.

'No, madam! Just my brother and me. In a village, the lineman is king. No, he's more than a king; he's God, madam – not just one but every god. He is Indra, the king of the gods, whose weapon is lightning, for what is lightning but electricity? He is the Yahweh of the Christians. The lineman says let there be light, and the lights come on. He is Varuna, the water god. The lineman waves his wrench and sweet water flows from pumpsets onto the fields.'

Shyam turned to look at Mrs Ali and she nodded, mollified. He went back to his work, using pliers to twist the end of a cable round a copper terminal.

'If my brother has to climb an electricity pole for a repair, the villagers pay him one hundred rupees. If there is a wedding in any house, he sets up a direct connection from the distribution lines, so they can have full lighting for the whole night without it being charged to their meter. The householder pays him two hundred and fifty rupees for this service. We grew up in a palm-thatched hut with a floor lined with cow dung, but now my brother has a pukka cement house on two floors, a television and a stereo, and he runs a motorcycle and has a mobile phone. My brother not only brought me up, but he made my life also, madam. He paid thousands of rupees in bribes to get me a job with the electricity board. Unfortunately, I didn't have the qualifications to become a lineman like him. So I became a meter reader. My brother and my sister-in-law are my true mother and father and I want to prove to them that their efforts in raising me have not been wasted.'

Mrs Ali nodded. She appreciated Shyam's motivation and had no problem with it – so long as her own household was not affected.

Two buses went past, one behind the other, so overcrowded that passengers were standing at the doors, holding on tightly with just one foot on the stairwell.

Shyam said, 'This road has become very busy, madam. Maybe that's why they are going to widen it.'

'Excuse me, what did you say?' said Mrs Ali.

'I was putting in a new fuse box at the municipal corporator's house yesterday and they were discussing it there. They are going to widen this road from the highway to the culvert by the Muslim graveyard.'

'But it is already eighty feet wide,' said Mrs Ali.

'There was talk of making it one hundred and twenty feet wide, madam.'

'What?'

She was shocked. An additional forty feet! If they took it equally from both sides, as was likely, that would be twenty feet from her land. A rock settled in her heart. The guava tree, the hibiscus, the henna, the curry leaf plants, the well that supplied their water; all would be gone. But their front yard was only twelve feet deep, which meant that most of this verandah would be gone too! The thought of workers using iron crowbars to break down the house was horrible. And where would her husband run his marriage bureau?

'How sure are you about the news?' said Aruna. 'Maybe you misunderstood what you heard.'

'Oh no, madam. I am absolutely certain. They had blueprints and everything.'

Aruna made a quick visit to the temple after she finished work. After praying to the Lord, she came out into the temple yard. If what Shyam, the meter reader, had said was true, the temple would be in trouble too. This yard and part of the platform would be lost, and the whole area so diminished that its capacity would be a fraction of what it was currently. I shouldn't spread rumours, she thought, looking at the people praying. I'd better keep quiet until the news is official.

Seeing her friend Gita laying out a grid of dots with rice

flour on the swept and washed floor on one side of the yard, she walked up to her. 'How come you are drawing muggu here?'

Gita looked up and smiled at Aruna. 'I do this regularly now.'

Gita started joining up the dots of flour in intricate patterns.

As Aruna watched, a flower took shape. 'That's lovely,' she said. 'Shall I help you?'

Like all girls, Aruna knew how to draw muggu and had done so regularly as she grew up.

'No, Akka! It'll take me just a few minutes.'

'How is Srinu? How are you both coping with city life?'

'Srinu is very happy with the way the business is shaping up. And by helping here, I have become friends with many people as well.'

A bearded man in saffron clothes walked up to them. Aruna felt uneasy when she recognised him as the temple official who had been told by Vasu that his mother was Muslim, but she greeted him respectfully. He acknowledged her with a dip of his head.

Gita greeted him by name. 'Namaskaaram, Narayana-gaaru.'

Narayana said to Gita, 'Can you come tomorrow as well? I need food prepared for some important visitors to the temple and I was wondering whether you could help.'

'Of course, sir. I'd be delighted to assist.'

Narayana turned to Aruna. 'Why didn't you tell me that you are Somayajulu's daughter when I saw you before?'

'I didn't think you would know my father, sir.'

'I've known your father for many years. Tell him that Narayana was asking after him. He doesn't come to our temple any more. But looking at your clothes and jewellery, I can see that he has married off his daughter into a wealthy house. Why would he want to come to our humble temple?'

Aruna was embarrassed. 'I can assure you, sir, that my father has not changed—'

'Your father has changed. Otherwise, he would not have allowed you to work, let alone in a Muslim household.'

Aruna flushed. 'It was our economic circumstances that compelled me to start working,' she said. 'There is no sin in that. And my father satisfied himself that Sir and Madam are good people, before letting me go there. That was the important thing for him, not whether they were Hindus or Muslims. And my in-laws think so too, which is why they have allowed me to continue to work there after my marriage.'

'The world has come to such a pass that young women can answer back to their elders in a temple,' he said.

Aruna bit her tongue and refrained from replying because that would have just validated his argument.

'Where is the boy who came with you last time? You should have brought him to the temple as well.'

'He was doing his homework,' she replied.

'I bet he wouldn't be doing his homework if it was time to go the mosque. The biggest problem we have in our community is not Muslims or Christians. It is we Hindus ourselves who are our worst enemies.' He turned on his heel and walked away before Aruna could reply.

'I'm sorry,' said Gita in a small voice.

Aruna frowned. 'You don't have to apologise for him.'

'He has very strong feelings about Hindus and their rights. But he is a good man – a strong leader, a very inspiring talker and he is totally dedicated to this temple.'

'He may be strong and committed to the temple but, with views like that, I wouldn't call him good. You know Mr and Mrs Ali and their son, Rehman. How can anyone imply that they are somehow unworthy just because of their religion?'

'That is true . . . ' said Gita slowly.

'People are good or bad by their thoughts and deeds, not by their faith.'

Working with Mr Ali had clearly rubbed off on Aruna and she was able to able to articulate philosophy in a way that she wouldn't have been able to a year before.

Mrs Ali, Pari and Vasu travelled to Azhar's house in a three-wheeled auto-rickshaw. They would normally have walked, but it was half an hour before sunset and the ladies were still fasting. Azhar had arranged an iftar party – a get-together for breaking the fast.

Soon Mrs Ali was in the kitchen, helping Azhar's wife roll out the dough to make the rotis. Wonderful smells from the lamb biryani, steaming quietly in a covered dish with a weight on top, filled the kitchen and made Pari's mouth water. Her empty stomach contracted painfully and she looked discreetly at her watch. Another twenty minutes to go. More than the food, it was the lack of water that troubled her. The hot air sucked moisture out of a body like a vice squeezing a sponge.

I ate a very nice meal before dawn and I worked today in an air-conditioned office, she thought. There are men and women out there who have nothing to begin their fast with but a grain of salt and a tumbler of water, and they then carry out heavy manual labour out of doors all day long. Compared to them, I have it easy, she thought, as she arranged dates and almonds on a platter.

Azhar came into the kitchen. 'Just fifteen minutes to go. The imam will be here at any moment.'

His wife said, 'Everything is ready, don't worry.' She turned to Mrs Ali. 'Bhaabhi, help me take the biryani out into a serving dish.'

'The imam always breaks his fast in the mosque. He is doing us a great honour by coming to our house today. Pyare Lal, the fan-shop owner, asked him but the imam said no. Siddiqui, the granite seller, asked him too. But the imam is coming here instead.'

'Sharif was telling me a story about the saint who is buried in the dargah in Faiz's village,' Mrs Ali said.

Azhar and his wife looked at her with interest. They still missed the granddaughter whom they had raised.

'Apparently, the sufi fasted throughout the year, not just during Ramzaan. He used to eat a couple of dates before dawn and his only meal was in the evening after sunset. His servant used to stand outside the house and invite any passersby to come in and break their fast with his master. The holy man would not eat unless he had at least one guest.'

'A great man . . . ' said Azhar.

Pari wondered why Muslims were so obsessed with feeding others. Food is extremely important to us, she thought, far beyond its value as fuel for the body. Inviting others, sharing food and water, giving grand feasts: is it because of our religion's origins in a harsh desert?

They took the platters of food into the living room, where the floor was covered with mats and sheets. The space had been divided into two with the help of a sari as a makeshift curtain down the middle. Mrs Ali was surprised and looked questioningly at her brother. They didn't practise purdah in their family, separating the men and women. He shrugged uncomfortably.

'The imam-saab insisted. He said that he could not break his fast in mixed company.'

The food was divided into two portions – one for the men and one for the women.

'Is Bhaijaan definitely not coming?' Azhar asked.

'No,' said Mrs Ali. Her husband did not feel comfortable attending an iftar party when he had not fasted during the day.

'Probably for the best,' said Azhar. 'The imam-saab would not have been happy.'

Vasu came running in from the front yard. 'The guests have come,' he announced.

The ladies quickly arranged the platters of food and retreated behind the curtain. Azhar and Vasu greeted the imam and three other elders from the mosque. Mrs Ali had her first look at the new imam. She had known Haji Saab, the old imam, quite well. He used to come to her home once a month to collect their mosque subscription, and stay for a tea and a chat. She knew his family – his wife, daughter and nephew too. The daughter, Jahannara, had been married to a good but poor motorcycle mechanic. A few years after the wedding, the son of an old friend of Haji Saab had helped the son-in-law to go to Saudi Arabia on a contract. Jahannara, who by now had a baby and was pregnant again, had shed many tears at being separated from her husband. The son-in-law had spent three years in Saudi Arabia and had come back, not only having done the Haj pilgrimage to Mecca, but also with enough savings to buy a small house and set up a motor-cycle repair shop. Over the years, the business had grown and they now lived very comfortably. Everyone said, and Mrs Ali agreed, that their story was a reflection of the pious and gentle life led by Haji Saab. It showed that Allah had not forsaken this world and that goodness was still rewarded in this world.

The new imam was very young. That's what her husband had said after his visit to the mosque and she now saw what he meant. In certain professions, such as the priesthood and medicine, there should be only mature people, she thought. It felt wrong to see a man in his twenties occupying such a post.

As there was not much time left before the moment came to break the fast, they all sat down quickly on the sheets around the food and drink.

'Fasting during the holy month of Ramzaan is one of the pillars of Islam,' said the imam. His voice had the timbre of youth but carried well. 'It was during the month of Ramadaan that the Qur'an was first revealed to the Prophet, peace be upon him.' He turned to Vasu, to ask, 'Do you know how to read and write?'

Pari caught her breath. Vasu knew Telugu, the language of the local Hindus, but did not know how to speak Urdu, the language of the Muslims. But to her surprise and relief, Vasu nodded. He had obviously been picking up more of the language by being around them than she thought.

'Mohammed, peace be upon him, was unlettered. The revelation came to him as burning letters in the sky and he heard a voice booming all around him that said, "Read!" He was frightened. "I don't know how to read," he said. "Read!" came the voice again.'

An alarm went off loudly. Azhar shut it off and turned to the imam. 'Sorry,' he said, 'but it is time to break the fast.' He held out the platter of dates and men took one each. On the other side of the curtain, the women did the same.

The young imam recited the dua. 'O Allah! I fasted for You and I put my trust in You and I break my fast with Your sustenance.'

Teeth tore through the brown parchment-thin skin of the dates and sank into the luscious flesh, releasing an intense sugary rush onto hungry tongues. Nothing tastes better than that first bite after a fast.

After the dates came cooling sherbet, followed by the biryani and the chicken curry. As usual at an iftar party, an enormous amount of food had been made, on the assumption that people would be hungry, but people's stomachs are surprisingly easily sated after the day's fast. Mrs Ali knew what Azhar and his wife would be using to break their fasts for the next few days.

'What's your name?' the imam asked Vasu.

'Vasu.' The namesake of the Preserver God of the Hindus.

'But that's . . . ' The imam turned accusing eyes on Azhar. 'Have I just broken my fast with an unbeliever?'

Mrs Ali could see her brother squirming. Finally, he said, 'He is my niece's adopted son. We were talking—'

'Looking after an orphan is the most virtuous thing a

Muslim can do. The Prophet said, "I and the guardian of an orphan will be like this in the garden of Paradise," and he raised his index and middle fingers held together.' The imam paused for a moment, then continued, 'It is not enough to look after the material needs of children. Parents are also responsible for their children's spiritual well-being. They must be taught the true path and given guidance in the way of our religion.'

'No,' said Pari, loudly. Before Mrs Ali could stop her, she brushed the curtain aside, went over to the men's area and hugged Vasu. 'Vasu is my son. But I will not take advantage of that to make him forget his parents' religion and raise him as a Muslim.'

The imam recoiled at the sight of a woman among the men. Pari turned on him. 'You may be a Hafiz, one who knows the Qur'an by heart, but you are still a young man who has much to learn about life. This is not Saudi Arabia where women have to hide away from men and Islam is the only religion around. We live in Hindustan and our well-being is promoted by remembering that fact.'

The imam stood up and his companions followed suit. 'The entire community has a responsibility towards individuals who stray. Your son will be brought up as a Muslim or you and your family will be thrown out of the mosque.' His gaze slid past Mrs Ali and settled on Azhar. 'The entire family,' he repeated and turned on his heel.

CHAPTER SEVEN

The big house in the posh suburb of Daspalla Hills was in uproar. In the large living room, servants rushed around, some rearranging furniture, others changing curtains, and a couple of men wiping the dust off the ceiling-fan blades. Smells and sounds of snacks being fried came from the kitchen and in the centre of it all, the old man sat still on a divan, holding a walking stick. Joining Mr Ali's marriage bureau had paid off and today a boy's family was coming to see Mr Koteshwar Reddy's granddaughter.

Mr Reddy's nephew, Bobbili, walked into the room and shouted at the men shifting a large sofa, 'Careful! Don't mark the floor.'

'Yes, sir.' the men nodded and made an effort to lift the sofa rather than just slide it along the marble tiles.

'Well?' said Mr Reddy when Bobbili stood in front of him.

Bobbili nodded. 'Sukumar is ready, sir. It took a bit of arm-twisting, but I managed it finally. I've also asked Venkatesh to stay with him and make sure that he doesn't find another bottle somehow.'

'You and your son are both so good for my house,' said Mr Reddy. He was determined that his son would not spoil the occasion this time.

Bobbili shrugged. 'We are just doing our duty, Uncle.' Seeing where the sofa had been moved to, he rushed up to the men shifting it. 'Orey, I think moths have eaten your brains. How can you have the sofa touching the cupboard? That's an antique piece inlaid with ivory. You can't get such a thing any more for love or money. Move the sofa to that side, carefully now.'

Bobbili came back to the old man and said, 'Don't worry, Uncle. We'll have everything shipshape before the guests arrive.'

'I am not worried. I know you will sort out all the problems.'

Mr Reddy sighed, thinking, if my son had a tenth of the sense that my nephew shows, I would have been a happy man. The women of the family never seemed to have much luck. His wife had died ten years ago, after a long life marked by much ill health. His sister had died five, no, six years ago now, after much unhappiness. Materially, she had never lacked for anything in his house, but she had become a widow as a young woman and was abandoned by her husband's family, cheated of the share of inheritance she should have received from her in-laws. But her son, Bobbili, had grown up to be a responsible person and her grandson, Venkat, was a smart young man, going to college, even if his marks were too low and his tastes a bit too rich.

If any woman could be said to have everything going for her, it should be his granddaughter, Sujatha. Good looks, charm, manners, intelligence, education: name the quality and she had it. But her family's curse seemed to have touched her too. Four – four! – marriage proposals had broken down at the last stage when he thought everything had been settled. One, he could understand, two he could explain, but four was ridiculous. He had sent Bobbili to talk to one of the parties after they had broken off the match. Did they want more money as dowry? Was it because Sujatha was studying for her MA? That was just something to pass the time and it could be stopped if necessary. Bobbili had come back with the news that they didn't want to take Sujatha because her father was an alcoholic. That had left Mr Reddy incandescent for weeks. Not only had his son destroyed his own life, but he was also casting a shadow on the next generation.

Mr Reddy wiggled his finger and a servant came running over. 'Ask the younger master to come down. I want to talk to him.'

Sukumar walked into the room. His once-sharp features had blurred like an out-of-focus picture from all the alcohol that he had consumed over the years. Mr Reddy tapped his walking stick on the floor.

'You will behave yourself,' he said to his son. 'No drinking for the rest of the day. No tantrums, no talking nonsense; you will sit quietly on that sofa like a mannequin in a shop window, when the guests come. You will not say a single word to jeopardise the viewing. Understand?'

'I don't think—'

'I don't care what you think. I don't want you to think.'

Sukumar shuffled his feet and muttered something indistinct. Mr Reddy turned to the young man hovering behind

Sukumar. 'Venkat, watch your uncle like a hawk. Don't let him give you the slip.'

'Of course, Thaatha. No problem.'

Mr Reddy turned to his son. 'All this wealth is going into a trust that will be controlled by your daughter. Your monthly stipend has to be released by her. If you cause any trouble for her now, think of the trouble she can cause you later.'

Sukumar sat on the sofa indicated by his father.

Mr Reddy shook his head. What had he done to deserve this? The family curse on women had struck Sujatha very early. Her mother had died giving birth to her. Would his daughter-in-law have survived if the childbirth had taken place in a hospital rather than at home, as he had insisted? He didn't think so. Everybody's lifeline was written at birth and when it is time for Lord Yama to collect your soul, no hospital or doctor can stop the God of Death. Sukumar had refused to talk to him or even to look at Sujatha's face for months. Only slowly did he become reconciled with the daughter who had caused the death of his wife. Sukumar had always had grandiose plans to make money, and now there was no one to control him. He refused to listen to Mr Reddy and somewhere along the line, as plan after plan failed, he started drinking.

Mr Reddy had tried hard to keep his son away from alcohol but, with a craftiness that he did not show in his business dealings, Sukumar always managed to lay his hands on a bottle or three. Mr Reddy glanced at his son and felt disgust at the sight of his shiny, bulbous nose and florid cheeks.

Mr Reddy turned to Venkat, who was standing behind Sukumar. 'Ask if Sujatha is ready.'

'Yes, Thaatha.' The young man smiled happily and left the room.

Six-thirty, the time for the guests to arrive, had come and gone but nobody had made an appearance.

'Hey, Bobbili, phone them and find out what's happening,' said Mr Reddy, tapping his walking stick on the ground in a staccato manner.

'It's not yet seven, sir. They'll be here soon. Let's not be seen to be hassling them.'

'Hmm ... Call up Mr Ali and ask him to find out. As the middleman who introduced us, he can phone them.'

Venkat came back into the living room. 'Sujatha is asking what's going on, Thaatha.'

'If I knew, I would tell,' said Mr Reddy, grumbling. 'These people have no sense of time. What kind of match will they make?'

'A good one, sir,' said Bobbili. 'You know how it is when trying to get everybody out of the house for occasions like this. Things always take longer than you expect.' He turned to his son. 'Orey, Venkat. Go and keep Sujatha company. It must be pretty boring for her to sit in her room alone.'

'Of course, Naanna.' Venkat jumped up and headed towards Sujatha's room.

It was almost seven-thirty and even Bobbili was getting anxious. At last the servant he had posted at the end of the street as a lookout came in with the news that a car had come.

Bobbili rushed out to greet the guests. 'Namaste, sir. Namaste, madam. How are you, young man?'

Seven people had turned up, in two cars – the second one had taken a slightly different route and arrived a few minutes later. Two parents, one uncle, one aunt, one sister, one cousin and, of course, one bridegroom.

Ajay, the bridegroom, was twenty-seven; his birth star was Mrigasira in Taurus, which had been checked by a priest and found compatible for happiness with Sujatha's Aswini, the Gemini twins. Ajay had studied in a 'donation' college – where one had to pay a fee to get a seat – which was a black mark against him, but he had done well afterwards. He worked for a company in Hyderabad called Oracle, which, as Bobbili had found out, was one of the biggest companies in the world and made something called databases. Neither Mr Reddy nor Bobbili understood what that was, but both Venkat and Sujatha had assured them that it was a well-known firm and the job was good. Ajay earned a salary of fifty thousand rupees a month, a fact that the elders understood and which impressed them. Beyond the salary itself, Ajay's family, like Mr Reddy's, were landlords and between them, the young couple would never lack for money.

After they were all seated and snacks had been served, Sujatha walked in and all eyes turned to her, making her self-conscious. She was wearing an aubergine-coloured sari with a pale-pink border that set off her fair complexion. A discreet brooch, in the shape of a butterfly with shimmering purple wings, pinned the edge of her sari to her blouse. Her hair was plaited with a matching purple ribbon and she wore thin, oversized gold earrings that emphasised her round face and complemented a plain gold chain round her neck. The final touch: pale-pink nail polish – she had gone for a facial, manicure and pedicure the day before at the Blue Heaven beauty parlour – made her look beautiful and elegant. Bobbili glanced quickly at Ajay and he was pretty sure that the young man was of the same opinion. Venkat was escorting Sujatha and Bobbili signalled discreetly to his son to come away.

Sujatha sat down next to her grandfather, took a covert peek at Ajay and was satisfied that he looked just like his photograph. He faintly resembled a Telugu film star – with wide shoulders, fair skin, a long nose that was neither broad nor thin, a strong chin, beautiful eyes and a rumpled over-the-ear hairstyle. His piercing gaze met hers and she glanced away, flustered. Her eyes fell on her cousin Venkat and when he smiled at her encouragingly her heart slowed down. She had grown disillusioned with the whole marriage-viewing rigmarole after the rejections, but this time was different – she could feel it. She twisted the tassel on the corner of her sari in the fingers of her right hand and glanced at Ajay again, immediately being captured in the depths of his eyes. Yet she felt that there was no lechery in them, probably because of his shy but confident smile.

Ajay glanced at his mother and Sujatha suddenly realised that her prospective mother-in-law was asking her a question. She shook her head. 'Sorry, Auntie. What did you say?'

'How are your studies going, child?'

'All right, Auntie. I am actually taking the course for the sake of keeping busy. I would like to do something practical, but Vizag is such a small city that it is difficult here.'

'I am not sure—' began Ajay's father.

'What would you like to do?' said Ajay, interrupting his father.

Sujatha seemed confused, her gaze flicking from father to son, not knowing whom to answer. Ajay raised his hand. 'Sorry, Naanna,' he said to his father. 'You were saying . . . '

'No, no,' said his father. 'I was just going to say that you don't need to do anything practical, but obviously it is up to the two of you. Whatever makes you happy is fine by us.'

Sujatha blushed. 'I love designing jewellery. I want to do a course to learn more about it.'

'That's a very good hobby. You could even turn it into a business if you wanted to,' said Ajay. 'I am sure that a bigger city like Hyderabad will be better than Vizag for that kind of thing.'

Sujatha smiled. 'Thanks!' she said.

Ajay's father asked Sujatha's father a question about their fields and how many bags of rice they got per acre. Sujatha's grandfather answered quickly before his son could say a word.

The conversation moved on to the dowry. 'Everything I have, I've put in a trust in Sujatha's name. She will inherit everything after I am gone,' Mr Reddy said.

Ajay's parents glanced at Mr Reddy's son, Sukumar. 'May you have a long life,' said Ajay's father. 'Why talk about such gloomy matters at an auspicious time like this?'

'But I will not allow my granddaughter to leave my house with nothing. I will give her a dowry of one crore and I will buy a flat for the couple in any part of Hyderabad that they choose. Of course, I will furnish the flat appropriately and she will bring all her jewellery with her.'

A dowry of ten million rupees was a handsome one indeed, and Ajay's family were cultured enough to recognise that and not quibble for more.

'Is any of that jewellery designed by you?' asked Ajay.

Sujatha smiled. 'No, Thaatha is talking about traditional gold stuff like the nav-lakha haar and vaddaanam.' She spoke of a diamond necklace supposedly worth nine lakhs of rupees and a lady's cummerbund made of gold.

'Lucky for him that you are slim,' said Ajay and everybody laughed.

'Uncle, is it OK if I have a chat with Sujatha?' asked Ajay.

Mr Reddy looked startled and then frowned. Her father, Sukumar spoke for the first time since the guests had arrived. 'I don't see a problem with that,' he said. 'Sujatha, why don't you show the young man the garden?'

She glanced at her grandfather for confirmation and when he didn't object – though he didn't quite agree – she stood up. Ajay rose as well and they walked out into the garden by the side of the house.

Bobbili turned to his son and nodded towards the young couple. 'Go with them,' he said, then added softly, 'but don't breathe down their necks.'

Venkat gave him a tight smile and padded out.

After the guests had left, Bobbili called up one of the bride-groom's uncles who had accompanied Ajay and through whom he had negotiated all the salient points before the actual viewing. He listened for a few moments, then hung up and turned to the rest of the family, beaming. 'They like everything they've seen. Very positive.' He turned to Sujatha. 'What about you, daughter? What do you say?'

'I like the match too,' she said, blushing.

'So the tour of the garden went well,' he said, his eyes twinkling.

'Yes,' muttered Sujatha, blushing even more.

'Fantastic.' He turned to Sujatha's grandfather. 'Congrats,' he said. 'We have good news.'

Mr Reddy smiled, but Sukumar said, 'We've been here before, so let's not jump ahead of ourselves and raise our hopes too much. That would be like the proverbial man who is still single but daydreams of naming his son Somalingam when his non-existent wife finally becomes pregnant and has a baby.'

Mr Reddy turned on his son. 'Don't open your mouth if all you can speak are inauspicious words,' he said.

'Yeah, shut me up. What else can you do?' he said.

Sujatha said, 'Please don't argue for my sake.'

Bobbili said, 'Our daughter is right. We shouldn't fight. Sukumar is also right. We've been disappointed before. But this time I do feel it is different. I've never been optimistic. The boy is great, the family is perfect – respectable and so nice. They didn't even object when Sujatha said she wanted to do a jewellery-making course. They are very good people.'

Sujatha's dreams that night were full of a wide-shouldered young man called Ajay with romantic eyes and a nice line in banter.

In another part of town, Mrs Ali and Pari were finishing preparing dinner. Most of the dishes had already been cooked, including tomato khatta – chopped tomatoes sautéed to a gravy with onions, chillies and mustard seeds; curried fresh whitebait – which Mrs Ali had made her husband get from the fishing harbour; and mutton-fry. The rice had been cooked too and they were just finishing off the rotis, Pari flattening the dough with a rolling pin and Mrs Ali cooking them on the hot iron griddle.

Pari suddenly realised that they were cooking all these dishes not just for breaking their fast but because Rehman was coming home today. Her lips tightened at the thought.

'Are you OK?' asked Mrs Ali.

Pari brushed a strand of hair away from her eyes with the back of her hand and nodded, glancing at her watch. Less than half an hour to go for breaking the fast. She was thirsty and the smell of all the food made her mouth water, but she nodded. 'When is Rehman coming?' she asked, keeping her voice as casual as she could.

'He said he'd be here before—' began Mrs Ali and was interrupted by Vasu running in.

'Rehman-uncle is here,' he shouted, holding up a toy car in one hand. 'Look what he got for me.'

Pari's heart lurched though she was careful to keep her expression completely calm.

A tall, young man with five-day-old stubble, wearing crumpled clothes that seemed too loose for his lanky frame, walked into the kitchen and smiled at the two ladies. 'Salaam, Ammi. Salaam, Pari. How is the fast going?'

Mrs Ali looked as if a hundred-watt bulb had lit up behind her. 'Wash your hands and feet quickly. We are breaking the fast soon.' They were not a very demonstrative family.

Pari couldn't stop smiling too. She said, 'Hello, stranger. Long time no see.'

Despite his unkempt attire and aversion to regular shaving, Rehman's intense eyes, high cheekbones and rich voice made Pari go weak at the knees. She gave the roti she was rolling an extra-hard shove and it tore where the pressure made it particularly thin. Luckily, nobody noticed and Pari quickly gathered up the dough back into a ball and set about rolling it again.

Mrs Ali said to him, 'Have you been eating anything in the village? You look starved.'

The food was soon transferred to the table and after checking that the sun had truly set, Mrs Ali and Pari broke their fast. Rehman, Mr Ali and Vasu joined them for dinner.

'Did you finish the work in that village?' Mr Ali asked his son.

Rehman was chewing a piece of roti. 'Sorry,' he said, swallowing hard. 'I just went to have a look around. They are doing some really impressive work and they offered me a job, so I accepted.'

'Congratulations!' said Mrs Ali and Pari.

'What's the pay?' asked Mr Ali.

'Not much,' conceded Rehman. 'And they needed a two-year commitment to which I agreed.'

'What are the hours?'

'There are no hours as such. I can keep coming back to Vizag every so often, but while I am in the village, I'll be working all hours.'

'Let me get this straight,' said Mr Ali, looking at his son. 'The pay is measly, you have to stay in a village and work long hours, and you have to sign up for a minimum of two years. Have I missed anything?'

Rehman grinned. 'Yes. After two years, the project will end or be taken over by the government. Either way, I'll be out of a job.'

'Why don't you go back to that builder you used to work for and ask him if he'll take you back?'

'Who? Mr Bhargav?' Rehman shook his head. 'He doesn't need an engineer. He just wants somebody who can push the papers through the municipal planning committees by hook or by crook. That's not a real job.'

'The money he paid was real enough.'

Rehman shrugged. 'I want to do this, Abba. Water management is very important for our country. Two thirds of all borewells in the world have been dug in India. We just poke holes into the ground and draw up the water. It is not sustainable. Surface water is the same. Many of our rivers have stopped flowing all the way to the sea ... ' He fell silent and went back to his food, as if he had said too much.

Mr Ali shook his head. He did not deny that water was an important problem, but why did his son have to fight the battles? One man couldn't change anything. Idealism was all well and good, but for that one needed a full stomach not just today but the confidence that it would be full tomorrow also. From the application forms that he received in the marriage bureau, he saw that young men of Rehman's age were earning great sums of money and building wonderful careers with national and international companies. Now that India's economy had opened up, the youth of today had opportunities that men of his generation could not even have dreamed about. But not his son. He looked around the table and knew the women would not support him, so he kept quiet.

A couple of minutes later, Pari turned to her son. 'Vasu, don't wolf down your food. Eat slowly.'

The boy nodded and popped the next mouthful of rice

into his mouth while still chewing his previous mouthful. Pari wagged her finger. 'That's exactly what I was talking about. Finish one morsel before starting the next one.'

'Yes, yes,' said Vasu, stuffing his mouth again with rice and whitebait curry.

Pari rolled her eyes and Rehman laughed. 'Don't!' said Pari. 'I am trying to teach him good manners and you are not helping.'

'Can I fast with you and Daadi?' Vasu asked Pari.

'No, you are too young,' said Pari firmly.

'A boy in my class says he fasts on Sundays,' said Vasu.

'Well, I don't think you should fast,' said Pari.

'Just on Sundays,' said Vasu.

'No!'

'Why not?'

'Because I say so.'

'That's your answer for everything. You don't let me do anything,' Vasu said, his voice rising.

When Pari looked miserable, Rehman said, 'That's no way to talk to your mother, young man. Apologise now.'

Vasu fixed his eyes on his plate, concentrating on his food. Rehman waited for a moment and then said, 'I must be going deaf. I didn't hear an apology.'

'Sorry,' mumbled Vasu.

After dinner, Pari and Rehman were left alone when Mr Ali went to his office on the verandah, Vasu made for the television and Mrs Ali slipped out to the front yard to watch the world go by.

'Thanks for your help with Vasu,' said Pari.

Rehman shrugged.

Pari felt flustered by his slow smile. A few months ago, a neighbour had seen them together on the terrace of the house and had spread rumours that they were lovers. Since then, they had been careful not to spend time together on their own. The ironic thing for Pari was that she really was in love with Rehman. But Rehman's parents had been good to her and they had been – and still were – a great support after she had been widowed and lost her father. Pari did not want them to feel that she was like a cuckoo's hatchling, who had taken advantage of their goodness and somehow trapped their son in an unsuitable marriage.

'I thought you were going to say something more when your father asked you about the job but you stopped yourself. What was it?'

'I can't keep anything from you, can I?' he said and grinned. 'Guess who I met on the train coming back?'

Pari thought for a moment and shook her head.

'Usha,' he said.

Her heart lurched. His ex. Did he really have to smile so much when he said her name? Usha's parents had found out about their engagement and made a condition that, if he wanted to marry their daughter, Rehman could not go on being a social activist fighting for the rights of poor farmers. He had to get a job, and buy a car and a flat. Rehman had agreed. All had seemed to go well for a while, but then, Usha had broken it off, telling Rehman that she loved him too much to change him.

Rehman had been plunged into depression and Pari had supported him in those dark days. He had recovered slowly and seemed to be forgetting his ex-fiancée. Until now.

'That's nice,' Pari said slowly, her expression sweet enough to cause problems for diabetics. 'What is she doing now?'

'She is working on a story about how the various political parties are deploying their cadres for the election.'

'Hmm,' said Pari. That seemed like an interesting, if not earth-shaking, story to follow up. A sudden intuition struck her and she looked at him more fully in the face. 'There's more, isn't there?'

'I agreed to help her.'

'Agreed . . . Help . . . How exactly?'

Rehman shrugged. 'Nothing serious.'

'How will you help?'

'Time to watch the news on the television,' he said, standing up.

'Rehma-a-a-an . . . Shall I call your mother into the room?'

He drew back in mock-fear. 'Oooh, I am scared. I think you are spending too much time with Vasu,' he said and laughed.

'I am serious,' she said. 'How exactly are you helping Usha?'

'Well . . . Just for a few days before I go back to the village.'

'Rehman!' Pari stamped her foot in frustration. 'Stop evading and just tell me.'

'You know the HUT Party, right?'

'The Hindutva Universal Truth Party? They are a religious organisation. What have they got to do with elections?'

'Usha has found out that they are training cadres of volunteers and sending them out to canvass for Hindu right-wing nationalist candidates.'

'How does that—'

'I am going to join them. Their next training camp starts tomorrow.'

Pari frowned. 'But you are not a—'

'Hindu?' Rehman shrugged. 'None of the volunteers are talking and in her report Usha wants to include a first-hand account of the training.'

'Won't it be dangerous? What if they find out that you are a Muslim? They'll probably beat you up. Or worse.'

Rehman waved dismissively. 'I am just going to attend the training camp. I am not going to be actually campaigning for fascist candidates.'

'It's too dangerous. Usha shouldn't have asked you to do it.'

'She didn't ask me. I offered to do it when I found out about her difficulties in getting a first-hand report.'

'And she accepted your offer?'

'She's a journalist and for her the story always comes first. But if she'd thought there would be real danger, she would have stopped me.'

Pari shook her head. You are a fool, she thought.

CHAPTER EIGHT

Pari had been as surprised as anybody else when she had received, the previous year, a proposal from an aristocratic family. She was a widow, an orphan of unknown parentage and also the mother of an adopted eight-year-old boy. But her fair complexion and long nose had trumped all those disadvantages. Her fiancé, Dilawar – handsome, considerate and well paid – worked as an executive in a multinational company in Mumbai. He was also gay, hiding his sexual leanings from his family and, indeed, everybody else in Vizag. He even had a secret boyfriend in Mumbai. Dilawar had finally come clean and broken off the engagement. Pari was quite sure that Dilawar's mother had always been aware that her son was not straight, but had seen it as a temporary weakness that would be 'cured' by getting him married to an attractive woman.

Despite their history, Pari and Dilawar remained friends and kept in regular touch. He was more emotionally attuned than most men that Pari knew – not that she actually knew that many – and he had figured out how Pari felt about Rehman.

'Have you told Rehman yet?' he asked that evening on the phone.

Vasu had gone to bed and Pari was relaxing on the sofa in the living room of her flat, sitting in a corner with her feet tucked up under her and a cup of tea on the table beside her. 'Told him what?'

'That you love him, silly.'

'No, not yet,' she said.

'What are you waiting for? Go on, tell him.'

'The tangerine curtains you suggested go well with the sofa cushions,' she said.

'I told you they would,' he said. 'But don't change the topic.'

'He came back just yesterday. And on the way he met Usha and he has offered to help her get material for a report she is working on.'

Dilawar went silent for a moment. 'You are miserable,' he said finally.

'No. Yes … Oh, Dee, I don't know what to think. He was so depressed when she broke off the engagement last time, but she may not end the relationship a second time. Maybe he'll be happier with her, and shouldn't I try to make him as happy as possible?'

'Rubbish,' he said, his voice reaching strongly across the two-thousand-mile expanse of India from Mumbai on the west coast to Vizag on the east. 'I tell you that he loves you too.'

Pari shook her head and then realised that Dilawar couldn't see her. 'No,' she said. 'He is still in love with Usha.'

'You are a foolish woman, but I suppose you've got to do it in your own time. How is Vasu?'

'He is good. He got ninety-five per cent in his last maths exam.'

'That's great.'

'Don't say that. I was telling him that he needs to work harder and get a hundred per cent next time.'

Laughter came down the wires. 'You have turned into a typical Indian mother. Ninety-five per cent is not good enough. It has to be one hundred per cent. And when he gets one hundred per cent, you will tell him to aim for something more – maybe one hundred and ten per cent if they'll give such a mark.'

'You don't understand, Dee.'

'I do understand,' he said. 'My mother used to be after me every day with the same refrain – study, study. Give the poor boy a chance to be a child. Let him enjoy life. There will be enough problems for him to face when he grows up.'

'If he doesn't study and do well, I'll put him on a train and send him to you. They say that anybody can make a living somehow or other in Mumbai.'

Dilawar laughed. 'Of course, he can come over to Dilawar-Uncle's house at any time. He's a clever kid – he'll be fine. Let's talk about your love life.'

'No,' said Pari. 'Let's talk about *yours*. How's Shaan?'

'You know Shaan. Always chasing something big – he reminds me a lot of Rehman, actually.' Shaan was Dilawar's openly gay boyfriend. 'We are planning to go to London soon.'

'Really? That's great. Listen, I'd love to continue chatting to you, but I have to wake up early to eat for the sahri, before the fast starts, so let's call it a night.'

The pre-dawn air was cool as Rehman kicked the stand down and parked his motorbike. There was little traffic and the streets were deserted except for milkmen on their rounds and a few housewives, washing the small patches of road in front of their homes with water and decorating it with patterns of powdered rice. Rehman stretched and yawned hugely. Ahead of him, a group of labourers in sarong-like lungis were cleaning their teeth with neem twigs. A bearded man in khaki shorts and a saffron T-shirt walked up and said, 'Are you here for the HUT training?'

Rehman nodded.

'My name is Narayana. Follow me.'

Rehman fell in behind him.

Rehman's mother, who had been heating up food, had been surprised to see him awake so early. 'Are you going to fast too?' she had asked, looking hopeful.

'I have to go out,' he had said, not mentioning that he was going on a training course organised by a Hindu religious organisation during the Muslim holy month of Ramzaan.

There were about thirty young men in the open area, limbering up for exercise. Some were stretching, trying to touch their toes with their fingertips; others were twisting their torsos and a couple of particularly keen men were doing push-ups. Most of them were in yellow T-shirts and khaki shorts. The man who had led Rehman in seemed to be some sort of leader because several young men broke off their exercises and came over to greet him.

'Namaskaaram, guru-gaaru,' they said.

Mr Narayana nodded to them, then turned to Rehman. 'What's your name?' he asked. 'Who sent you here?'

Rehman was suddenly glad that he had practised this with Usha, but his throat was still dry as he answered, 'My name is Raghu. I've heard about you from the priest at the Hanuman temple in Steel City.'

Steel City, the colony that housed the employees of the Steel Plant, seemed distant enough from town.

The man nodded. 'I like the fact that you are not ashamed to wear our traditional Indian clothes.'

Rehman looked down at himself. He wore his habitual kurta pyjama – a long shirt that came almost to his knee and thin trousers, made from rough hand-loom cloth. He hadn't given it much thought, then suddenly remembered how Usha had once tried to get him to change to more 'modern' clothes. He had proposed to her in that shop and she had agreed. How simple life had been then . . .

The guru clapped his hands. 'Right, form into lines, boys. We'll start our Surya Namaskaaram now.'

The men quickly formed into lines six deep, facing east. Rehman found a place at the back of one of them. The guru went to the front and faced east too, then raised his right leg and placed his foot against the knee of his left leg. His hands were placed together, palms joined in salutation. Rehman and the other young men imitated the leader. The guru must be quite fit for somebody of his age and size, thought Rehman in surprise. Standing on one leg wasn't as easy as it looked, but Mr Narayana stood rock steady, unlike several of the younger men behind him, including Rehman, who wobbled like the knock-down clowns beloved of toddlers.

As the first rays of light filtered through the trees, and smoke rose from a nearby kitchen, the guru said loudly, 'Aum suryaaya namah.'

They were worshipping the sun, reciting verses from the three-thousand-year-old Rig Veda with accompanying yoga stretches. Rehman was sweating and muscles that he didn't know he had were screaming for attention before the guru stopped. The young men sat down on the ground, legs folded in the lotus asana – each foot tucked over the other thigh, spine straight, arms on knees. The guru turned to face them.

'I can see that we have a few new men here today. So, before we start practising karrasaamu, fighting with sticks, I want to talk about why we are here and what we are trying to achieve.'

A cool breeze, passing over the open ground, felt very pleasant to Rehman. He looked at the youths around him – he was one of the older men, in fact. Most of the trainees seemed to be no older than twenty.

'India is not called Bharat Mata for nothing. She is, indeed, our mother. She has given us life and she sustains us. She gives us food to eat and water to drink. She does not protest when we tear open her body to get iron and coal to build our industries. In truth, she asks for very little. But if we are her children, what is our duty to our mother?' The guru stared at the orderly group of men.

The youths remained silent.

'Our duty,' continued the guru, 'to our mother is very simple. It is respect.' His voice grew louder. 'Respect. And how do we show our respect?'

He pointed his finger to the young man sitting on the left of Rehman. The young man glanced around and said, 'Me?'

The guru nodded.

'Erm ...' Everybody turned to look at the young man, who blushed uncomfortably and stammered. 'Er ...'

The guru let the moment linger and then continued, 'This is the problem with the education system in our country. We have lost sight of the important things.'

Rehman smiled sympathetically at the young man and said out of the corner of his mouth, 'It is like being back in school, isn't it?'

The young man grimaced and whispered back, 'This is worse than school.'

Rehman grinned.

The young man said, 'My name is Babu. Did you say your name was Raghu?'

Rehman nodded and looked away, unable to meet Babu's guileless eyes while confirming the lie.

'Do I know you? I think I've seen you before somewhere.'

Rehman's heart gave a jolt, and he had to fight to keep the shock off his face. 'No...' he muttered. 'You couldn't have.'

Luckily, the guru's voice reached a new level and everybody's attention shifted back to the speaker. The guru seemed to have forgotten his own question, however, because his next words had no connection to what went before. 'We are an ancient culture. Sanskrit is the oldest language in the world. The Vedas are the repository of much wisdom – philosophy, law, even mathematics. But have any of you studied the Vedas in school?'

The young men shook their heads.

'How many of you have studied Shakespeare?'

Quite a few of the trainees raised their hands. The guru shook his head. 'We have been free for over sixty years, but we have not let go of our colonial attitude. We are like a dog that keeps following its master even though he is kicking it.'

In the silence that followed, Rehman thought that while the guru was probably right about the hangover of colonialism in the Indian psyche, he was being a little unfair too. The men's familiarity with Shakespeare was probably no greater than their acquaintance of Kalidasa, the greatest Sanskrit playwright. Surely, following the guru's logic, knowledge of *Macbeth* was cancelled out by a familiarity with Kalidasa's masterpiece, *Abhijñānaśākuntalam*.

'Is this how we show respect to our mother?' The guru's voice was a whiplash. 'No!' He answered his own question. 'We should teach our children the eternal values of our dharma, our religion. We do not covet an inch of another country's territory. We never have and we never shall. But by God, we should be ready to tear the heart out of any enemy who dares to lay covetous eyes on motherland.'

That's true, thought Rehman. India had been invaded many times over the millennia starting with the Aryans and followed by the Greeks, the Mongols, the Turks, the Persians, the Portuguese, the French, the British and finally the Chinese, as late as 1962. But, almost uniquely among the nations of the earth, Indians had never attempted to conquer other lands. It is not that they were not militaristic; they had fought pretty hard but only ever among themselves, leaving the way open for foreigners to take advantage. India's stormtroopers into the outside world had not been her soldiers but her religions; her philosophy, shoonya; the number zero of the decimal system; and, more recently, her software engineers and call-centre operators.

'Max Mueller, the German orientalist, said, "If I were asked under what sky the human mind has most fully developed some of its choicest gifts, has most deeply pondered on the greatest problems of life, and has found solutions, I should point to India."'

It's funny, thought Rehman, that somebody who was insistent on Indian pride and breaking colonial mindsets still looked to foreigners for validation.

'If you study the Vedas, all knowledge will be yours – from the deepest philosophical thoughts to town planning, from your responsibilities as a husband and parent to mathematics. If you study the scriptures, they can tell you the future and more.'

Rehman's mind wandered. Why did all these religious types want to read more than there already was in the books? Wasn't the poetry and the great truths in the books enough? It wasn't just the Hindus. He knew Muslim 'scholars' who said the same about the Qur'an, while the crackpots were legion who claimed to have decoded the secrets of the Bible.

'The knowledge of the ancient Aryans was not restricted to our subcontinent.' The reasonable-sounding voice of the guru carried on. 'Do you know that there is a mountain range in Europe called the Alps?'

Most of the men listening had indeed heard of the Alps. Weren't they the white mountains that provided the backdrop to all those romantic Hindi movies filmed in Switzerland?

'The word Alps comes from alpa, a Sanskrit word meaning

lesser or smaller, because, you see, the Alps are not as high as our own Himalayas. The city of Amsterdam gets its name from antardham, which means below the sea. And if you look it up on Google, you will find that Amsterdam is indeed below sea-level. Let's go to London . . . '

The guru peered at them and several of the young men sniggered; going to London was a common euphemism for going to the toilet. The older man waited patiently until the titters died out. 'London is named after Nandi – Siva's mount, the bull. It's original name was Nandinyam.'

By now, it was getting hot. The sun had risen over the roofline. Rehman could feel its rays burning his skin. Luckily, the lecture came to an end soon after and they were then taught how to wield a stick in ritualised combat exercises.

'Remember, your body is your temple. Treat it with respect. And discipline is the foundation of all good things in life. The biggest problem we Hindus have is our lack of unity. We don't think of ourselves as Hindus, we think of ourselves as Andhras and Tamils, as Brahmins and Shudras. And political parties take advantage of this fact – they emphasise our differences and ignore our common gripes. The parties appease minorities because they vote as a bloc and give all sorts of advantages to Muslims that are denied to Hindus.'

Rehman almost shook his head before he realised the company he was keeping and stopped himself. The guru was now doing exactly what he had accused the mainstream politicians of doing: dividing Indians in his bid to create a common Hindu front. If Muslims were so advantaged by the system, why were Muslims still the least educated and among the poorest people in India? The fact that Muslims were overwhelmingly self-employed in small businesses showed that they were failing to break into mainstream jobs.

Anyway, the idea that one community had to be promoted over another was silly. Again and again, people all over India had shown that they hungered for an efficient administration that provided sadak, bijli, paani – roads, electricity and water. For some reason, politicians seemed to find that very hard to provide, and instead played complicated games, using caste and religion, to get votes.

That evening, Mr and Mrs Ali were watching the news on television in their living room with Pari. Vasu was in the bedroom doing his homework.

'Where is Rehman? Why didn't he come home for dinner?' asked Mr Ali.

'He said he was meeting a friend,' said Mrs Ali. 'He is eating out.'

'Who is this friend? At least during Ramzaan, he should eat with you when breaking the fast.'

Pari knew who the friend was, but she didn't reply. Rehman was meeting Usha, his ex-fiancée, and apparently giving her a report on the training session at HUT, the Hindu religious organisation. It's all a farce, Pari thought. Rehman was a fool not to see that getting him to infiltrate the training camp was not only dangerous but also a flimsy excuse for his ex to keep in touch with him. After all, why did they have to have dinner together to exchange a report?

'What did you say?' asked Mrs Ali.

Pari shook her head. 'Nothing,' she said. Had she muttered her thoughts out loud? That woman would leave him again and Rehman would once more become unhappy. That was clear – why couldn't Rehman see it?

Pari sighed. Why couldn't *she* declare her feelings for him? It wasn't so easy. She was a widow, dependent on the good-will of his parents. She couldn't jeopardise that, regardless of what Dilawar said, from the safety of a large city like Mumbai. Small towns were different and she had to live by the rules here.

The doorbell rang and Mr Ali went out to the verandah. Pari heard the surprise in his voice as he greeted whoever was at the door and her eyes met Mrs Ali's. The older woman looked baffled too. Who could be coming here at this hour?

Pari peeked out from behind the curtain. A large number of men, at least ten or fifteen of them, were at the door, led by the young imam. They all appeared to have come directly from the mosque, as they were wearing flowing white kurta-pyjamas and some of them still had lace skullcaps on their heads. Mrs Ali's brother, Azhar, was standing with the crowd as if he was an outsider and not a family member. Pari frowned. Azhar's eyes met hers and he quickly looked away, his face frozen. Her disquiet increased. This was definitely not a routine social visit.

Usha's turquoise dress looked black in the sodium-vapour lamps that lined Beach Road. The sun had set more than an hour ago and the crowds around Rehman and Usha, who were sitting on a low wall facing the beach, were thinning. Usha had been telling Rehman about the progress of her article, which her editor had asked her to cut by three hun-dred words.

'So what else did the guru say in his speech?' she asked.

Rehman, who had already mentioned that the knowledge of the ancient Indians had encompassed all of Europe, thought for a moment. 'Oh, yes!' he said. 'According to the guru, Muslims and other minorities are being appeased at the expense of the Hindu majority.'

'Did he give any examples?'

'Yes,' said Rehman. 'The fact that Muslim men can have four wives while a Hindu man can have only have one apparently shows that Hindus are being discriminated against.'

Usha snorted. 'If there is any discrimination in the personal law, it is against Muslim women, not Hindu men! Why are all these religious types so sexist? They talk as if only men count and women are chattels to be passed around.' She stopped to take a deep breath. 'Did anybody tell you what the point of all this training is?'

'Not in so many words, but it is very clear. They are targeting young men, mainly unemployed or those struggling in jobs for which they are overqualified, and feeding their sense of injustice. They are showing them a higher purpose and drilling them in obedience in the name of discipline, to form a cadre that can then be used as cheap fodder for enforcing strikes – hartals – and supporting their favoured candidates in elections. It's hardly unique. I'm sure this is exactly what is happening in Pakistani madrassahs with Muslim boys, for example.'

Usha nodded. A strand of hair fell over her forehead and Rehman almost reached out and to brush it back, as he had done, several times, while they had been engaged. Her eyes caught his. As if she knew exactly what he was thinking, she flushed and looked away, pointing to the tireless waves pounding the sandy beach. 'Do you remember how you once told me that the sea was a lover trying to visit its beloved, the city?'

Rehman smiled at the thought, although he could no longer recall the name of the medieval Arab poet who had made the comparison. The sea rushed forward to meet its love but fell back when it saw the city's guards, but it continued to try, again and again, for ever.

'I remember it every time I come to the beach. It tells me that love is not enough on its own. The sea has been trying to enter the city for aeons.'

'Well, if the scientists are correct and global warming causes the sea levels to rise, the ocean will eventually overwhelm the city's defences and force its way in.'

Usha jumped up from the low wall on which they had been sitting. 'What a cheery companion you are!' she said. 'Let's go home.'

CHAPTER NINE

The verandah filled up as the men from the mosque crowded in. 'And to what do I owe the honour of such a visit?' said Mr Ali.

Only the imam, Azhar and an elderly gentleman, respected not only for his age but because he was a retired senior state government official, sat on the sofa. The rest remained standing. Mr Ali reclaimed his seat. Vasu came out with a tray of glasses of water, but everybody declined and the tumblers stood abandoned on the coffee table. Everybody was silent until Vasu went back inside.

'Is the boy's mother here?' asked the imam, finally.

Mr Ali nodded and Pari's face peeked out from behind the curtain, like a disembodied djinn from a fairy tale. 'Salaam A'laikum,' she said.

A volley of salaams followed from the assembled men. The imam spoke again. 'The mosque committee met today to discuss what should be done about your son.'

Mr Ali frowned. 'How can you people discuss my family

just like that? Has our reputation sunk so low that any random person in the bazaar can hazard an opinion about us?'

'This was not the market, but your local mosque. And you too would have been part of the discussion if you had bothered to attend the prayers like a good Muslim. It's especially inexcusable that an elderly man like you, whose thoughts should be focused on how he is going to meet his maker, doesn't bother to come to the mosque even during the holy month of Ramadaan.'

'What is it to anybody whether I come to the mosque or not?'

'It should be every person's responsibility to make sure that his neighbour is acting like a good Muslim. But that's not what we are here to discuss.' The imam turned to Pari. 'We have decided that your son should be raised as a Muslim. If you send him to the mosque with one of his uncles or great-uncles, we will give him the shahaada, the oath, so that he can become a true Muslim, and we can start teaching him the Kalma and the Qur'an. And what better month to start it than this holy month?'

'No,' said Pari.

The imam looked flustered. 'What do you mean, no?' he said.

'No means that I am not sending him to the mosque.'

The young imam's face turned a beetroot red. He had clearly not expected to be turned down so flatly in front of a large audience.

Azhar spoke up. 'Don't be silly, Pari. Don't you know who you are talking to? The idea of a Muslim raising a kafir, an infidel, is unthinkable. Apologise to the imam now.'

'Don't *you* all realise who you are talking about?' said Pari. The curtain dropped as she came forward onto the verandah. 'Vasu is not a kafir. He is my son and I decide how to bring him up.'

Mr Ali stood up from his chair and raised his hands in a placatory fashion. 'Pari,' he said, 'don't take offence now.' He turned to the men. 'Azhar, you are family. Razzaq, we have known each other since before you started your seat-cover business. Pervez . . . ' Mr Ali shook his head. 'I see my brothers in front of me – men I have known for years – whose salt I have eaten and who've eaten in my house, but I don't recognise your words. What are these demands that you place upon me? Who among you has a perfect family? Some of you have sons who are going out with girls . . . '

Razzaq flushed. His son Sajid was known to be living it up as a university student, even if he regularly attended the mosque. 'How—'

'I am just talking in general terms. But it is said that when the guard asked who had the pumpkins, the thief checked his shoulders.'

'Are you calling us—' said another man loudly.

Pari said, 'Please stop, everybody. Chaacha and Chaachi are giving me great honour, but I am not their daughter. There is no need for them to lose their age-old friends and spoil their reputations as gracious hosts by fighting with their guests.' She turned to Azhar. 'Am I not related to you too? Don't I have my own house? Why should anybody else be affected by my decisions? I will take my son to my flat and you can visit me there and tell me what you think.'

Mr Ali said, 'No, Pari. Every family has some weakness or

the other, because families are made up of human beings and humans are imperfect. It is sheer arrogance to point fingers at other people. Anyway, I don't think what you are doing is wrong; they are only picking on you because, as you are a single woman, they think you are an easy target. I promised your father before he died that I would look after you; don't make me a liar.'

'The consequences of your rebellion won't be good,' said the imam. 'Umar bin Khattab, the Prophet's companion and our second caliph, was very clear – a Muslim's duty is to preserve the unity of the ummah. Recant before you are thrown out of the community.'

Vasu pushed through the curtain and hugged Pari. 'I am sorry,' he said, tears flowing down his cheeks. 'I don't mind becoming a Muslim, but I don't want to leave you.'

Pari immediately engulfed him in her arms. 'Oh, baby. Nobody is going to take you away from me. Don't cry, please.'

Vasu's sobs increased even more, prompting Mrs Ali to come out of the house and take Pari and Vasu back inside.

Mr Ali turned to the men. 'It is said that an economist is a man who knows the price of everything, but the value of nothing. Similarly, you call yourselves Muslims and know all the rules, but you have none of the spirit behind our religion. You quote Umar bin Khattab, but what about the Prophet's own example? He had two grandsons, as you know – Hasan and Hussein. They used to clamber over his shoulders when he prostrated himself in prayer, but when the people round him wanted to chastise the boys, he would stop them. They were children, and he didn't want to cause them unhappiness. You made a boy cry today in the name of religion. Is that what the Prophet would have wanted? Think about it.'

The gate to the front yard rattled and Rehman came in. He looked at the assembled men in surprise for a moment, before turning to close the gate.

'Leave it open, Rehman,' said Mr Ali. 'The guests are leaving.'

In the large living room of the big house on Daspalla Hills, Mr Koteshwar Reddy and his granddaughter, Sujatha, were playing chess. They were in mid-game and on equal terms, both having lost two foot-soldiers (or pawns) and a horse (or knight) each. Mr Reddy was playing white, and it was his turn. He frowned at the board, as if willing it to tell him the right move.

'Come on, Thaatha. It's too early to think so long.'

'I have to be careful with you,' he growled. After almost another minute of thought, he moved a piece and said, 'Aha! My minister checks you.'

Chess was invented in India, and Indians have their own, far more logical, names for the pieces. For example, the most powerful members of the opposing armies are the two ministers, not queens. After all, whoever heard of a queen going out to battle while the king cowered in his castle?

Sujatha's horse jumped two squares to the right and one forward to land in front of the king to shield him from the enemy minister.

Mr Reddy glanced at the board and, horror-struck, raised his eyes to Sujatha, who stuck out her tongue and laughed. 'Your elephant, or rook as they call it in the books, is mine,' she said.

Mr Reddy saw that she was right. There was no hope – he would lose either his minister or his elephant. He heard a noise at the door and looked up as his nephew came in.

'Aye, Bobbili. Come here,' he called out and then turned to Sujatha. 'Sorry, baby. We have to abandon the match here.'

'Cheating, Thaatha. Concede that you've lost,' she said.

He shook his head. 'Lost? What a joke! This is just the beginning, but Bobbili is here and that means I have to discuss business with him.'

'Cheater, cheater, pumpkin eater,' she chanted.

'I am not a cheater and there's nothing wrong with a pumpkin, especially if you sauté it with red chillies and dhal,' Mr Reddy said hotly. He then inclined his head towards her and said, much more softly, 'Whom will I play against when you are married and gone, baby? The others are all nincompoops and it's no fun checkmating them in ten moves.'

Checkmate, a nonsense word, is a corruption of shahmat, literally, the king's death, signifying disaster.

Sujatha laughed. Mr Reddy gazed on her fondly, thinking that she looked at her youthful best. The man who married her was lucky indeed. She had intelligence, character and wealth in a beautiful package: what more could anybody want? He was quite sure that he was not biased.

Bobbili came and stood in front of them. Mr Reddy's smile faded at the sight of his expression. 'You look like a man who has bitten a sour gooseberry. What's the problem?'

'They ...' said Bobbili and tailed off. 'They ...' he repeated.

Mr Reddy frowned. 'Don't bleat like a goat.' He twisted

and shouted towards the door, 'Somebody, get a glass of water.'

Bobbili sat down on a cushioned pouffe. A maid ran in with water and Mr Reddy told her to give it to Bobbili. 'Drink it,' he said, gruffly.

Bobbili swallowed the cool water in one big gulp, then said, 'They called,' getting out twice as many words as before.

'Who? And what did they say?'

'The b-boy's family,' he said.

Sujatha looked up from the chess pieces that she had been rearranging. 'Yes?' she said tonelessly.

'The boy's family called. They've rejected us. The boy said he was not interested any more and they couldn't convince him otherwise.' The words tumbled out quickly.

Sujatha went rigid for a moment and then she screamed, a keening, animal-like noise that went on and on. Bobbili and Mr Reddy, turned to stone by her anguish, could only stare in dismay. Sujatha suddenly stopped wailing and, sweeping the chessboard and its pieces to the ground, she ran out of the room.

Mr Reddy turned to his nephew. 'What demon has wrapped its claws around our house?'

Bobbili just shook his head, like a confused bullock plagued by flies. His son came running in. 'Who was crying, Naanna?'

'Venkatesh, the people who came to see Sujatha the other day have rejected the match. Go and comfort her.'

'Yes, Naanna.' The youngster hurried away.

Aruna was typing up the list of Christian brides. Mrs Ali was sitting in the wicker chair, turning the pages of the newspaper listlessly. It had been so hot all day that the road in front of the house had been deserted. It was now five o'clock and the traffic had picked up only in the last hour. Mr Ali came out of the house balancing in his hands three bowls of diced watermelon. Mrs Ali took one and he handed another to Aruna. He then handed out three forks.

'Take a break,' he said to Aruna.

The bright-red pieces felt grainy on the tongue, but cool and refreshing in the heat.

'Pari told me about last night's visit from the mosque committee,' Aruna said.

Mrs Ali sighed and tossed the paper onto the coffee table. 'It's a worry,' she replied. 'We can't afford to antagonise family and friends. It's our mosque after all. At my age, I don't want to have to leave my house and move somewhere else.'

'Nonsense,' said Mr Ali. 'Why should we have to move? This is just a temporary insanity that'll blow over, once they have something more substantial to deal with. The imam is young and he is trying to show that he is making a change, that's all.'

Mrs Ali said, 'It won't blow over. When even my own brother is against us, what hope do we have of convincing anybody else? Maybe we should ask Pari to send Vasu to the mosque. After all, what harm is there in that? He can also go to the temple. That way, he'll learn about both religions.'

'Why should he do that? His parents were Hindus and Pari doesn't want him to lose touch with his culture. Doesn't the Qur'an say, "Lakum Dinakum, wa liya din"?' Mr Ali saw the puzzled look on Aruna's face. 'Your religion for you and my religion for me – that's what the Qur'an says. The mosque committee has probably recited that phrase a thousand times in their prayers over the years, but they don't think about what they are saying.'

Mrs Ali shook her head. 'For a man who never goes to the mosque, you can out-argue any religious scholar. I am not saying that you are wrong. I am just worried. We are ordinary people and we cannot go against powerful forces. You are the one who keeps saying that Muslims consider only their enthusiasm when picking their enemies and not their strength. Isn't that what you are doing, too?'

'What would you have me do? Throw Pari to the dogs? I cannot do that.'

'No, I am not saying that. But I can have a chat with Pari. I'll tell her that we will support her but at the same time convince her that going head-on against all our family and friends is not wise.'

Mr Ali turned to his wife. 'You will not do that. Swear on my life that you will not have any such talk with Pari.'

Mrs Ali stared out at the road for a long moment. At last she said, 'All right. For all your fights, you and your son are both alike. I promise. I won't mention any of this to Pari. But let me warn you – losing all our family and friends won't be easy.'

'We won't lose all our friends. They'll see sense soon.'

'There are none so blind as those who won't see,' said Mrs Ali in English.

Mr Ali raised his eyebrows. 'An English proverb! Somebody's going posh.' It was rare for his wife to use any English words in her conversation.

The phone rang and Aruna answered it. She exchanged

greetings and listened for a moment, before holding out the handset to Mrs Ali. 'For you, madam.'

Mrs Ali took the phone, surprised. Most people called her on her mobile phone because the landline was always busy with the marriage bureau business. 'Hello,' she said cautiously.

'I told Daada that he was being foolish. Family should come before anything else. What can you expect from a bunch of senile men sitting on their own? There is no need to worry at all—'

Mrs Ali removed the phone from her ear and looked at it, puzzled. 'Excuse me, who are you?'

'Have you already forgotten me, Naani? It's Faiz.'

Azhar's granddaughter! 'Faiz, sorry, I didn't recognise your voice. Go back to the beginning again. What are you talking about?'

'I was talking to Daada and he told me how he and members of the congregation came to your house about Pari's son.'

'Ah! Now I understand. We were discussing the same thing here. I don't know what to do, to be honest. We are not at an age where we should be picking fights with the people around us.'

'Naani!'

Azhar was Faiz's paternal grandfather, so she called him Daada. Mrs Ali was naani, or maternal grandmother, because if she was daadi, it would imply that she and Azhar were husband and wife, when in fact they were brother and sister.

'Naani, are you there?'

Mrs Ali sighed. Why was she thinking about silly, simple things, such as whether she was Faiz's maternal or paternal grandmother, when there were more complicated issues to worry about? 'Sorry dear. My mind wandered. One of the hazards of old age, I am afraid.'

'I called up Daada to tell him to take the microwave away and you could have knocked me down with a feather when he told me what he had done.'

Mrs Ali remembered the microwave that she and Azhar had delivered to the village and the incident with the eggs exploding inside it. 'Why do you want him to take the microwave away? I thought you and your in-laws were quite proud of it.'

Faiz laughed. 'The microwave started stinking – such a horrible smell that you couldn't stand within six feet of it. In the end, we took it out of the living room and dumped it in the old storeroom, but the smell of the decomposing eggs attracted rats. They ate through a gunny sack and the rice inside it spilled everywhere. My sisters-in-law started teasing me – it's all very horrible. So I told Daada to take the microwave away and bring us a fridge instead.'

Mrs Ali laughed. 'What a sensible girl you are turning into,' she said. 'Dikhawa – showing off – never leads to anything good.'

Faiz said, 'Yes, the fridge will be much more useful, especially in the summer. We can give cold water to any guest who comes to our house.'

Mrs Ali shook her head and smiled. Oh well, there was some progress . . .

'Anyway, as I was saying, Naani, don't take Daada's words last night amiss. I'll talk to him again and convince him that families should always stick together – right or wrong.'

'Thank you, dear. That's very nice of you. Let's hope my silly brother comes to his senses. Give my salaams to your husband and your in-laws.'

She hung up, feeling much better. Not everybody had abandoned them.

Calm descended once more in the office of the marriage bureau. Aruna went back to her typing and Mr Ali to preparing ads for the weekend papers. For a long time, as it went about its business the gecko on the wall of the office heard only normal, everyday sounds – the clicking of the computer keys, the scratch of the pen as Mr Ali pared down the ads to their bare essentials – he had to pay for them by the word – the whirr of the fan above them and the noise of the traffic outside.

A grating noise disturbed them, making Aruna wince. The gecko quickly scurried away behind the meter cabinet. Mr Ali looked up, frowning. The iron gate of the front yard had been pushed open so violently that it had gone past its usual stopping place and ended up scraping the cement yard. A thickset man with wild hair shambled up the path and onto the verandah.

'Ish thish the marriage bureau for rich people?' he asked.

'No,' said Mr Ali and waved discreetly to Aruna when she looked at him in surprise.

The newcomer stood unsteadily, the top half of his body swaying. He stared at them owlishly for a moment. Aruna noticed that his eyes were red and baggy. He seemed at a loss for words. After a long moment, he steadied himself and stood up straight and tall.

'Shorry,' he said and stumbled out.

'Why—' said Aruna.

'Do *you* want to take him on as a client?' asked Mr Ali.

Aruna nodded and went back to her typing, pleased that Mr Ali, with his quick thinking, had been there at the time.

Mr Ali finally put down the pad of advertisements. 'If the boy from the newspaper comes, give these to him,' he said.

Aruna smiled and continued typing. She was given these same instructions every week without fail. Mr Ali closed the front gate and went back into the house through the side alley.

About five minutes later, the front gate was again pushed wide open, causing Aruna to wince as it scraped on the ground. The sound seemed to grate on her very soul, like nails going down a slate. She looked up to see the shambling man returning. He came straight towards the table and leaned over it, pointing a finger at her over the computer monitor. Aruna held her breath and tried to not to show her disgust as the smell of alcohol washed over her. The man wagged his finger and Aruna finally had to breathe in to avoid fainting. Nausea rose in her and she hurriedly stood up.

'You lied!' said the man, breathing another bout of alcoholic fumes in her face.

She gulped and clenched her fists tightly, digging her nails into her palms. A sheen of perspiration appeared on her forehead that had nothing to do with the heat.

'You—' said the man.

'Excuse me,' said Aruna and, pushing past him, she ran off the verandah.

'Hey!' shouted the man. 'Where are you going? Where is everybody?'

Aruna heard no more because she was throwing up over the potted plants in the small front garden. She was barely aware of Leela, the maid, calling out for Ali Madam.

Mrs Ali came and gave her a glass of cool water from a bottle that had come straight out of the fridge. 'Wash your face,' she said. The splash of water felt good.

'I am sorry,' said Aruna, looking at the mess over the plants.

'No, no, don't worry about it. Leela will wash it off.'

The maid was already drawing water from the well as Mrs Ali led Aruna back into the house. As they crossed the verandah, she saw Mr Ali talking to the drunk.

'You shouted at a pregnant woman,' said Mr Ali. 'That's not acceptable.'

'How was I to know that she was pregnant? I just thought she was chubby.'

Aruna stopped and glared at the man, but he had his back to her, facing Mr Ali. Mrs Ali dragged her away. 'Come on now, it's not good for you to get stressed.'

'I am not stressed,' said Aruna in a fierce whisper. 'But how dare—'

At that point the man turned towards her and, if looks could kill, Leela would have been drawing many more buckets of water from the well to wash away the pile of ash that he would have formed.

'You lied to me,' said the man to Mr Ali. 'This is the marriage bureau and you said it was not.'

'Oh! *Marriage bureau?* I thought you said Marigold Row.'

'There is no such place as Marigold Row,' said the man, peering at Mr Ali suspiciously.

Mr Ali returned his gaze with a guileless look. 'What do

you want, anyway?' he said. 'I don't think we have any suitable matches for you.'

'I don't want you to send any more matches for my daughter.'

'Your daughter?' Now Mr Ali was puzzled. 'What has your daughter got to do with us?'

'My father who is my daughter's grandfather . . . ' began the man.

'Yes, I can understand that bit. Go on.'

The man either was not aware of Mr Ali's sarcasm or, if he was, he ignored it. 'My father has joined your bureau on behalf of my daughter.'

Mr Ali went to the computer that was still switched on. He minimised the file that Aruna had been working on and said, 'What's your daughter's name?'

'Sujatha.'

A few keystrokes later, Mr Ali remembered the rich, older man who had been accompanied by his nephew. He hadn't met Sujatha, but, judging by her photo, she was a beautiful girl. Mr Ali remembered what a surprise it had been that somebody like her had to become a member of the marriage bureau.

'Are you Sukumar?' he asked.

The man nodded. 'I want to withdraw my daughter's membership. We are not interested in getting her married any more.'

'Why not?'

'What's it to you? I am the girl's father and I say that I don't want to belong to your agency. That's it. I shouldn't have to argue with you.'

'You didn't become the member. Your father did. So only he can withdraw the membership.'

'She's my daughter and if I say no, it is no, do you understand?' Sukumar's voice rose until at the end he was shouting. His eyes bulged and his expression became choleric as he brought his hand down hard on the table, making Mr Ali jump, along with the computer screen. Sukumar continued, 'I don't want any more matches coming for Sujatha. I've had enough of that nonsense.'

Mr Ali said, 'Uh, your father—'

That was evidently the wrong thing to say because it enraged Sukumar so much that he grasped Mr Ali by the collar and tried to lift him off the floor.

'What are you doing? Let go of me. Violence is not the way we do things here.'

'I'll show you how things are done,' said Sukumar, withdrawing one hand and forming it into a fist.

Mr Ali wriggled, trying to free himself, but Sukumar's grip was strong. Mr Ali kept silent because he was afraid that if he made a sound Aruna and his wife would come out onto the verandah, face to face with this madman. Where was Rehman? What good was a son who wasn't around to protect his aged father?

Sukumar drew his hand back like a boxer, ready to deliver a knockout blow. Mr Ali's eyes closed involuntarily, unable to watch it approach, but still he stayed silent. His collar was suddenly released and Mr Ali winced, expecting the blow, but unable to move and evade it. One second, two seconds, three . . . A noise of something being hit reached his ears, but he felt no pain. He cautiously squinted out of one eye and peeked out, then snapped both open when he appeared miraculously to be alone on the verandah. 'Where—'

Sukumar lay on the floor, having passed out.

Mr Ali's legs felt as weak and wobbly as a piece of Madugula halva. He simply had to sit down. I must call the police, he thought. He had been threatened before, most memorably by Aruna's father-in-law, before the rich man had been reconciled to his doctor-son marrying a girl from a poor family, but this was the first time that he had come face to face with physical violence. The English were right – a man's home was his castle and anybody who threatened it had to face the consequences. He reached for the phone.

'Thank you for not involving the police. The shame would have been too much to bear,' the older man said, leaning on his stick. Within twenty minutes of receiving the call from Mr Ali, Sukumar's father, Mr Koteshwar Reddy, had come with his assistant-nephew and the nephew's son.

Mr Ali nodded. 'It's all right,' he said. 'Luckily nothing happened.'

Bobbili, the nephew, and Bobbili's son, Venkat, hooked Sukumar's arms over their shoulders and lifted him up. Sukumar was still unconscious but his expression had a placidity that belied its earlier passion. The two men dragged Sukumar out to the car.

'You have put my family in your debt,' Mr Reddy said. 'Thank you. I've always known that my son's alcoholism was ruining Sujatha's marriage prospects, but I never thought he was spoiling his daughter's future so directly.'

'Why would he do that?'

'I've always said that once Sujatha was married, she would inherit all my wealth and that Sukumar would have to go to her for his allowance. Money is a bad thing, Mr Ali. It can make even parents turn against their children.'

'It's pretty drastic, though, putting a daughter in control of her father's money. He could not have been happy about that.'

'My son has no control. I've given him chance after chance. He has always lost money by the truckload. I've given him perfectly running, profitable businesses and he has run them into the ground. He has started his own ventures and I've backed him, but they've always failed. And as for the money he has wasted on the demon drink, don't even ask. He takes loans everywhere in town and Bobbili runs around sorting out the debtors. But I never realised until now just how low he has fallen – wrecking my granddaughter's future for his selfish purposes. That I cannot forgive.'

Bobbili came back. 'Let's go, Uncle,' he said, taking Mr Reddy's hand.

Mr Reddy nodded. His body seemed to sag and he looked older than before.

Mr Ali stared after them as they slowly made their way off the verandah, into the yard and out of the gate – Mr Reddy limping on his bad hip and the faithful assistant keeping pace with him.

A Hindi phrase came to Mr Ali's mind: bhoot sowaar, which literally meant, demon ride. There were many demons riding the tormented Sukumar, he thought, and frowned.

CHAPTER TEN

The supporters of the ruling party thronged down the road in a noisy procession, as if they were a bridegroom's family going to a wedding hall. Several motorbikes and three-wheeled auto-rickshaws came past, festooned with banners, flags, slogans and almost life-size pictures of the party's leader looking down on a smaller picture of the candidate. The last vehicle in the group loudly played songs from Telugu films, interspersed with snippets of speeches from the party's state leader.

Mrs Ali came to the gate when they stopped outside her house.

'Please vote for us, madam,' said one young man, in jeans, T-shirt and a bandanna.

'Why should we vote for you?' said Mrs Ali. 'Once the election is over, you'll all disappear and won't be seen again until the next election. The mango season comes every summer, but politicians are seen only once every five years.'

'Aye, oldie—' began the brash youth, before he was pushed aside by an older man.

'Namaskaaram, Amma,' the old man said, with a practised smile and a respectful bob of his head. 'Ignore the young man's rudeness, madam.'

Mrs Ali softened and asked, 'Aren't you the corporator for this ward?'

She had seen him the previous year, walking down the road with a municipal engineer and inspecting the storm drains. She had also seen him on television, being interviewed about using a fogging machine to kill mosquitoes.

'Yes, madam. This time, both the municipal and the state elections are being held together. I hope you'll vote for our party again.'

'What's this I hear about the road widening?' she asked.

'How did you find out about it? The news is not supposed to come out till later,' he said. 'I mean—'

Mrs Ali frowned. 'Till after you have been safely elected, you mean. If the road is widened, we'll lose half our house. Where are we supposed to move to at our age?'

'We are trying our best to stop it, madam. But it is a central government order that all roads connecting to the national highways have to be one hundred and twenty feet wide. And we are not trying to hide the bad news till after the election. After all, the ruling party in central government is different and it is they who are to blame.'

'I don't understand all the politics. I'll vote for anybody who'll protect my home.'

'We understand, madam. There are many houses and shops down this road and it is wrong to demolish them. That's what we are trying to tell the central government.'

The procession had moved on and the candidate hurried to

rejoin them. Mrs Ali turned back, distraught. As there had
been no news about the road widening programme, she had
convinced herself that Shyam, the meter reader, had been
mistaken and that it was just a rumour. But the corporator's
response showed that their house could indeed be demolished
soon. On her left grew the guava tree that shaded the front
and, underneath the tree, several curry-leaf plants and a henna
plant. The house would lose a lot of its beauty and value, and
the government would give them a pittance as compensation.
What a disaster to strike in their old age!

Left to his own devices, her husband would have been
content to continue living in a rented house all his life. It had
been Azhar who had pleaded and cajoled, persuading him to
buy this strip of land all those years ago. At that time, all the
area around them had been vacant and only one bus route
served this neighbourhood. Many people, including her husband's sister, Chhote Bhaabhi, had told them at that time that
they were paying far too much for a small piece of land far
from local markets and other amenities. But Azhar's predic-
tions had come true and now their house was in a busy part
of the city with all conveniences near by. The land value had
shot up two-hundredfold. Only the other day Chhote
Bhaabhi had been saying that they were so lucky to have
invested in real estate at the right time and got it so cheaply.
Maybe, Mrs Ali thought, it was her sister-in-law's evil eye that
had brought this calamity down on them.

On her right was the well that supplied their water. When
they had saved up enough money to get the house built, the
very first thing they had done was to get this well dug. She
remembered how the old imam of the mosque, Haji Saab,

had come with his nephew, Nasrullah, and read a dua, a prayer from the Qur'an, over the spot. Then the well-diggers, a trio of brothers, had marked the circumference of the well, three feet in diameter. Placing a stone at its centre, they had asked her husband to break a coconut on the stone and spill its water around it. After that was done, they had lit a packet of incense sticks, stuck them into the white flesh of the broken coconut and prayed over it to their Hindu gods. Mrs Ali had raised her eyebrows at the imam, but he had shrugged. 'They are praying to their gods for success and safety. That's nothing to do with us.'

She wondered how the new imam would have reacted. If he had objected to the ritual, the diggers might have balked and walked away from the job — after all, digging a well was dangerous. The sides could cave in at any time, burying the men underground, and they wouldn't have wanted to undertake such a hazardous venture without first propitiating their deities.

It didn't matter whose prayers had been answered, but they had struck water fairly quickly. The well had never gone dry even in the harshest summers, though it had come pretty close a couple of times. It was unimaginable that the faithful well would be closed up — tears came to her eyes at the very thought. And on top of that, she would become dependent upon an unreliable municipal tap for water — and have to pay for the privilege, too.

On the verandah, her husband looked up as she joined him. 'I've been thinking about that drunken man who came in the other day, Sukumar. I am sure—'

Mrs Ali turned towards him, her eyes flashing. 'Do you ever think about anything other than your stupid marriage bureau? There is a shahmat, a catastrophe, coming down on our heads and all you can talk about is some client of yours.' She suddenly sat down on the wicker chair and covered her face in her hands as sobs racked her.

Mr Ali thought that she was laughing and looked at her in puzzlement. After a few seconds, he realised that she was crying and stood up, alarmed. 'What—' he said. 'Why are you crying?'

He came round the table and stood awkwardly in front of his wife, scratching his head. What did she mean by catastrophe? His wife was a strong woman and it was not like her to burst into tears.

The bulldozers came in the night with the roar of an angry elephant and the smoke of a demon's belch. Two-hundred-watt bulbs, jerry-rigged on long leads, cast a harsh light on the carnage. The bulldozer's heavy arm had already knocked down the front wall and it now pushed against the guava tree. The thin trunk resisted for a moment with its supple strength but the bulldozer reversed a foot, digging its claws into the ground.

Mrs Ali stifled a cry as the valiant tree collapsed with a crack against the house. The bulldozer then, surprisingly gently, picked up the tree and laid it aside. A young construction worker (should that be a destruction worker?) casually reached out, plucked a ripe fruit from the fallen tree and bit into it. Mrs Ali could not even protest.

The bulldozer now assaulted the main house itself. The front wall came down with a resounding roar and a neighbour shouted from an upstairs flat: 'Why are you guys making such a racket? I have to go to the office tomorrow.'

Workers quickly separated the iron grille from the masonry. It would be recycled and, hopefully, protect somebody else's house better than it had done for the Alis. The front yard was churned up, its red soil scattered with rootballs and shards of shattered terracotta. The bulldozer roared again and carved through the verandah, cracking the granite floor tiles and bringing down the far wall. Mrs Ali could have sworn that they had cleared her husband's office the previous day, but she could clearly see the computer crushed and the wooden wardrobe that he used as a filing cabinet turned into kindling. Photos of handsome young men and beautiful women spilled on the ground, reflecting glossily the industrial strength electric light, while dust motes jumped crazily in the air above them.

Mrs Ali's eyes snapped open and she lay still for several moments, disoriented by the sudden silence, her mouth dry and her heart thudding with fear. What a nightmare that had been! She didn't move for a few minutes, staring in disbelief at the familiar solidity of the house around her. She got up shakily and stepped outside, surprised that it was still early afternoon and bright.

That evening they had dinner at Pari's house, on Pari's insistence once she heard of Mrs Ali's nightmare and had seen her distress.

'Rehman-Uncle, see this painting I drew for my homework today.'

Vasu pushed an A4 sheet of paper into Rehman's hands. It was a coloured-pencil drawing of the view from the flat's balcony, showing the road in front with shops on the other side.

An electricity pole looked like a brown smear and the sky was filled with blue lines. There were even dark smudges representing pedestrians and traffic. The Alis' house could not be seen but the guava tree made an appearance on the edge of the picture.

Rehman patted Vasu's head and said, 'Lovely.'

Vasu leaned over and pointed to the bottom right-hand corner. 'See the sweet shop ... ' Under his finger, past the Alis' house, on the other side of the road, was a blob of white.

The shop sold khajas from Kakinada, halva from Maluguda, savoury chaegodis and roasted chilli-dusted cashew nuts. Rehman handed the picture to his mother, who had been listening to their conversation.

She silently glanced at the picture and saw the ribbon of black road not as a pleasant byway but as a hungry snake that was just waiting to swallow her home. She shuddered and passed it on to her husband.

Soon, they were at the table eating. Pari had made sautéed soya beans and lamb with spinach. Buttermilk slaked their thirst. They were almost at the end of the meal when Rehman's mobile phone rang. The number was familiar but wasn't in his address book, so he ignored it. A couple of minutes later it rang again and Rehman answered it.

'Hello.'

'Raghu? This is Babu.'

'I am sorry—' Rehman started saying before he bit his tongue. He suddenly remembered the early-morning exercise sessions organised by HUT that he had attended for Usha's story. Babu was the young man who had sat next to him at the lectures and had been caught out when the guru had asked him questions.

'Yes, Babu. This is Raghu.'

His parents looked at him. His mother frowned and his father opened his mouth to say something. Rehman held his hand up, palm facing out, asking him to stay silent.

'Tell me, Babu. We are just having dinner.'

'So early?'

'My mother's just break—' Rehman stopped himself. He had to be careful not to reveal that he was a Muslim. 'Nothing . . . What's up?'

'You said you live near the Ram temple by the National Highway, didn't you?'

'Yes. Why?'

'There is a Muslim woman there who is forcibly convert-ing a Hindu boy to her religion. The guru wants all of us to go there, protest and rescue the boy.'

Rehman's mouth went dry and he had to force the next words out. 'What is the woman's name?'

'I don't know. But the boy's name is Vasu. We'll be there in fifteen minutes. Join us there.'

'I am not sure. I'll try. But what do you mean by "rescue"?'

'We'll take the boy away from such an unsuitable atmos-phere, of course. We'll trace his family or put him in a good Hindu orphanage. OK, got to go. It's the third building after the Ram temple. Be there. Bye.'

Rehman pressed the red button on his phone and slowly put it away. Was there such a shortage of unloved children roaming the streets in India, scavenging for scraps from dust-bins and rubbish heaps, that these people could get so worked up about a boy who was cherished and cared for in a loving environment?

'What is it?' said Pari.

'What did you mean by calling yourself some other name?' said his father.

'Don't worry about that for now, Abba. This is serious.' He quickly related what Babu had told him.

'What do we do?' said Pari, wringing her hands.

Vasu ran to her and hugged her tightly. 'It's OK, Amma. When those men come, I'll tell them that I love you and that I want to stay with you. Then they'll go away.'

Pari smiled with tight lips even though her heart was breaking and she twisted her fingers in his hair. She glanced up at the other adults in the room and silently mouthed, 'What should we do?'

'Let's go,' said Rehman.

Before they took a step, however, there was a loud banging on the front door.

'Get into the bedroom and close the door,' said Rehman. 'Quickly!'

Rehman went to the door and, looking out through the peephole, saw the building's watchman on the other side.

'What is it?' Rehman said.

'Men have started gathering downstairs, sir. I've locked the gate and my wife is standing guard.'

Rehman opened the door. 'How long can you hold them off?'

'Not long, sir. I had a chat with some of those men. They belong to a religious party and have come to take away Madam's boy.'

Pari and the others must have been listening behind the bedroom door because they now came out. The watchman saluted them and continued, 'They are waiting for their leader. As soon as he comes, they will ask for the gates to be opened.'

'Can you refuse to open them?' said Pari.

The watchman shook his head. 'Sorry, madam. I met the building society secretary on the way up. He said that I should open the gates when they asked. Otherwise they might damage the property.'

'Thank you for coming and warning us,' said Mrs Ali. 'You've kept faith with us.'

'I've eaten your salt over the years, madam. How could I do anything else?'

The watchman, poor as he was, represented the true values of India, thought Mr Ali: loyalty and tolerance. Unlike the braying mob filled with hatred, though they too were India – a nasty and voluble part but thankfully a small one.

The shouts from downstairs grew louder and could now be heard through the windows. 'Sri Ram ki Jai.' Victory to Lord Ram. It didn't feel like such a small part of the nation's psyche when the rabble was directly below them.

'Could we go into one of the neighbour's flats?' said Mr Ali.

Mrs Ali shook her head. 'They may refuse out of fear. We can't put them in that position.'

Rehman was thinking hard. 'We can't go down because the men are already there. We have to go up.'

Mrs Ali said, 'We'll just get trapped on the terrace.'

'Probably,' said Rehman. 'But we can't stay here like mice in a trap. We'll be caught for sure.'

'I'll tell them—' began Vasu.

'Shh,' said Pari.

The voices below reached a new pitch. The watchman glanced fearfully towards the stairs. 'I have to go, Amma. I'll delay them as much as I can.'

Mrs Ali thanked the man again and he left. She turned to Rehman. 'Take Pari and Vasu with you to the terrace. The three of you are young and can somehow escape. Your father and I are too old to jump from roof to roof like monkeys. We'll stay here.'

Mr Ali took a deep breath and sat down on a nearby chair. 'That makes sense. Go, there's not much time.'

'No!' said Pari, her voice sounding strong suddenly. 'I am not going to be driven away from my own home by thugs. Rehman, some of the men downstairs will recognise you and who knows what they'll do then? You can't stay here. And I don't want Vasu here for them to kidnap. Go, don't argue. We'll be fine. What can they do to us?'

The watchman's voice floated up from below. 'Be patient, please. I am opening the gate. Just one second.'

Rehman thanked the watchman silently for the warning. 'Vasu, come on.'

Pari hugged the boy fiercely. 'Go, my son. Follow Rehman-Uncle. Listen to what he says. We'll meet up soon again.'

Rehman quickly hugged his mother. As he walked past Pari, he put an arm around her shoulders. 'You are a brave woman. Take care.'

Rehman and Vasu ran up the stairs hand in hand, without looking back. Behind them, the two mothers' eyes filled with tears.

A tumult rose below them, jolting Pari back to her senses. She slammed shut the door of the flat and bolted it from inside. She knew it wouldn't hold the men back if they were really determined to break in, but that didn't mean that she had to make it easy for them.

In the living room, Mr and Mrs Ali were sitting stiffly in two chairs, staring straight ahead. A wave of gratitude, and sympathy, rolled over Pari at the sight of them. Mr Ali, in a white shirt and white trousers, was thin although his white hair was still thick. His cheekbones had become prominent as the years had melted away his fat. Time had had the opposite effect on Mrs Ali, who wore a dark-green cotton sari, the colour of mango leaves. Her hair was darker, as was her skin, and she was pleasantly plump, about half a foot shorter than her husband. Pari knew that her air of being an unassuming housewife hid a keen intelligence and knowledge of people.

'Who wants tea?' Pari asked, her voice artificially bright.

Voices could be heard outside.

Mr Ali smiled at her. 'Why not? Make ten cups of tea.'

'Ten?' said Pari, surprised.

Mrs Ali looked at her husband quizzically.

Mr Ali said, 'Hospitality is equivalent to godliness. Hindu–Muslim traditions are agreed on this topic.'

Pari went into the kitchen. The first knock came before the water had become lukewarm in the pan.

Within seconds, the knocks became much louder and reverberated through the flat. Pari came out of the kitchen, but Mrs Ali waved her back, while Mr Ali went to the door. 'I am not deaf,' he shouted. 'You don't have to knock so loudly.'

There was a silence on the other side for a moment. Then a shout, 'Let us in now, or we'll tear the door down.'

'Who are you?' said Mr Ali. 'What do you want?'

'We are the Hindutva Universal Truth Party members, reclaiming the rights of the majority Hindus in our own country. Open the door now.'

Mr Ali looked through the peephole. 'Atidhi daivo bhava,' he said in Sanskrit – a guest is like God – before switching back to Telugu. 'But this is a small flat and cannot accommodate so many people. I'll open the door, but only five of you can come in.'

'We'll break down the door, you Turkish pig.' Someone must have kicked the door because it boomed loudly and the hinges rattled.

Mr Ali moved back hurriedly. Another kick – Mr Ali's worried glance took in the door frame. A small silvery sticker on the top right-corner read, 'Vizag Woodworks'. Mr Ali wondered whether the door makers knew that their product would be tested so thoroughly, so many years after they had made it.

A deeper voice spoke softly on the other side and the banging stopped. The same voice became louder. 'All right. We agree to just five of us coming in. But no tricks, do you understand?'

'How can we trick you?' said Mr Ali. 'The rest of your men will be just outside, by the door.'

'All right,' said the same voice.

'Do I have your word that only five of you will come in?' said Mr Ali.

'Yes.'

'On the Gita?'

'What do you think this is? A court of law? Should I put my hand on the Bhagavat Gita and say, I will speak the truth and nothing but the truth? But remember, if you play any tricks, I will consider that I am not held by my oath any more.'

'No, no. Your word is enough. Stand back, I'll open the door.'

Mr Ali glanced back into the living room. Mrs Ali was sitting on the chair where he had left her. She inclined her head a fraction of an inch, and he turned to the door again. Taking a deep breath, he slid the bolt back and turned the lever.

There was a mass of men outside, filling the corridor between the flats, with some youths spilling down the stairs. The flat diagonally opposite had two doors, an outer one with bars for viewing visitors and letting in the breeze on summer days, and a standard wooden inner one behind that. The inner door was open, allowing a middle-aged, pot-bellied, bare-chested man to follow the proceedings with interest. As Mr Ali watched, the neighbour's wife hissed a sharp warning to her husband, pulled him back into the flat and slammed the solid inner door shut.

The men in the corridor raised a cheer as Mr Ali opened the door. Most of them were lanky and young, teenagers or in their early twenties, but the man standing at their head, waring saffon robes, was stouter, his hair streaked heavily with grey and his beard grizzled.

'Namaste,' said Mr Ali and stood to one side.

The older man nodded and walked in. Four of his men followed. Mr Ali moved to close the door but an angry growl issued from the crowd as if it was one animal, rather than an assembly of individuals. Mr Ali left the door open, wishing they had the same two-door system as the flat opposite.

Mrs Ali now stood up, vacating her chair, and said politely, 'Please sit down.' Pari was nowhere to be seen, but there was a noise from the kitchen of pots and pans.

The men took their places on the sofa and two chairs. Mr Ali pulled out a dining chair and sat down too. 'What can we do for you gentlemen? To what do we owe the honour of this visit?'

'Don't try to act smart, you—' said the young man sitting nearest to the door.

The older man raised his hand to silence the youth, then looked around with interest. Mr Ali had the sudden realisation that he had probably never visited a Muslim's house before.

Mr Ali tried to view the flat through the other man's eyes. They were in the largish rectangular living room, its walls painted yellow with distemper. Facing the men, behind Mr Ali, was the dining table, with a wooden display cabinet on the other side. In the middle of the wall facing the road a door led to the balcony. Two windows with iron grille-work framed the door. On one wall hung a calendar and photos – of Pari's ex-husband and her parents, as well as of Vasu's parents and grandfather. So far, so ordinary – except for the large number of pictures of dead people on the wall. Above

the door to the balcony was a banner that would definitely
not be seen in a Hindu household. Arabic calligraphy, in gold
on green silk, proclaimed the first sentence of the Qur'an:
Bismillah . . . In the name of Allah, the merciful, the beneficent.

Mr Ali saw the leader of the men frown when he noticed
the banner. 'Where is the boy?' the man said.

'What boy?' said Mr Ali.

'Don't play games with us, sir. We have information that a
Hindu boy is being brought up as a Muslim in this household.
We want to talk to him.'

'Why?'

One of the young men banged his fist on the coffee table.
'The guru is being polite. Don't take advantage of it. We will
rip this flat apart brick by brick if necessary.'

Mrs Ali spoke for the first time. 'My niece is only renting
the property. The flat actually belongs to Mr Rao – a devout
Hindu man who takes his entire family on a pilgrimage to
the Tirupati temple every year. He will not be happy to
learn that a Hindu religious organisation has damaged his
property.'

The guru waved his hand dismissively. 'There is no need
for any damage if you bring the boy before us. And where is
your niece?'

'Tea,' said Pari, coming out of the kitchen carrying a tray of
cups.

The men looked at her curiously as she put the tray down
on the coffee table, then moved back to join Mrs Ali, pulling
the edge of her sari protectively around herself. Her voice was
clear. 'What do you want with my son?'

'The boy is a Hindu. We do not want a Muslim to raise him. We've come to take him away.'

'Vasu is my son. How would you feel if some strangers barged into your house and threatened to take away your children?'

'It's not the same at all. My children are mine – and I am bringing them up in their tradition. I am not creating some kind of hybrid like a farmed chicken.'

'I am not forcing Vasu to be anything that he is not. See that picture.' Pari pointed to the photo of Vasu's parents on the wall. 'Those are his birth parents. My boy knows where he comes from. Nothing is being hidden from him. Have no fear that he is being raised as a Muslim.' She folded her hands in supplication. 'I am a widow. I don't have a powerful family to protect me. I am just trying to do the best for myself and my son. Please leave.'

The guru sat silent for a moment. 'It's good that you've told the boy who his parents are. But just as the water of even the Ganges needs to be stored in a silver pot to retain its purity, the boy cannot be raised in a Muslim household without some of your beliefs rubbing off on him. See, you are probably a nice person. I don't have anything against you personally. But your forefathers abandoned their original faith and converted to an alien religion. I was willing to take a long view on how the boy was being brought up, but I heard that the people of your mosque are demanding that Vasu should be converted. So we can't take the risk of leaving him with you any more.'

'How—' began Pari before biting her tongue.

There was a sudden noise outside the flat and a man came

rushing in. 'Sir, guruji. The man in the flat opposite says that he saw the boy being taken away by this old couple's son. Up the stairs, towards the terrace.'

The guru stood up, his face tight with anger. He wagged his finger in the Alis' and Pari's faces. 'You've not heard the last of this by any means.' He turned to the man who had come in with the news. 'What are you still doing here, standing like a statue? Go! Find that boy and bring him back to me.'

'What about the man who is with the boy, sir?'

'Do I look as if I am worried about him? Beat him and throw him off the roof for all I care.'

There were squeaks from Mrs Ali and Pari as the guru and his men stalked out.

CHAPTER ELEVEN

The grey concrete slab of the terrace was still warm from absorbing the sun's rays all day. It was bordered by a waist-high wall and punctuated at regular intervals by half-raised pillars. Between two of them, somebody had strung a line on which a yellow sari had dried to a crisp. The only other structure was a water tank on short stilts at the far end. There was no place to hide here and ... Rehman had a sudden thought and went back to the doorway. He grimaced when he saw that the bolt was on the other side of the door, which made sense. Why would anybody want to lock themselves out on the terrace?

The building faced east and he didn't dare to go that way in case the men gathered on the road below saw him. Along the length of the left-hand edge was the roof of his own house, but it was two storeys below and inaccessible. To his right was another building of equal height, but because the land sloped that way, it was at least seven or eight feet higher than where they were standing – not to mention the fact that there was at least a ten-foot gap between the two buildings.

He rushed to the far end, or the backside, as the watchman would call it, squeezed past the water tank and looked out. The land behind belonged to a widow who lived there with her daughter-in-law. Despite the land being worth millions of rupees, she survived on the money she made by grinding batter for dosas and the coconuts she sold from her own trees. The canopy of one of them leaned close to the wall.

Rehman studied the coconut tree carefully and turned to Vasu. 'What do you think?'

Vasu shook his head. 'If you are thinking what I think you are thinking, you are mad. We'll both break our necks.'

'Did you get that dialogue from a movie?'

Vasu nodded.

Rehman said, 'If . . . no, *when* we get out of here, I need to have a word with your mother about how many movies you are watching.'

If only it was any other tree, thought Rehman, they could have tried to climb down its branches. A coconut tree, however, is just a single cylindrical trunk with a crown of leaves on top. It was impossible to either ascend or descend it unless you were a monkey or a trained coconut picker – and even they used a special sling made of hemp rope and rubber to move up and down. Vasu was right: the coconut tree would lead to a broken neck faster than it led to freedom.

He and Vasu went back to the stairs. They could hear the heavy feet of the activists coming up the stairwell. Rehman became desperate. He was under no illusions what would happen. Once they recognised him, they would think that he was some sort of agent sent to infiltrate their ranks and, if he wasn't actually beaten to death, he would be left fairly close to it. What could he do?

With a sudden thought, he made for the dried sari. Before he reached it, Vasu shouted, 'Don't touch it.'

Rehman jerked his hand away in surprise. 'Shh!' he said. 'Don't talk so loudly.' He cocked his head to check whether the men below had heard Vasu, but luckily, they were making so much noise with their slogans that Vasu's voice had been drowned out. 'Why can't I touch it?'

'It is madi-battalu,' said Vasu.

'Oh!' said Rehman, laughing. 'I don't care. I thought you were worried about something important like stealing or something.'

There must be a Brahmin family in the flats. Only they were strict about madi. In Brahmin households, a woman was considered unclean while she was menstruating and was not allowed to enter the kitchen. After her period ended, she would take a ritual bath to purify herself. The clothes she wore before that bath were unclean too, and nobody was allowed to touch them.

'If we don't use it, it is our blood that will be spilled,' said Rehman.

Vasu looked blank. Rehman realised that while Vasu might have known about madi and avoiding such clothes, he didn't really understand what lay behind the prohibitions.

'Take the other end of the sari and twist,' said Rehman.

Once the cotton sari resembled a rope, he knotted the two ends together, so that it formed a loop. Rehman unhooked the clothes line from the pillars, his fingers clumsy and stiff with fear. He could not believe that such an obvious hiding place as the terrace would remain unsearched for long.

'Come on,' he said. 'We don't have time to waste.'

Vasu eyed the flimsy cotton loop and the thin nylon rope with misgivings. 'I don't think—'

'Didn't your mother tell you to listen to me?'

'Yes, of course, but still . . .'

They reached the far end of the terrace again. As Rehman looked at the gap between the wall, the coconut leaves near them and the long, slim trunk of the tree, he could understand Vasu's reluctance. Trying to descend the tree was a quick way to commit suicide.

'Give me your chappal,' he said.

Vasu took off his flip-flops.

'Just one, keep the other one on,' said Rehman.

He flung the rope around one of the coconut branches. It took three goes before he was able to snag it and tie the ends to the nearest pillar. A thin nylon bridge now closed the gap to the tree.

Rehman took careful aim with Vasu's flip-flop – he would get only one chance to do this – and threw the slipper onto the widow's land. He twirled the looped sari like a lasso in his right hand and pointed with his left. 'You first. I'll follow.'

'Are you sure?'

The noise from the crowd, which had died down a bit, now rose again. It also seemed to be coming closer.

'Quick,' said Rehman, unable to keep the worry out of his voice or his eyes from flicking towards the stairs. 'I think they are coming up.'

His last view of the terrace before it dropped out of his sight was the door swinging open.

The men stumbled out of the doorway and spilled out on the terrace, like water from a broken pipe. 'They are not here,' shouted one of them.

'The neighbour said he had seen them go up on to the terrace. They must be here. Look everywhere.'

They spread out, peering over the edges and behind the pillars. 'Guys, come here . . .'

The men rushed to the far end by the water tank. A blue rope, most of its colour leached from long exposure to the sun, trailed from an iron rod sticking out of a pillar to one of the branches of the coconut tree.

'It looks so thin . . .'

'It's nylon, very strong. Look, down there.'

It was already getting dark and they had to squint. A boy's lone rubber flip-flop lay halfway across the neighbour's land. 'But how can anybody get down a coconut tree?'

'That's how,' said a third man, pointing.

A yellow cotton sari, faded from repeated washing, twisted to form a rope and knotted into a loop, lay like a three-day-old marigold garland at the base of the tree.

'Go. Run down. That way – round the block. Ask if anybody's seen a man and a boy leaving. Come on, come on, move it.'

The men rushed away and then stopped as their guru came out onto the terrace. The man who had given the earlier orders tugged the nylon rope away from the tree and took it to the older man. 'They've managed to escape, sir.'

'They can run but they can't hide. Keep the men looking for the boy, but once they find him, just keep an eye on him. Don't bring him back.'

'Why, sir, won't the boy be in greater danger then? We might lose track of him again.'

The guru stroked his beard. 'The elections are still several weeks away. This will give the story wings. Call your tame reporters and tell them that a Hindu boy has been kidnapped by Muslims. After all, if they didn't have anything to hide, why would they spirit him away?'

'You are a genius, sir. It'll be in all the newspapers tomorrow.'

'I don't care about the English papers – the people who read them don't vote anyway. It's the regional papers that are important. Let's go.'

The men had their mobile phones out before they reached the stairs. Silence again descended on the terrace and it grew steadily darker. Several minutes passed before the galvanised iron sheet covering the water tank slowly rose on its hinges. The only witness was a bat flying past. Just at that moment it dropped a half-eaten fruit of a wild almond, the shell making a loud metal ping. The lid fell back with a jerk.

It was another five minutes before the lid rose again and two wet figures climbed out of the tank, resembling water-logged kittens. 'Are they g-gone?' said Vasu, his teeth chattering in the evening breeze.

They were lucky that the water had absorbed the heat of the sun all day, but the soaking still left them shivering.

'Let's go down,' said Rehman. 'But be careful. We don't want anybody to see us – not even the neighbours.'

★

When Mrs Ali was a girl, everybody would meet up in her grandparents' house at lunchtime for Eid. 'Everybody' meant her parents and siblings, four of her five uncles and aunts, several cousins and her grandparents. Her eldest uncle, who had spent half his life in a faraway mining town, leaving his wife and kids behind in his parents' house, had come home after retirement, by which time Mrs Ali was ten or eleven. He always had a huge smile on his face and was beloved by all the children because he was generous with his 'eidi', the money the men gave the women and children after returning from the festival prayers at the mosque.

'Isn't this the happiest day ever?' he would say. Mrs Ali could still remember his red paan-stained teeth. 'I am sure that on this day everybody in the world is joyous.'

Even as a child, Mrs Ali knew that it wasn't true. Her uncle had only to look at his own house to see it. His wife invariably looked frazzled, cooking a festive lunch for so many people. And her grandparents were always melancholy despite their smiles. One Ramzaan her grandmother had let slip the reason: one of their sons had migrated to Pakistan after the Partition and on this day of the year they missed him the most.

If Mrs Ali didn't believe in a day of universal happiness, she did think of Eid as a day when the whole family got together. The festival this year would be horrible: Rehman and Vasu had fled to Vasu's grandfather's village to escape the vigilantes who were still hunting for the boy. Azhar would probably not come to their house. Her eldest sister was no more. Mrs Ali felt heartsick at the thought of Eid.

She was standing at the gate, barely noticing the world go

past, when Mr Ali came back from the butcher's. 'I managed to get the meat,' he said. 'But are you sure the festival is tomorrow? Hasn't it been only twenty-nine days since you started fasting?'

'It's possible. Not all months have thirty days; some have only twenty-nine.'

Mr Ali handed the thin polythene bag of mutton to his wife. 'I'll go to the mosque and check,' he said.

'Are you sure? After all, the imam—'

'We are still members of the mosque. Why shouldn't I go there?'

'I suppose so . . .'

The traffic had picked up and Mr Ali had to walk along the dusty edge of the road. He thought about what his wife had said: that some months just had twenty-nine days. The Muslim calendar is a purely lunar one – and, depending on the exact time of day that the new moon is born, some months end up shorter than others. But beyond that astronomical fact, there was another reason for twenty-nine-day months.

Once upon a time, the Prophet, peace be upon him, had been dismayed by the squabbling of his wives and declared that he would stay away from them for a month. He moved to his daughter's house and returned after twenty-nine days. The Prophet's youngest wife, Ayesha, had teased him that it wasn't yet a month and he is said to have replied, 'Some months have only twenty-nine days.'

Mr Ali usually took the same route to the fish market and, by habit, he almost walked past the mosque before doubling back. A large number of men were crowded near the entrance, each with just one question on their lips. 'Has the moon been sighted?' and 'Is it Eid tomorrow?' Actually, that was two questions, but they both meant the same thing.

Mr Ali noticed among them Razaaq, his friend with the seat-cover business. Razaaq had been in the crowd led by the imam, demanding that Vasu be converted to Islam. But Mr Ali wasn't one to hold grudges. If you were a member of a committee, you had to go along with it – collective cabinet responsibility and all that. After all, even his own brother-in-law had accompanied the visitors. It's funny, he thought, that the mosque committee and that Hindu organisation had come up with pretty much the same demand.

He made his way through the crowd and said, 'Salaam A'laikum, Razaaq mian.'

Razaaq made a face as if he had just bitten into a peanut and found it foul-tasting. His eyes slid away and he moved off with a cough.

Mr Ali showed no reaction, but he was deeply hurt. He and Razaaq had known each other for a long time. Almost thirty years ago, Mr Ali had been posted to Pithapuram, Razaaq's native town. While he was there, Razaaq's parents had needed a residence certificate because their ration card had been accidentally put in the wash and they had to apply for a replacement. It had been a trivial matter for somebody like Mr Ali, working in a government office, to cut through the bureaucracy and get the certificate issued, but it had saved Razaaq's parents a lot of hassle. Later, when Mr and Mrs Ali moved to Vizag, they had asked them to look up their son. Razaaq's parents were no more but the men's friendship had remained strong since then – until now.

As he moved towards the edge of the throng, somebody tapped him on his shoulder. He turned around to see Razaaq. His friend didn't meet his eye, but whispered, 'Go back home. There'll be trouble.'

'Why should I—' began Mr Ali, but Razaaq slipped away.

What did Razaaq mean by trouble? Before Mr Ali could think further about it, he was face to face with a group of young men, ostentatiously religious, with beards, skullcaps and long-flowing Arab robes. 'You are not welcome here, old man. Go away,' said one of them.

Mr Ali peered at the speaker and said, 'Saajid! What do you mean by being so rude? Don't you know who I am?'

'You are the man who defies our imam and goes against our Prophet's sunna, his teaching. You are not welcome here.'

'Does your father know you are here?'

'Of course he does. He is happy to see me on the true path.'

Mr Ali remembered the rumours about Saajid spending time with girls and drinking. If religion put a stop to that, any father would be glad. But if it made a young man talk rudely to his elders, that wasn't so good, was it?

Mr Ali tried to pass him, but found himself blocked by Saajid and his friends. Mr Ali said, 'Since when have you become the watchman of the mosque, Saajid?'

The youth flushed and one of his friends shoved Mr Ali. Mr Ali stumbled back, rubbing his chest where he had been struck. 'Hey!' he said. 'This is a religious place, not a dance hall to keep people out.' Mr Ali suddenly realised that a circle had opened in the crowd and he was in the centre of it.

'Men who side with the infidels, the kafir, are not welcome here.'

'Then you should go to Pakistan or Saudi Arabia where there are only Muslims,' said Mr Ali. 'We live in Hindustan, in case you've forgotten. And anyway, what's it to do with you? I've been a member of this mosque for years. And regardless of that, I've never heard of a Muslim being denied entry to any mosque anywhere. What kind of sunna is that?' Mr Ali's voice rose and his face turned red. 'I don't believe what the world is coming to.'

Since when did young men care so much about religion anyway? Youth was a time that people spent carelessly, in the way that a farmer with a riverside field used water, knowing that more would flow his way the following day. As the years passed and there was less time left to them, people started facing up to what came after and turned more religious. He himself had never had the urge, but that's how his brother-in-law, Azhar, had changed – from a fun-loving man who enjoyed a joke and laughed heartily with a wide circle of friends, to a bearded, serious individual who spent an awful lot of time in the mosque. But that, at least, was the natural order of things. That's how people had always behaved. This new trend for young men to be more religious than their fathers was odd – and dangerous, Mr Ali couldn't help feeling. He thought again of Azhar, who, in his twenties, had flirted with communism. Mr Ali remembered a dinner at his in-laws' house soon after he had got married at which Azhar had argued that religion was a tool to subdue the poor – a drug to keep them compliant. Mr Ali wondered whether Azhar remembered those days any more.

Somebody shoved Mr Ali again and he snapped out of his reverie. The crowd around him had grown and he suddenly felt alone and vulnerable. The young men nearest to him suddenly parted and the imam, Azhar and a few other older men were standing in front of him.

'I've come to find out if Eid is tomorrow,' said Mr Ali.

'I don't know which mosque you belong to, so I can't say what your imam has decided.'

Mr Ali's eyes slid from the imam's face to Azhar's. Azhar turned red and looked away. Mr Ali's attention flicked back to the imam's youthful face.

'I belong to this mosque.'

'You are not welcome here. You will not be allowed entry on the day of Eid. When you die, nobody from this mosque will come to your house for the burial. Maybe your family can use the government crematorium.'

Mr Ali flushed. Hindus burned their dead. Muslims buried theirs.

'Hasn't your study of the Qur'an taught you that tomorrow is guaranteed to nobody? I am older than you, but I might still be alive twenty years from now while tomorrow night your family might be wailing over your body.'

The imam inclined his head. Saajid roared, thrusting his face close to Mr Ali's, 'Hey, oldie! Are you threatening the imam in front of his own mosque?'

Mr Ali was glad to see Saajid's father, Razaaq, pull his son back and was then shocked when Saajid brushed his father's hand away brusquely.

Mr Ali raised his voice. 'If you will not bury my body in the graveyard, I will arrange for people to break in overnight and bury me just inside the mosque by the entrance so you will all have to step over me on the way to your prayers.'

There was a shocked silence and the crowd parted as Mr Ali turned away.

The imam's voice was soft behind him. 'There is no festival tomorrow. The moon has not been sighted. I suggest that you use the day to fast and show your gratitude to Allah for the gift of this duniya, this world, and the faith that He has given you.'

At ten the next morning, Mr Ali was sitting in his living room with his wife and Pari.

Mrs Ali said to him, 'The imam was right about one thing, anyway. You should fast during Ramzaan. All over the world, Muslims fast in this month. And they have much more physically demanding jobs than you – farmers, soldiers, rickshaw pullers, manual labourers. Many of them don't have proper food to start the fast either. They just eat a few grains of coarse salt, drink a bit of water and that's their preparation for the day. You sit at the front of the house, under a fan, talking to a few people and scribbling a few lines on paper. How hard can it be for you to fast?'

'Don't get started on that now,' said Mr Ali. 'It doesn't matter whether I was fasting or whether I had been to Mecca on the Haj, they would still have kicked me out.'

'Chaacha is right,' said Pari. 'It is about politics, not religion.'

'Take his side,' muttered Mrs Ali.

'What did you say?' said Mr Ali, just as the doorbell rang.

'Nothing,' said Mrs Ali. 'Go and see who it is.'

Mr Ali came back within seconds with Azhar's granddaughter and her husband in tow. Mrs Ali's face broke into a smile. 'When did you come from the village? What are you doing here? Does Azhar know that you are here?'

'My grandfather is a fool,' said Faiz.

Mrs Ali blinked in surprise. 'Faiz—'

Faiz turned to Mr Ali. 'It is true. I couldn't believe it when I heard what happened yesterday at the mosque. He taught me that family always comes first. How could he stand there watching while you were insulted?'

Mrs Ali said, 'These things are complicated, Faiz.'

'Nothing could be simpler. You all are coming with us to the village now.'

'What? How come you are in Vizag anyway?'

'I came to take you away as soon as I heard what happened. You cannot spend the day of Eid on your own.'

Mr and Mrs Ali glanced at Faiz's husband. 'I agree,' he said. 'If you are here, it will just create more trouble. My parents invite you as well.'

'I've spoken to Rehman. I know that he and Vasu are not here either. So what's holding you all back?' said Faiz. She turned to Pari. 'You are coming too, of course.'

'I don't think—'

Within the hour, all of them were squeezed into a taxi, going to Faiz's village.

CHAPTER TWELVE

When they reached their destination, Mrs Ali remembered her previous visit to Faiz's house with Azhar. Had that been just a month ago? Usually, the month of Ramzaan brought her peace because the troubles of the world would be sublimated in its familiar patterns: the need to get up early to eat, then the low-level hunger and thirst that became easier to handle as the month went on, but was always present just below the surface; the routine of the prayers that punctuated the day; and the anticipation of the first sip of water and the first bite into a date as the sun dipped in the west. The spring-cleaning of the house, the making of the sevian, the fine vermicelli noodles that are eaten only at Ramzaan, the new clothes and a host of other details that come with the festival, marked the passage of the holy month. This year, however, had been anything but joyous. First, the news had come of the road widening and the worry over its impact on the house, then the kerfuffle with the Hindu organisation about Vasu, and finally their dreadful excommunication from their own mosque . . . None of these problems had been resolved, either. What was Allah thinking of, burdening them with all this at their age?

'Daadi, don't look so glum. Tomorrow is the festival. Think about that.'

Mrs Ali smiled at Faiz. 'You are right, my dear. I've fasted for thirty days and tomorrow is the feast. Allah has given us one day to enjoy and forget our anxieties. We might as well make use of that.'

'Thirty? We've fasted only for twenty-nine, because we started one day later.'

'Yes, I'd forgotten about that. So, is Eid definitely tomorrow?'

'I am not sure, but everybody is saying so. Even the government has announced that the public holiday is tomorrow. But we have to wait and see what the imam decides.'

'Don't talk to me about imams,' said Mrs Ali.

'Did you know that yesterday we took the microwave with us to Grandfather's house and dumped it there?'

The thought of a stinking appliance in Azhar's house, just in time for Ramzaan, cheered Mrs Ali. Serves him right! she thought. A tiny twinge of conscience pricked her, but she suppressed it ruthlessly. Her brother deserved it.

'Let's go to the dargah,' she said. 'There's still an hour before sunset.'

'There won't be anybody to offer the prayers at the saint's tomb,' said Faiz.

'That doesn't matter. I just want to visit it.'

Faiz told her mother-in-law where they were going and they set off. They asked Pari whether she wanted to come too, but she was talking to Vasu on the phone and stayed behind. It was a short walk to the dargah and once there they sat on a cement bench in the shadow of the onion-dome surmounting the saint's tomb. Their own heads were covered by the ends of their saris, to show respect for this holy place.

'The microwave oven was a gift from your father. It's a pity that you had to return it.'

Faiz shrugged. 'The microwave is a silly thing to bring to a village like this. There are four ladies and a number of serving maids always in the house. We cook every meal from scratch. All our pots and pans have to be big enough to hold food for at least a dozen people. The microwave was just a show-off item – something to impress visitors with. I am done with such things.'

'Maasha' Allah!' God has willed it! Mrs Ali cracked her knuckles on the sides of her head. 'You are growing up to be a sensible woman. You will have a wonderful time in your in-laws' house, I am sure.'

'I know that I am a lucky woman,' said Faiz, blushing. 'In all the time that the microwave was smelling bad, my husband didn't say a single word. In fact, he defended me whenever his sisters or any of the others tried to make fun of me.'

Mrs Ali smiled. 'He loves you. Anybody can see that. A woman with a loving husband is lucky indeed, for what else can God give her that's a bigger boon than that?'

The ladies ate at home while the men went to the mosque to break their fast, coming home half an hour later with the dishes in which the food had been taken to the mosque.

'Where is the big aluminium pan?' asked Faiz's mother-in-law.

Faiz's husband said, 'The dish with the chicken curry?

There was still some left and the Ibrahim brothers were late and still eating, so we left it there.'

'Left it there? We'll lose it, for sure. Last year, my deep ladle, which I had brought from my mother's house when I got married, went missing when you men left it at the mosque.'

Faiz and her sisters-in-law looked at each other and suppressed smiles. They had heard their mother-in-law moan about the missing ladle at least thirty-six times in the preceding twelve months.

'Is it Eid tomorrow?' asked Faiz.

They had received a phone call from her father in Bangalore and her grandfather in Vizag, and in both places the festival was being celebrated the next day. A short message had been broadcast on television from the imam of the Jamia Masjid in Delhi, congratulating Muslims all over India on enjoying the blessing of another holy month that had given them an opportunity to wipe out their sins, and wishing them a happy Eid. The newscaster had said that the festival was also being celebrated the following day in Saudi Arabia and most Middle-Eastern countries.

'Well, there's not much doubt about it. The whole world seems to agree on the date, for once.'

'But we've fasted for only twenty-nine days,' said Faiz's mother-in-law.

'We started late; it doesn't mean we also have to finish late,' her husband said. 'The discussions were still going on when we left the mosque. We are going to the imam's house now to find out what's been decided.'

The men, including Mr Ali, went out again.

After a few minutes, Faiz's mother-in-law said, 'I am sure they'll forget to bring back the big aluminium dish. The servants have retired for the day. Shall we go too?'

Faiz agreed, and the women also left for the imam's house.

In the hour since the sun had set, darkness had fallen and they had to carry a kerosene lantern to light their way.

'Careful, there might be snakes,' said one of Faiz's sisters-in-law.

'Foolish girl, don't mention those creatures after dark. They know when they are being called and they'll make a beeline for you. Refer to them as ropes, instead, and we'll know what we are talking about but they won't.'

'Sorry.'

'Look, Faiz, your friend's house is dark.'

'They are Hindus, so this is a free holiday for them. They have gone to Vizag.'

'The fragrance of the night-queen plant in their garden is pretty strong, isn't it?'

Faiz's sister-in-law piped up, 'Isn't that plant supposed to attract snak— oops, ropes?'

'Yes,' said Faiz's mother-in-law and turned to Faiz. 'You should tell your friend to chop the plant down.'

Mrs Ali enjoyed the walk with the other ladies, but the village was small and it took them just a few minutes to reach the imam's house, hard by the wall of the mosque. All the Muslim families of the village must have been represented because about thirty or forty men were standing outside.

Faiz's husband saw them and walked over. His mother said to him, 'Get the vessel from the mosque.'

'The imam's wife has taken it for cleaning.'

'There must have been a lot of curry left for her to do that,' said Faiz's mother-in-law, darkly.

The ladies laughed. The imam's wife acted as if she were superior to all her neighbours because of her husband's job and most of the local women disliked her.

'There's a very interesting discussion going on,' said Faiz's husband. 'The Ibrahim brothers claim that they've seen the moon but the imam refuses to believe them.'

'But they said on TV ... Come on, ladies, let's go to the rear entrance.'

They knocked on the wooden door until the imam's teenage daughter opened it.

'Is your mother in?'

'Yes, Auntie.'

Faiz's mother-in-law walked in before the young girl could say anything more. The others followed. The teenager stood by the door, undecided whether to stay and latch the door or to rush into the house and announce the visitors.

'Salaam A'laikum, sister,' said Faiz's mother-in-law.

'Wa'laikum as'salaam. There was no need for your whole family to come over just to take the dish back. I would have sent it over later with the men.'

'Oh, do you have the dish?' Faiz's mother-in-law waved her hand dismissively. 'I didn't even realise that it hadn't been brought back. We came here to find out whether tomorrow is Eid or not.'

'Have you left your menfolk cooking in the kitchen?' the imam's wife said and laughed.

Mrs Ali and Pari exchanged glances. Mrs Ali shook her

head almost imperceptibly. Pari smiled tightly and looked away, not wanting to betray herself by laughing out loud. Why would she want to intrude on a confrontation between two queen bees? Had a rabid dog bitten her and sent her mad?

'We made a lot of chicken curry. It will probably be useful for you tomorrow – whether it is Eid or not.'

'I—' began the imam's wife, but a loud shout in the front of the house interrupted her. The ladies exchanged glances and made for the doorway, from where they could see the men.

The imam was standing with his back to them, with the other men clustered in front of him in a semicircle. Mrs Ali could see Faiz's husband and his brothers on the edge of the crowd, looking uncomfortable. Two tall men stood directly in front of them, leaning towards the imam. 'The Ibrahim brothers,' whispered Faiz to Mrs Ali, who nodded. The brothers who had come late to the breaking of the fast at the mosque.

The brother on the right wagged his finger in the imam's face. 'I tell you, we saw the moon. It was bright as a silver sickle. Eid has to be tomorrow.'

'Weren't the two of you seen drinking alcohol in the market town last month?' asked the imam.

'That's a lie. Who's spreading these calumnies about us? And anyway, what has that got to do with us seeing the moon today?' The brother on the right, who seemed to be the younger one, was the more forceful. His nose glowed red and sweat glistened on his forehead. 'And they've announced the news on television as well. The government has declared tomorrow as a holiday. If we don't celebrate tomorrow, I'll lose three days' pay, because the weekend will also be counted as time off.'

'That's no reason to say that Eid will be tomorrow. The government can declare anything they want. I'll go by our traditions. Eid is either the day after the moon is sighted or when we have fasted for thirty days. Neither is the case now.'

Several other men joined in the argument. 'Don't be so old-fashioned. Do you think the imam of Delhi would have come on television if he was not sure?'

The imam was inflexible. 'Delhi is far away and in this mosque I am the imam.'

The mood grew angrier as the realisation spread that a delay would mean taking an unpaid day off from work.

'Are you saying that the whole world is wrong and only you are right? We agreed to delay starting the fast because you didn't see the moon until it was so plump that it was clearly a second-day moon. Now you are saying that we should delay the festival just because you didn't see it again. What kind of imam does that make you?'

'A blind one,' shouted the older Ibrahim brother and the crowd laughed.

Behind the curtain, the imam's wife turned to her daughter and muttered, 'People will happily fast for twenty-nine days, but they get upset at having to fast on that last day.'

Mrs Ali kept silent, but she agreed with the observation. She too had noticed the same thing over the years.

'If a Haji, a person who has been on the pilgrimage to Mecca, swears on the Qur'an that he has sighted the moon, then I will agree to celebrate the festival. Otherwise, we fast tomorrow. That's my final word as the imam. Now, leave me alone to prepare for the night-time prayers.'

He turned his back on the assembly and came into the house. The ladies retreated to the backyard, collected the aluminium dish – devoid of curry – and made their way home. This time the lane was crowded with men. Most of them seemed resigned to the decision, but the Ibrahim brothers were still annoyed.

'He called us liars to our face,' said the older one. 'The festival has got to be tomorrow.' He made his way to an older man in the middle of the crowd. 'Uncle, what do you say?'

'I think we started fasting a day late and tomorrow is the festival,' said the old man and shrugged. 'But as there is no Haji in the village, there is no way we can satisfy the imam and so I guess we should just leave it till the day after tomorrow.'

'The imam knows as well as everybody else that the only man to have gone to Mecca from our village is your brother, and he is in heaven, by God's grace. The imam was taunting you because you have not been able to go on the pilgrimage.'

'I say, I am sure that's not what—'

The men turned off down a side lane and their words were lost to Mrs Ali, who focused her attention instead on what Faiz's mother-in-law was saying.

'Did you see how that woman didn't return the leftover curry?'

It was eight-forty-five in the evening, and Pari, the Alis and all of Faiz's family were gathered in the living room.

'I love the turquoise border on your sari,' one of the women said to Pari.

'Oh, it's not a new sari—'

'—she doesn't use ginger. Tell me, how can upma taste good without ginger in it?' said Faiz's mother-in-law.

Mrs Ali nodded and barely suppressed a yawn. She wasn't a late-night person at the best of times, and the month of getting up early and fasting had taken its toll. She wondered how Rehman was coping in the village with Vasu. Vasu's grandfather's hut was small and basic. What were they doing for food?

'South Africa were good, but I thought India could have easily beaten them if they had batted more intelligently.'

'But their bowlers—'

Mr Ali didn't understand the mania for cricket, not just among the youth, but among many older people too. He looked across the room to his wife. 'Tomorrow will be your thirty-first day of fasting, won't it?'

'Yes,' said Mrs Ali. 'In all my years, I've never had to do that. I'd better go to bed. Otherwise, I won't be able to get up tomorrow at four in the morning.'

She stood up and Faiz's mother-in-law turned to Faiz. 'Go with your great-aunt and make sure the bed is made up.'

As Faiz also stood, there was a loud knock at the door. Every eye swung involuntarily towards the big clock on the wall: old and made in England, as Faiz's father-in-law was proud of pointing out. Faiz's husband jumped up, opened the door slightly and peeked out.

'Come in. What's the matter?' he said, opening the door more fully. The younger Ibrahim brother was standing there.

'Sorry, I don't have time. I need to tell all the families in the village. Eid is tomorrow.'

Mrs Ali stopped in her tracks, as did Faiz. 'What?' said seven voices, in a chorus.

'Has the imam changed his mind?' said Mr Ali.

'Yes, the imam is convinced. Sorry, got to go. The khutba, the festival sermon, starts at eight-thirty.'

They woke up to a beautifully overcast day, the sun shooting luminous arrows through breaks in the clouds, like a painting in which the artist is trying to depict heavenly beneficence falling on a bonny child in front of a copy of the Qur'an.

'Eid Mubarak,' they greeted each other.

There was a mad rush for the bathroom because everybody had to take a head-bath. 'Why can't I wear my new clothes now?' said Faiz's nine-year-old nephew.

'Eat your breakfast first. Otherwise you'll drop it down the front of your new shirt before you've even gone to the mosque,' the boy's mother said.

'But Chaacha has worn his new clothes,' the boy said, pointing at his paternal uncle, Faiz's husband.

'Just *sit down* and eat. I have a ton of work,' said his mother crossly. The boy started crying.

Pari sat down next to him. 'Shall I feed you? What are you going to do with your eidi – the money you get today?'

The boy wiped his eyes with the back of his hands and said, 'My mother takes it all away. She says it is to pay for the eidis that my father has to pay to the other boys. That's not fair because my cousins can keep their money.'

'I'll tell you what. Let's bargain with your mother so that you can keep some of it.' She gathered the first spoon of the vermicelli with milk and fed him with it.

The boy's mother patted Pari's shoulder with gratitude and disappeared into the kitchen.

Mrs Ali took a bath, changed into a new sari and came back into the room given to her and her husband, to find him standing by the suitcase.

'What are you doing?' she asked. 'I packed all the clothes neatly. Don't pull them out like that. You'll make a mess.'

'I am looking for a handkerchief.'

She pushed him out of the way and took out the kerchief from a corner. 'Did you take your cap?'

'No.'

'OK, I'll get it. Go and eat your breakfast quickly. You have to leave for the mosque soon.'

As if on cue, an electrically amplified voice boomed through the village.

Hayya 'ala salat,	Make haste towards worship,
Hayya 'alal-falah.	Hasten towards the true success . . .

'See, the muezzin has already started his call.'

The men and the children, both boys and girls, were soon assembled at the front of the house – the older men wearing silken Nehru suits, taken out after a year in storage, pressed and smelling of mothballs, and the youngsters wearing brand-new clothes, stitched and delivered just a couple of days ago. Faiz came out with a bottle of ittar and a ball of cotton with which she applied the traditional perfume to all the men's clothes.

A sudden calm descended on the house as the men left. The ladies sat down in the living room, taking the opportunity to catch their breath before starting their own prayers and beginning the cooking. Mrs Ali, aware that Pari was not with them, went to investigate. She found Pari sitting on her bed by a window, looking out, her face blank and impassive. Mrs Ali tiptoed in, though it was doubtful whether an elephant tramping into the room would have disturbed the young woman. She sat beside Pari and laid her hand on her shoulder. Several moments later, Pari turned towards Mrs Ali, who realised that she had been wrong about the lack of emotion on Pari's face. Two unshed tears had gathered in the corners of her eyes, glittering like diamonds.

'Everybody leaves you,' Pari said. 'Nobody stays.'

Mrs Ali gulped. She couldn't think of a word to say, even if her throat had been capable of saying it. Pari had lost her husband a couple of years ago; then the previous year, her father too had passed away after being bedridden for more than ten months. The poor girl had seen more tragedy in her young life than those who had lived far longer.

'Those whom God loves, He takes to his fold early,' said Mrs Ali finally.

'I loved my husband and my father too. Then why was He so selfish? Of all the people in the world, why did He have to take from me the two men I loved the most? Does He have a shortage of people in heaven? Tell me, Chaachi, is there such a shortage of people in heaven?'

Mrs Ali blotted Pari's tears with the edge of her sari. 'Who knows why God does anything? He is not human, after all, and our minds can't fathom His reasons.'

Pari shook her head and turned back to the window. 'If only Vasu was here. He would have enjoyed all the hubbub of a festival in a large household.'

'Yes, it's a pity that he is not here. You wouldn't have felt so lonely then.'

Pari turned suddenly to Mrs Ali. 'Oh, I am sorry for being so selfish. You must be missing Rehman terribly too.'

Mrs Ali shrugged. 'Just keep busy and it will be all right. And of course you don't have to apologise. You have more to miss.'

The two women sat in companionable silence, listening to the sounds in the background of the ladies of the household. Pari raised her head, alert as a hound that had caught sight of a rabbit. 'I hear Vasu,' she said.

'Don't be sil—' began Mrs Ali, just as Vasu burst into the room and jumped into Pari's lap.

Pari nuzzled her face into Vasu's neck. 'My baby . . . my baby.' Now, the tears flowed freely down her cheeks.

Mrs Ali heard a noise and turned. Rehman was standing there, tall and lean. She got out of bed and hugged him, tears in her own eyes. 'How . . . When . . . '

Mrs Ali soon stepped back. 'Go to the mosque. Hurry. It hasn't been long since the muezzin called out the azdan and the prayers won't have started yet.'

At the mosque, Mr Ali and the rest of Faiz's family had been among the early arrivals and had found a place near the front, as intended. Other families trickled in and slowly took their places. There was one question on everybody's lips. 'Why had the imam changed his mind about the day of the festival?'

There were all happy, of course, that Eid was today, though some of the children wished it were not, as that would have meant two days of holiday instead of one: the official one today and the real one tomorrow. But new clothes, the prospect of receiving money later on and the smell of rich food being prepared was enough to make everybody festive. The pleasant cloudy weather was a welcome bonus and, everybody said, a sign of Allah's favour.

'The imam is gone . . . '

'What do you mean gone? Who's going to lead the prayers? Who's going to give the sermon?'

'I went to his house this morning and the door was wide open. The house was bare.'

'Have you been drinking, like the Ibrahim brothers?'

'No, it's true, I tell you.'

'The chai-shop owner said that he saw the imam leaving the village in a bullock cart late last night with his wife and daughter. He said the cart was loaded with what looked like all their belongings.'

'Don't be ridiculous. How can the imam leave the village the night before Eid?'

Rumours swirled through the crowd. A middle-aged, barrel-chested man sitting next to Mr Ali in the front row suddenly stood up. 'Silence,' he shouted. His voice carried like that of an army sergeant and after a couple more such admonitions the congregation became quiet.

'Yesterday evening, most of us were at the imam's house. He was adamant then that since the moon had not been sighted in this village, the festival would not be celebrated today. After that, we were all informed that he had changed his mind. And now I hear that the imam is not in the village at all. What's going on? Have we been played for fools?'

At this, the men started talking to their neighbours again.

'Who told you?'

'The older Ibrahim brother.'

'And you?'

'The younger one.'

It was soon clear that they had all been called to the mosque by one of the two brothers.

'Where are the brothers?' The barrel-chested man was speaking again. 'I have not missed a day's fast since I was eleven years old, even during my college years when the fast coincided with my degree exams, or in my thirties when I was very ill one Ramzaan. If those brothers are the cause of my missing today's fast, I will thrash them and make them eat burning coals. Religious matters are not to be trifled with.'

The brothers were not in the congregation. Several men stood up and everybody started talking loudly, half of them saying, 'Sit down. Stop shouting.'

An older man made his way to the front and stood facing the congregation. He raised his hands until one or two people in the front noticed him, then he signalled with a motion of his palms for them to sit. Gradually a few others picked up the signal until eventually the mosque was quiet again. Mr Ali recognised him as the man that the Ibrahim brothers had been talking to the previous evening, who had agreed with them that Eid should be today.

'That's Musa,' whispered Faiz's father-in-law to Mr Ali.

Musa had a good public-speaking voice and a lovely old-fashioned Urdu vocabulary.

'My dear men, the Ibrahim brothers have played a trick on us. The imam could not be persuaded to change his mind, so the brothers chased him out of the village overnight.'

The congregation erupted into shouts again.

Mr Ali leaned towards Faiz's father-in-law and whispered to him. Faiz's father-in-law nodded and urged Mr Ali to stand up.

Mr Ali shook his head. 'I am an outsider here. It's best if you do it.'

Faiz's father-in-law stood up next to Musa.

'Friends, brothers ... quiet!' Once the noise levels had died down, he started speaking again. 'We have two choices before us now. We can all lament that we've lost a day of fasting. Or, we can join the rest of the country and celebrate today. Our womenfolk must already be praying in our houses and getting ready to make a festive lunch. Our children are in their best clothes and anticipating an afternoon of fun and sweets. What's the point of throwing it all away? We are gathered in the mosque. I say to you all, Eid Mubarak! I wish you all a happy Eid.'

'How can we celebrate the festival without an imam?'

Faiz's father-in-law pointed to Musa. 'A well-respected and good man is standing right here. I have known him as boy and man, and can heartily recommend him to lead us in prayers today and, insha'Allah, God willing, for many more years.'

Everybody quickly agreed, partly because no man really wanted to go back home and face his wife's disappointment or his Hindu neighbour's scorn at being unable to organise a prayer in a mosque.

Faiz's father-in-law sat down and Musa bent his head for a long moment, before looking up at the crowd. 'I am honoured and humbled by your trust in me. Insha'Allah, I will lead you in prayers today. But I am not a trained imam and we should either try to get back our old imam or find a new man in the longer term.'

He nodded to a young man in the front who jumped up and put his hands to his lips. 'Hayya 'ala salat, make haste towards worship . . . '

When Rehman walked into the mosque, the men were standing in rows. He joined the last line.

'Fill up the lines in front. There should be no gaps,' shouted a man in the front.

There was a tiny space ahead of them and the man on Rehman's left moved forward. Another gap appeared ahead and the man moved forward again, leaving a gap behind him. A couple of minutes later, the last line in which Rehman was still standing had shrunk to less than half its original size, but the lines ahead all occupied the full width of the mosque.

'Straight lines, please.'

The namaaz, ritual prayers, first designed by the Prophet fourteen hundred years ago and followed ever since all over the world, began.

Ten minutes later the namaaz ended and the straight lines dissolved into groups as the men sank to the floor to sit cross-legged. Rehman could finally see his father and Faiz's family in the front row, but decided to stay where he was for the moment when he saw that there was little space near them. A chair was brought and Musa sat facing them. Some men near Rehman half stood and were about to leave the mosque when Musa said, 'Listening to the sermon is as much a part of the Eid worship as the actual prayers. Don't worry, I won't talk for long!'

Several people laughed and the men were embarrassed into sitting down again. Rehman got distracted by a line of ants walking along the narrow gap between two mats in the row in front. Eid or no Eid, life carried on as normal for many of Allah's creatures.

By the time he started paying attention to Musa, the sermon was well under way.

'The people of Israel were led to freedom from the Pharoah by Musa, the prophet whom the Christians call Moses.'

'That's your name, isn't it, Uncle?' said a boy sitting with Faiz's family. Rehman recognised him as Faiz's nephew.

'Shh,' said the boy's grandfather. 'Don't interrupt the sermon.'

Musa smiled gently and didn't seem to mind. 'Yes, I was named after that Prophet, peace be upon him, and maybe that's why his story has always spoken to my heart. In the course of leading his people to the Promised Land, Musa went up a mountain by himself and actually saw God. It seems so simple when you say it like that – he saw God. But very, very few of the thousands of prophets down the ages have physically seen God. Adam, Noah, Abraham, Moses, Jesus and Mohammed – that's it, I think. Musa saw God as a burning bush and that rattled him to his core. He started saying that *he* was God! And that is why Musa himself never reached the Promised Land. There is a deeper truth in this story than first appears.'

Musa, the temporary imam, looked around the crowd and wagged his finger, before continuing.

'The word of God is like a fire on a winter night. If you

stray too far from it, your heart becomes cold and numb. And if you go too close to the fire, your heart gets consumed and you end up doing terrible things, for the word of God is more than most human beings can safely handle. Stay the right distance, however, and God will provide you with warmth and comfort, light and guidance. Amen.'

CHAPTER THIRTEEN

The next day, back in Vizag, Mrs Ali gave the rope one last pull and reached down to grasp the handle of the metal bucket. She was drawing water from the well for the plants. They had become quite dry and looked sadly wilted after the two days she had spent at Faiz's village. She was determined to water them properly now. By the time the bigger plastic bucket was full, she was out of breath – she wasn't as young as she used to be, that was for sure.

She took a mug and started with the potted plants. She couldn't imagine losing all this area when the road was widened, watching while rough men with iron spikes and shovels broke down something that she and her husband had built with so much care and affection. She had personally watered the wall for two weeks after it was built, to cure the cement and make it strong.

'This house will last a hundred years, Amma,' the maestri, or master builder, had assured her.

She plucked a yellowing leaf and cut away another that appeared to have been half chewed by a caterpillar. Some people, she wouldn't name any names, might call her foolish to be tending to a garden that would be soon gone. *She* would take care of it until the last possible day.

The gate opened and the noise made her look up. 'Why have you come?' she asked, frowning when she saw who it was.

'Namaskaaram, madam,' the man said, his smile making his mouth as wide as the gate behind him.

She flinched inwardly but did not let her expression change. She realised that she had not been gracious to a guest, however unwanted he might be, but there was no point in letting him know that.

'Well, every time you come here, it costs me money and you bring me bad news.'

'I am sorry you feel like that, madam. I just came by to greet you on your vermicelli festival. I came yesterday but the house was locked.'

'We were out for the festival. Have you run out of houses to fix electricity meters in?' She knew why he had come, but she would not make it easy for him by giving him an opening.

'I just do what is good for the department, madam. But today, I have come for the maamool.'

The man was shameless – he didn't need an opening to ask for a bribe. Well, it was not quite corrupt practice, she supposed. After all, she had given saris and money to the maid, Leela, and to her daughter, who sometimes filled in for Leela when she was ill. It was an expected part of life: that on big festivals you gave something to servants and others who did things for you.

'Did I miss the Dusserah celebrations?'

That was the big Hindu autumn harvest festival when every single person who had even raised an eyebrow over the past year expected to be given a 'gift'.

Shyam, the meter reader, laughed. 'You are Muslims, madam. We want to feel happy along with you when you celebrate your festival.'

Mrs Ali tightened her lips and went inside for her purse. Trying to evade greedy workers was as pointless as trying to escape blood-sucking mosquitoes – and just as successful.

'A hundred rupees?' Mrs Ali was scandalised. She took out another ten-rupee note from her purse and added it to the one that she had already put in Shyam's hand. 'We don't need another meter put in.'

'Seventy-five, at least, madam. You have a commercial meter – you need to pay more.'

'You made us pay thousands of rupees for a commercial meter that we didn't need and now you want me to pay you a bigger maamool because we have a commercial meter. What cheek you have!' She gave him a twenty-rupee note and tucked the purse under her right arm with finality.

Shyam waited hopefully for a moment, but eventually put the money away in his pocket.

Mrs Ali said, 'Have you heard anything more about the road widening?'

'Yes, madam. I was at the corporator's home only yesterday and saw the papers. The press announcement is going to be released on Monday.'

'Monday?' Mrs Ali was dismayed. A butterfly was fluttering up from a small pink grass-rose flower towards a white guava blossom. Her eyes misted over when she realised that the ground-hugging grass-rose and the tall guava tree would soon be gone. And then, would she ever see a butterfly?

'Yes, madam. Monday.'

'Every time I see you, I hear bad news and lose money. I hope I don't see you again for a long time.'

'You'll see me in a few weeks, madam, for Dusserah.'

'Another maamool? You are asking for money now to feel happy along with us when we celebrate our festival. What will your excuse be then?'

Shyam laughed, his teeth bright and his mouth wide. 'To make *you* feel happy along with us when we celebrate *our* festival, of course.'

Mrs Ali watched him walk away. A man like Shyam would always do well in life – he was an entrepreneur and always had a ready answer for everything. Unfortunately, her own future wasn't looking so bright.

On the verandah, the marriage bureau was open for business as usual. The postman delivered the letters; Aruna reorganised some files, weeding out old members' details; Mr Ali filled in the paying-in slips for the cheques that had come by post; two potential clients came and one became a member, but the second could not be convinced despite their best efforts; a fishwife came to the gate, shouting that she had large fresh-caught prawns for sale, and Mr Ali called out to his wife to handle the woman.

The phone rang and Mr Ali picked it up. 'Hello, the Marriage Bureau for Rich People.'

A voice came down the wire.

Mrs Ali nodded. 'Yes, sir. Of course I remember. Your son Sukumar was here. How could I forget?'

Mr Ali had always thought himself a brave man – though his wife would probably describe him as foolishly naive – but his domain was words, and physical violence was something he was not used to. Sukumar's threatening behaviour had left a big impression on him.

Aruna could hear the tinny squawk at the other end of the line, but could not make out any more than the fact that the caller was excited. She remembered his name, however: Mr Koteshwar Reddy, and his granddaughter's name was Sujatha.

'That's great news, sir,' said Mr Ali finally. 'Congrats and I hope that it all goes well.' He put the phone down and gazed into the distance as if lost in thought. After a moment, he turned to Aruna and said, 'Can you take out the papers for Raju?'

Aruna went to the wooden wardrobe and handed the folder to Mr Ali. He flipped through the papers and looked up with a big smile. 'Bingo!' he said.

'I don't understand, sir,' said Aruna. 'Raju is a Christian. Mr Reddy seemed like a very orthodox gentleman – not somebody who would want his granddaughter to marry outside his religion.'

'Aha,' said Mr Ali. 'They are actually the same caste. Didn't you see?'

'Yes, but—'

Aruna bit her tongue. She was pretty sure that the caste wouldn't matter when the religions themselves were different.

Pari had just come back home from her call-centre office and was wondering what to make for dinner. Vasu would like bone soup, she thought, before she remembered, with a pang, that Vasu was not here. Rehman and Vasu had returned after the festival to Vasu's grandfather's village to stay away from the clutches of the Hindu activists. And she didn't have bones either, she realised.

She might as well make a dhal and eat it with rice. What was the point of cooking nice meals for just one person?

She picked up her mobile phone and opened the list of recently called numbers. If she couldn't see her son, she could at least speak to him. And Rehman, of course. It was always fun talking to him. Before she dialled the number, a knock came at the door. She put the phone down, puzzled. Since the day that the group of men had come to take Vasu away, her neighbours had avoided her and she had stopped receiving any visitors.

There were two constables at the door, wearing khaki and carrying bamboo lathis. 'Are you the mother of the Hindu boy?' one of them asked rudely without any introduction.

Pari nodded mutely.

'You have to come to the police station.'

Pari almost agreed, but then remembered what she had heard many times: that it was not a good idea for a single woman to go alone to a police station. She shook her head and said, 'Have you got a warrant?'

The constable spoke into a radio walkie-talkie. 'Sir, the party is here. She is asking for a warrant. Shall we bring her in anyway?'

She heard the squawk of a negative. Boots sounded on the steps and a police inspector appeared. His uniform was khaki too, but the cloth was more expensive and crisply ironed. He carried a short, smooth, mahogany-varnished baton rather than the long iron-banded bamboo sticks of his men.

'May we come in, madam?' he said.

Pari stood aside and the men tramped in. Pari was torn between keeping the door open and closing it. Finally, her sense of caution won over the need for privacy and she left the door wide open.

'Do you want tea or coffee?' she asked.

'No, madam. It's very simple. We have received information that you are a Muslim and you are bringing up a Hindu boy.'

'I don't know anything about Hindu or Muslim,' she replied. 'Vasu is my son, legally adopted. Do you want to see the papers?'

'Legally?'

'Yes, at the registrar's office.'

She took a photocopy from a drawer, thanking Rehman for his foresight in asking her to do this, and handed it to the inspector.

'Hmm ... I see ...' The inspector seemed a bit deflated.

'My uncle, Azhar, is a good friend of the inspector in the three-town police station. I think his name is Bhaskar. I can call my uncle and you can speak to his friend,' she said, hoping sincerely that he wouldn't take up her offer. Mrs Ali's brother wasn't currently talking to any of them, which would complicate things slightly.

'Oh, Inspector Bhaskar is a friend of the family?'

She saw the constables exchange glances. The inspector frowned in thought. 'See, I will ask Guru-ji to withdraw his complaint. I am sure we don't need to do this formally. But I need to see the boy and talk to him myself.'

'Why?' said Pari. 'Isn't the certificate good enough?'

'It should be, but this is election time and I don't want to clash with politicians.'

'Do you want me to give up my son? What kind of cruel man are you that would tear a child away from its mother?'

The constables stirred but the officer remained calm. 'In the course of our duty, we policemen do not have the luxury of worrying about kindness or cruelty. I have received a formal complaint and I have to investigate. I want to see your son and talk to him myself. Where is he?'

'He is not here.'

The officer frowned. 'I can arrest you for obstruction of justice, young lady. Don't play games with me. I expect to see your son produced at the police station within a week or the consequences will be dire.'

He strode out and his men followed him.

Pari went after them to close the door. At the steps, the inspector turned and said, 'Don't think of running away, madam. You can't escape from us.'

Pari stood at the door until they disappeared from view. Seeing movement out of the corner of her eye, she noticed the man in the opposite flat staring at her through the bars of his outer door.

'First rioters and now policemen . . . What is our building coming to?' he said.

Pari slammed the door shut and sank to the floor behind it. Priests, imams, police, neighbours . . . She stayed there without moving as the room slowly grew dark. The phone rang and her stomach growled but she didn't answer either call.

*

After a while, Pari didn't know how long, she became aware that somebody was knocking on the door. She could feel the vibration of the wood on her back. It's surely a man rapping on the door, she thought. A woman's touch would be different – softer, not so peremptory. She thought of her husband, but to her horror she couldn't recall his face very well. She could still see the curve of his smiling lips, but the rest of his features had somehow faded away. She frowned and concentrated, snapping out of her fugue when the face of her dead husband was replaced by Rehman's: his thin, curved eyebrows – a look that many women would pay beauticians good money to achieve, his high cheekbones and deep-set eyes. How could that be? How could she forget what her husband looked like? She was a horrible, horrible woman, faithless, inconstant, flighty . . .

A feminine voice called out her name. Sheer surprise shifted Pari's thoughts away from herself. She had been so sure that it was the knock of a man. She stood up and opened the door. Aruna and Gita, together with their husbands, were standing there.

Aruna came forward and hugged her tightly. 'You look as if something terrible has happened. Are you all right?'

They passed into the house. Pari finally came to her senses about her duties as a hostess, asking, 'Do you want tea or coffee?'

Gita jumped up. 'Don't worry about it. You sit there with Akka. I'll make the drinks.'

Gita and Aruna were not related. They had met in the forest when both women – along with their husbands, plus Rehman and Pari's ex-fiancé Dilawar – had been kidnapped by Maoist insurgents. It was then that Gita had started calling Aruna akka, elder sister, and she had continued to do so. Aruna seemed quite happy to be referred to as elder sister, though what Vani, Aruna's real younger sister, thought of it, wasn't clear.

Srinu, Gita's husband, had followed his wife into the kitchen. It was quite sweet how he helped her with all the housework.

'How come you are all here?' asked Pari.

'Why didn't you pick up the phone? Rehman was trying to call you and got worried when you didn't answer. So he asked us to check on you. We were together so we all decided to come,' said Aruna.

'Oh. I'm sorry that I broke up your evening.'

'Don't be silly,' said Aruna. 'The evening is still going and now there are five of us, instead of four.'

Pari smiled wanly. She didn't particularly feel like company at the moment, but she didn't want to be alone with her thoughts either.

Gita came out of the kitchen and whispered into Aruna's ear. Aruna turned towards Pari. 'You haven't had dinner, have you?'

'No, but . . . Have you all eaten?'

'Not yet.'

Pari got up from her chair. 'Let me cook something up. Nothing elaborate.'

Gita spoke. 'Don't worry about it. Just tell me where the rice, vegetables and the pans are and I'll make something.'

'This is the first time you've come to my house. I can't let you do that.'

Eventually, Pari had to give in and Gita rejoined Srinu in the kitchen. It was so strange to hear the noise of pots and pans in her own kitchen, while she was sitting in the living room, that she got up, unable to help herself. 'Let me go and help Gita and Srinu first with making the dinner. My mother used to say that all problems are easier to solve when your belly is full.'

Aruna followed Pari into the kitchen and they chased Srinu out. It didn't take long for the three young women to whip up a simple meal of rice, dhal and aubergine-fry. At the last minute, Pari filled a small wok with oil in which she fried poppadums and a few sundried gourd vadiyams as an accompaniment for the meal. She turned to Gita. 'Please slice a couple of onions and cucumbers for the salad.'

Gita soon had rings of red onions and ovals of greenish-white cucumbers arranged alternately on a steel plate, with wedges of lemon in the middle.

Pari removed the last of the vadiyams from the hot oil with a slotted spoon and glanced at Gita's work. 'That looks very pretty, Gita. The green chillies are in the brown paper bag – put them on the plate in case anybody wants to eat them.'

The table was set and dinner was relatively quiet, though Ramanujam, Aruna's husband, tried to enliven it with a tale about a tout who had recently been caught outside the district hospital where he worked.

'I don't think he's studied beyond high school, but he probably knows more about medicine than most house surgeons and even some of the experienced doctors. A family of villagers come to the hospital looking confused. He goes up to them and asks, "Who's ill?" The villagers might reply, "My son is not well." He will say, "What's his problem?" "My boy has headaches and keeps vomiting." "He needs to be seen by a neurosurgeon. If you give me a hundred rupees, I'll get him admitted. I know the porter in the department."

'And that's how I saw the patient today. I too have noticed before that he directs the patients perfectly: whether to cardiology, ENT, dermatology or renal. As far as I can tell, he takes people to the right department just by asking a couple of questions.'

'What would have happened if the tout had made a mistake and taken your patient to the cardiology department?' asked Gita.

'Then, heaven help the patient. They would probably have carried out open-heart surgery on him.'

They all laughed, even Pari; but silence descended again until the meal was finished.

'How do you solve a problem like Vasu?' asked Ramanujam.

Pari, who hadn't seen many, or actually any, English films, bridled. 'Vasu is not the problem. It's those stupid priests and imams.'

'Pari is right,' said Aruna, glaring at her husband. She hadn't seen any English movies either.

Ramanujam threw up his hands in despair and bit his tongue at the last moment before he landed himself in greater trouble with his wife.

Srinu said, 'I don't understand something. You said that Rehman has taken Vasu to his village where his uncles and other relatives live.'

'Yes,' said Pari. 'What about it?'

'Forgive me for this doubt, but if he has family members in his own village, why aren't they looking after him? Why is he being brought up by you?'

Gita hit Srinu on the shoulder. 'What kind of question is that? Pari . . . '

Pari held up her hand and looked at all of them. 'You don't have to walk on eggshells around me. I'm Vasu's adopted mother. I know that, Vasu knows that, and I willingly declare it to the whole world. It's not a secret.' She took a deep breath and closed her eyes. 'Rehman knows Vasu's story from the beginning and I know of it only through him. It seems strange, doesn't it, that somebody else knows more about a boy's past than his mother? But that's the difference between a natural mother and an adopted mother.'

Pari smiled. Aruna thought that she looked both beautiful and ineffably sad.

'Vasu's parents were classmates of Rehman's and they were his good friends. Vasu's mother was a girl from Vizag – the daughter of a rich, high-caste family. Vasu's father, the son of an illiterate farmer, was the first person in his family to go to college. Vasu's mother's parents were naturally against the match. Most parents become reconciled to such situations after a child is born, but her mother and father were adamant. Anyway, when Vasu was still quite young, his father died in an accident at work.'

'That's terrible,' said Gita, her eyes round.

Pari gave her a tight smile. 'That's just the beginning. Vasu's mother went into a depression. She asked her parents for help, but they refused to have anything to do with her. Vasu had been born prematurely and they accused her of having premarital sex. Insulted, and as Rehman found out later, hoping that once she was gone, they would take their grandson into their fold and raise him as they had raised her, she killed herself. But she was mistaken and her parents refused to care for her son. Vasu was finally taken to his father's village by his paternal grandfather, who had a small farm on which they lived from harvest to harvest. Rehman went and helped them sometimes. Anyway, Vasu's grandfather made a mistake and was about to lose even his tiny field to pay off a debt, so he drank pesticide and committed suicide.'

'Oh my God . . .'

'Yes, Vasu's short life has been full of tragedies. After the grandfather's funeral, Vasu's uncles and caste-men refused to take Vasu into their houses. They said that he was an ill-starred boy who brought misfortune to whoever was his guardian. So Rehman brought him to Vizag and then I adopted him.'

Aruna and Ramanujam knew the story but this was the first time that Gita and Srinu had heard it.

'So much trouble in such a young life,' said Gita.

Pari said, 'In his eight years, Vasu has had to face so many changes, and now that he has found a bit of stability, the priests and the imams want to disturb him again. Useless do-gooders – why can't they keep their noses in their own kitchens?'

Ramanujam laughed at Pari's fierce expression. He remembered an old saying: for the sake of its calf, even a cow will fight like a tigress.

A knock came at the door and they looked at each other in surprise. Who could it be? Fear replaced the anger on Pari's face.

Ramanujam stood up and said, 'Let me see who it is.' Moments later, they all heard the surprise in his voice as he said, 'Come in. Please!'

Pari exchanged a puzzled glance with Aruna before twisting round to see Mr and Mrs Ali walk in. Pari exclaimed, 'Chaachi, Chaacha! What are you doing here at this time of the evening?'

'Rehman called us and said he was worried about you,' said Mrs Ali.

'I am all right. You shouldn't have troubled yourselves.'

The older couple were offered dinner, which they refused, as a matter of course. Finally, cups of tea were made and they all sat sipping it.

Aruna turned to Pari. 'So, tell me. The house was dark, there was no dinner being prepared and you were not answering any phone calls. What's going on?'

Pari remembered a long-ago afternoon that had been spent in just such a way with her husband. Of course, the reason then was romantic. The following day the housewife next door had asked Pari much the same question with a knowing look, causing her considerable embarrassment. Pushing the thought aside, Pari told them about the police visit.

'That's ridiculous,' said Ramanujam. 'Let me call police-uncle.' He saw Pari's puzzled look and explained, 'He is a very good friend of my father, who has just been promoted to superintendant. He will sort it out in a moment.'

A superintendant outranked a police inspector by two or three levels at least.

Mr Ali frowned. 'The police are mere agents – they are just doing their duty and chasing up on a complaint that somebody's filed.' He turned to Pari. 'Who did you say it was?'

Pari replied, 'They didn't say, but I guess it was HUT, the Hindutva Universal Truth Party, Chaacha. The people who came barging in here the other day.'

Mr Ali nodded. '*They* are the people who need to be silenced. Otherwise this tamasha, this spectacle, will go on.'

'They are just rabble-rousers,' said Ramanujam. 'Religious parties might do very well in parts of North India, but they'll never be popular here. We South Indians are much too sensible for that.'

'There are none so sensible that they can't be turned,' said Aruna.

Ramanujam laughed and said to Mr Ali, 'My wife has been working too long with you, sir! She's become philosophical!'

A smile finally came to Pari's face.

Aruna continued talking. 'In the Mahabharata, Arjuna doesn't want to fight because in the army opposing him are members of his own family and friends – his great-uncle Bheeshma, his guru Drona and many others. But Lord Krishna tells him that he must fight because that is his dharma, his duty, as a warrior to fight. And so it is with politicians – their dharma is to fight elections and get into power. If that means they have to bend the truth, sell their grandmother or take a child away from its mother, they'll do it.'

The smile faded from Pari's face. 'You are scaring me now,' she said.

'Sorry, I didn't want to do that. But Sir is right. We have to somehow solve the underlying problem. We can't just hide from it. After all, how long can Rehman and Vasu stay away?'

Pari said, 'Yes, it's not fair on Rehman, or Chaacha and Chaachi either.'

Mrs Ali waved a hand dismissively.

Pari shook her head. 'Don't lie, Chaachi. I saw how much you were missing Rehman on Eid. It was very lucky that Rehman came to the village to celebrate it.'

'I still think we should go to Police-Uncle,' said Ramanujam. 'I am sure that he will sort out the problem.'

Mr Ali was frowning. 'No,' he said slowly. 'A needle can sometimes accomplish what a sword cannot do.'

Everybody in the room was looking at him.

'What are you thinking, Chaacha?' said Pari.

'The government order to widen the road is being released on Monday. It's not just our house that will be affected, but the temple too.'

'Yes,' said Mrs Ali, whose face had turned stony when reminded about the impending doom of her house. 'But what has that got to do with Vasu and Pari now?'

'I think it is time to call Rehman and Vasu back to town,' said Mr Ali.

'What? They'll just take Vasu away and then what'll we do? You can bet that the police won't search very hard for him when powerful people are involved,' said Mrs Ali.

'Listen to me.' He leaned forward and laid out his plan.

'I don't know ... Sounds very risky to me,' said Pari.

'I think it'll work,' said Gita. 'I know Mr Narayana, the guru-gaaru, and he is a very superstitious man.' She turned to Aruna. 'The other day, I sneezed as I was leaving the temple and he stopped me from going straightaway because it was bad luck.'

Aruna thought back to the temple official who had told her that her father had changed because she had married into a rich family. It was easy to believe that the man would be superstitious. She added her weight to Gita's argument.

'All right, it might work,' conceded Pari. 'But I still don't trust those men. What's to stop them from just spiriting Vasu away so I don't see him ever again? Also, Vasu is not a parcel to be handed from person to person. He won't like being with strangers and I won't force him to go.'

Mr Ali leaned back. 'You are correct, of course.' He thought for a moment, then smacked one hand against the other and grimaced. 'We'll have to somehow make them take responsibility without giving them Vasu.'

For a while, as they mulled over the idea, the only sound in the room was the noise of a TV elsewhere in the building and the traffic on the road.

'What if—' began Gita, and shook her head. 'Vasu could stay with me and Srinu . . . But then Mr Narayana won't believe—'

'That could work,' said Mr Ali. 'We'll simply have to say that he is merely staying at your place and the responsibility still lies with the temple.'

Pari thought for a moment. 'It's a risk,' she said finally. 'But we can't just sit with our hands in our laps and do nothing. Vasu's already missed several days of school and we need to present him at the police station within seven days anyway. We have to get them to come back.' She picked up the phone. 'Let me call Rehman.'

CHAPTER FOURTEEN

Aruna and Ramanujam went to the temple on Sunday afternoon, where they prayed first to Lord Rama, then moved to the side of the temple. There Aruna bowed low to the idol of the monkey-headed Hanuman, who had become worthy of worship by being himself devoted to Ram.

'Oh Lord, help Pari and Vasu just as you helped Ram and Lakshman in their time of need. They need your strength to keep them safe.'

Gita met them in the courtyard. They followed her into a small room with a table and three chairs with strung seats, the nylon broken in places. Gita left and they waited in silence. Aruna couldn't stop biting her lips.

About five minutes later, Mr Narayana joined them in his usual saffron-coloured robes. After the usual greetings, he said, 'Gita tells me that you have some sort of proposal for me.'

Ramanujam said, 'You are a man of God, who seeks to promote goodness in the world.'

'That's right,' Mr Narayana said. He glanced briefly at the

clock on the wall behind Aruna and Ramanujam. 'The evening prayers will start soon.'

Ramanujam's eyes met Aruna's. He looked back at Mr Narayana. 'We won't take up much of your time. I am told that you are looking for a boy called Vasu.'

Mr Narayana's face took on a sharper look of interest. 'The boy being raised as a Muslim? Yes.'

'We know the family, sir, and can assure you that Vasu is not being raised as a Muslim. In fact, he's even come to this temple with Gita and my wife,' Ramanujam waved his hand towards Aruna.

Mr Narayana smiled and rubbed the stubble on his chin. 'I know for a fact that the mosque has asked the woman to convert the boy to Islam. Did you say that you were a doctor?'

Ramanujam was dizzy at the sudden change of topic. 'I didn't say that but, yes, I'm a doctor at KGH.'

King George Hospital was the government district hospital in Vizag. The man before them was far more worldly than the average holy man at a local temple — no wonder he had gone into politics.

'You are a good man and an innocent. You don't understand how these Muslims work. They came to our country, ransacked our temples, stole our women, ruled us and converted our people.'

That was hundreds of years ago, Ramanujam wanted to say. And during all those centuries of empire, if they could convert only a small percentage of the population to Islam, they were either not very motivated or had been spectacularly unsuccessful. The Portuguese had converted a larger percentage of the population of Goa to Roman Catholicism in a far shorter period of time. But he kept silent. He was not here to argue.

'And even now the minority community are pandered to by the politicians. The Muslims have their own personal laws; they have driven Hindus out of Kashmir; Assam and the north-east is being overrun by refugees from Bangladesh but the government doesn't do anything. And why is that?'

Ramanujam and Aruna shook their heads.

'Because they want the Muslims' votes. And we Hindus are too divided and too weak to stand up for ourselves. That is the fundamental problem.'

It was clear that once he had climbed on his soapbox, the man could talk for hours.

Ramanujam said, 'Um ... about the boy. The mother is willing to give him up temporarily so that you can check that he is not being brainwashed.'

'We need to be united ... er, what did you say?'

'The mother is willing to give him up temporarily.'

'Temporarily? What good is that?'

'As I said, you can make sure that Vasu remembers his parents and their heritage. And at the moment, you don't even know where he is. So that's got to be an improvement.'

Mr Narayana stroked his stubble, weighing up some unknown pros and cons that Ramanujam and Aruna were not privy to.

'All right ...'

'But she has some conditions.'

'Aha! I knew there would be a catch.'

'She doesn't want the boy to stay with strangers. That's understandable, isn't it? He is only eight years old, after all. She suggested that the boy stay with us, but my parents wouldn't like it, so we made another suggestion. We said that Gita and Srinu could look after the boy and she's agreed to that.'

'Hmm ... That might work. Gita comes to the temple every day. What does she say?'

'Gita and Srinu don't know about it yet, sir. We thought we'd speak to you first and see whether the idea was acceptable to you.'

The priest nodded. Aruna took her phone out of her handbag. 'Let me call her.'

Aruna spoke as soon as Gita came into the room. 'Gita, will you look after Vasu?'

Gita pulled the edge of her sari out of her waistband, where it had been tucked while she was working, and wrung out the cloth in her hands. 'Don't take this the wrong way – I like Vasu as a boy, but I can't look after him.'

'Why not?' said Mr Narayana.

'He is a very unlucky boy. Whoever looks after him dies.'

'That's not a very nice thing to say, Gita,' said Ramanujam. 'There is no need to be so superstitious.'

'You are a doctor, Ram-babu. I am a simple village woman. I've only just moved to town with my husband and we are trying to make our life here. We can't afford any bad luck.' She turned to Mr Narayana. 'He is a yamadoot, sir – a foot soldier of Yama, the Lord of Death. His father died, then his mother and then his grandfather – three guardians in eight years. Tell me, sir, what you would call that?'

'How do you know all this?' asked Mr Narayana.

'They told me,' said Gita, pointing to Ramanujam and Aruna. 'Isn't it true?'

Ramanujam hesitated. 'Er . . . '

Aruna spoke up. 'Yes, we told you, but we didn't expect you to turn it against us like this.' Aruna threw up her hands and turned to her husband, 'Why hide the facts?' She then addressed Gita once more. 'I can understand your reluctance. I would be unhappy to take the boy into my house too.'

'Aruna!' said Ramanujam, his voice rising. 'I am shocked that you can say such a thing!'

'I am sorry, but the truth is the truth. Vasu will be staying in your house, Gita, only because he can't live in the temple. The temple will take all responsibility for the boy.'

'I don't understand,' said Gita. 'My married life began with my husband and me being kidnapped. I don't want to tempt fate again.'

Aruna turned to Mr Narayana. 'Sir, Gita's concern is understandable. It has been proven, not once but three times, that whoever is responsible for Vasu ends up dead. You cannot expect anyone to be brave enough to disregard that. You might as well expect a deer to take in a lion cub.'

Mr Narayana seemed perplexed. 'I didn't know all this,' he said. 'But if Gita doesn't want to look after him, that's fine. I know an orphanage where we can place him.'

'No, sir,' said Ramanujam. 'There is no way Pari, or any mother in fact, would allow her son to be sent to an orphanage. That's a horrible idea.'

'But he is an orphan, isn't he?'

Aruna made a slight signal behind the table to Ramanujam to keep him silent, and said, 'He has a mother, sir. So how can he be an orphan? But there is another way out. If we all agree that this temple is the rightful guardian of the boy and that Gita is taking him to her house only to feed him and give him a place to sleep, then I am sure that Gita won't have a problem with Vasu.'

Gita said, 'Yes, that would work. I don't mind that. But we can't just agree among ourselves. We have to swear by the Lord.'

That, of course, created no difficulty in a temple.

While Aruna and Ramanujam were talking to Mr Narayana, the doorbell rang at Pari's flat. She opened the door. 'Vasu!' she screamed, sweeping the boy into her arms. 'Oh, I missed you, darling. How are you?'

'Mum, we spoke only two hours ago on the phone,' said Vasu.

'I know. But this is different.' She gave him a kiss.

Vasu pulled himself out of his mother's embrace, looking embarrassed. Pari finally noticed Rehman, standing behind Vasu, and smiled at him. 'Boys!' he said.

'Yes, and I bet that you would do exactly the same if Chaachi hugged you.'

Rehman laughed and Pari's heart did a backflip. Already speeding like a car, it now started racing like a rocket and she had to put a hand on the door frame for support because her legs felt as if they might collapse for some reason.

An older man stepped out from behind Rehman and Pari's eyes widened in surprise.

'Hello, Naidu-gaaru. I didn't know you were coming too.'

The man shrugged. 'If I ever had any doubts whether Vasu has found the right home, they've been dispelled. My cousin's soul must be at peace in heaven.'

Mr Naidu's cousin was Vasu's grandfather, whose suicide had led to Pari adopting Vasu.

Before long, Vasu was eating halwa – sweet semolina with raisins and cashew nuts – and the adults were sipping tea.

Mr Naidu said, 'Tell me what I need to say to the priest and his men. I'll happily tell any lies that are necessary.'

Rehman smiled. 'No lies are necessary, sir. Just tell them the truth as you see it.' His phone rang and he looked at the caller's name on the screen. 'It's Ramanujam,' he told them and answered the phone. 'Hi, how's it going?' He listened, nodded several times and finally said, 'All right. Ten minutes.' He hung up and turned to Pari. 'They can't see me, otherwise I'll get in trouble with the HUT activists. I'll go home and see my folks. You take Vasu and Mr Naidu to the temple.'

The cup in Pari's hand shook, almost spilling the tea, and she hurriedly put it down.

'Are we doing the right thing?' she asked. 'What if I lose . . . ' She wiggled her eyebrows towards Vasu.

Rehman put a hand on her shoulder and squeezed gently. 'Be brave,' he said.

Much later that evening, there was a knock at the door and Srinu answered it. He was so surprised to see Mr Narayana and two of his men that he just stood there, mouth gaping.

After a moment, the priest smiled at his young host and said, 'May we?'

Srinu jerked back into life, apologising. 'I am sorry, sir. Please come in.'

Srinu seated the men in the living room and rushed into the kitchen. His wife wasn't there. He went into the second room. Vasu was sitting on a beanbag, watching a cartoon on TV, but there was no sign of his wife. That left only the bedroom. When he didn't find Gita there, Srinu went out onto the terrace. They lived on the first floor of a house that belonged to the pharmacist who had a shop on the main road. When they had first come to town Mrs Ali had put them in touch with the pharmacist once she found out, while picking up medicines for her arthritic knees, that the house was available to let.

The downstairs was bigger than the upstairs, which meant that a section of the roof, above the rooms on the ground floor, formed a wide balcony that was used for drying chillies, poppadums and many other things. A canopy of coconut trees overlooked the roof like peeping Toms. Gita was in the backyard, taking down clothes that had dried during the day.

'Mr Narayana has come,' said Srinu.

'Here?' said Gita, looking alarmed.

Srinu nodded. They both rushed back into the living room where Mr Narayana was gazing in approval at a garlanded picture of Lord Ram that hung in an alcove.

'Would you like tea or coffee, sir?' asked Gita. 'We also have coconuts that our landlord gave us from the trees, if you'd prefer them.'

'Yes, that would be good. It's been very hot all day,' said the priest. His men, of course, agreed with their boss.

'I'll get them,' said Srinu and went into the kitchen.

'He doesn't trust me to use the machete properly to take the tops off the coconuts,' said Gita.

She didn't want them to think that she always sent her husband off to do the work while she sat talking to guests.

'Is the boy inside?' said the priest, gesturing with his head towards the sound of the TV.

'Y-yes,' said Gita, 'but you can't take him away.'

'I am not sure about that,' said Mr Narayana.

'No, I will not allow it,' said Gita.

Mr Narayana's companions bridled. 'If it's what the guru wishes, then who are you to stop him?' said one of them. The other nodded, looking stern.

Ignoring them, Gita addressed Mr Narayana. 'I am sorry, sir. I mean no disrespect, but we swore an oath in front of the Lord in the temple not to allow Vasu to leave my house. His great-uncle placed the boy's hand in mine only after the oath.'

Mr Narayana nodded, remembering the villager who had come to see him earlier in the evening.

'I hear that you are interested in my great-nephew,' Mr Naidu had said after the introductions.

'Yes, though why should it matter to you?' the priest had said, rather rudely, not having expected the boy to have any kin.

The villager sighed. 'Yes, I suppose I deserved that question. You must understand, sir, that all the Naidus of our village are conscious of how badly we have acted by driving out a boy of our caste when his grandfather died. We fully deserve any opprobrium that you may cast on us – no one more so than myself. Vasu's grandfather was my cousin and my greatest friend. We grew up together, living side by side all our lives, and when he finally died I refused to look after his grandson. That makes me a traitor and I know it. So I am really grateful that he has found a good home and I don't want anything to jeopardise that. The boy has a good life, and

I tell myself that my own karma is not as bad as it could have been, because of that fact.'

'But he is with a Muslim family—'

'Hindu, Muslim — what's the difference, sir? The boy is being well looked after and that's the important thing. My cousin always wanted his grandson to have a good education, which he is getting. The boy even knows how to read and write English. He is happy. Everything else is a dream within a dewdrop, isn't it?'

Mr Narayana, who obviously didn't agree with these views, had looked sharply back at the villager. Hinduism was born in India and India was born of Hinduism: the two were inseparable. Both words were derived from the same root — the river Sindhu. Islam was an interloper, the religion of invaders and conquerors. Sixty years ago, Muslims had split the motherland in two with their demand for a separate nation of Pakistan — literally, the land of the pure, as if Hindus were somehow unclean. Well, if that's how they felt, they should all have left India. But even though he felt that the old man was wrong, Mr Narayana was still proud that even an illiterate Indian had a grasp of philosophy and could argue about such metaphysical matters.

'Why did you and the other Naidus send the boy away? He could have helped any of you in your homes and fields.'

'I wanted to keep him with us, very much. But my wife and my sons were against me. They did not want me to take him in.' Mr Naidu closed his eyes for a moment and then opened them. 'Who am I trying to fool? This is a temple and here at least men should not lie. It's true that my wife and sons told me not to take in my cousin's grandson but, really, I was scared too.'

'Gita told me that the boy was unlucky. But surely that's an exaggeration. You should have asked the priest in your village to say some prayers and break the gandam – the obstacle – and then taken him in.'

Mr Naidu laughed shortly. 'Of course I thought of that. I asked the Brahmin who came to officiate at the funeral rites of my cousin, but . . . ' Mr Naidu shrugged. 'He said that some misfortunes are external – brought on by doing something; a woman of childbearing age cutting down a green tree and becoming barren, for example, or a young man disturbing a snake on a holy day and failing to find a job. Such matters can be resolved by prayers and offerings to the gods.'

Mr Narayana nodded.

Mr Naidu went on, 'The Brahmin said that Vasu's misfortune was intrinsic to him. Only such a powerful characteristic could kill not one, not two, but three of his guardians before the boy had even turned nine years old. That's why I was very happy when Rehman took the boy away.'

'Maybe the ill luck has waned. The Muslim woman who looks after him seems all right.'

'I initially thought that maybe Muslims were immune to the boy's ill luck. After all, they don't believe in our gods, so why should they be affected? But that was just a faint hope and now I am sure that all people, regardless of religion, are the same. You see, Vasu's adopted mother is a widow. Do you think she could have paid the price even before she became his guardian?'

'No, no. That's silly,' said the priest.

Mr Naidu leaned forward. 'Then what do you think of this? I heard that a few months ago they had almost settled her marriage. It was all decided and they were just about to fix the wedding date. Her would-be husband came to our village with Rehman and I met him. I couldn't help wondering why a rich, handsome man like him would marry a widow rather than a virgin, but Muslims are funny that way. I'm told that their Prophet married only widows so some of them consider it a duty to do the same. Anyway, soon after the man left the village, his father died suddenly and the marriage was called off.'

Mr Narayana was startled. 'Is that true?'

'Oh yes, sir. So do you still think the boy's bad luck has broken? Trust me, sir. You have disturbed something very powerful by taking the boy under your care. I would be careful if I were you.'

'Don't be silly,' said Mr Narayana, but there was a tremor in his voice. People came to him to cast horoscopes and determine auspicious times, for he was the most knowledgeable local authority on the ancient Sanskrit shastras. In all his experience, he had never encountered such malevolence as this boy seemed to represent. His voice grew stronger as he said, 'Anyway, the boy is not under my care. He is under the care of the temple.'

Gita's voice broke in on his reverie. 'As I said, sir, I swore an oath in the temple to keep Vasu here and I can't break that.'

The priest smiled. 'You are a good woman,' he said. 'Let it not be said that a good Hindu woman's word spoken in the hearing of the gods was worthless. I just want to see the boy who's caused us so much trouble. I am not going to take him away.'

Srinu and Gita exchanged glances and Srinu nodded. Gita

went to fetch Vasu. A brief exchange of words was heard, in which the boy seemed to questioning why he had to leave in the middle of the cartoon.

Vasu was soon at the door and Gita pushed him further into the living room. Mr Narayana was surprised to see an ordinary-looking boy. After all the talk about the ill fortune that he brought, he had been expecting to see some sort of raakshas, or demon. The boy was dark and scrawny, more like a servant despite his good clothes. Actually, he resembled the son of peasants, which, of course, he was.

'Can I go now?' Vasu said to Gita, twisting back to look at her.

She nodded and he rushed back to the TV.

After a quick tea and snacks, the men took their leave, Mr Narayana wondering how to turn Vasu into a good-luck charm for the candidates that he supported in the forthcoming election – candidates who had proven by their word and deed that they would not be pressurised into appeasing minority communities for short-term electoral gains. He had first taken up Vasu's case because his blood had boiled with indignation on hearing about the demand from the mosque for Vasu's conversion, but now Mr Narayana's busy mind was focused on how to gain all the advantage he could from the situation.

CHAPTER FIFTEEN

The Tirupati temple, on the seventh peak of the Tirumala mountains, is the most popular and richly endowed Hindu temple in India. When Lord Vishnu decided to descend to earth in the avatar of the boar, his mount, the celestial eagle Garuda, brought down the heavenly mountain, Vaikuntha, for His residence. On that mountain, the idol of Venkateshwara (another name for Lord Vishnu) spontaneously manifested itself and, over the centuries, a magnificent temple complex has been built around it. The temple day there starts at three in the morning when the priests begin chanting the Venkateshwara Suprabhatam to wake up the Lord from His yogic sleep, as they have done every single day since it was composed seven hundred years ago by Sri Prativadi Bhayankaram Annan Swami.

Five hundred miles to the north of the temple, in the town of Vizag, which lay at sea-level, the day started a couple of hours later. At five in the morning, an electronic switch tripped and M. S. Subbalakshmi's definitive rendition of the same Suprabhatam filled the room, escaping through the open windows. Mr Narayana opened his eyes and lay for a moment, listening to the clearly enunciated words.

Kausalyasuprajarama!	O Rama! Kausalya's auspicious son!
Purva sandhya pravartate,	Twilight is approaching in the east,
Uttistha! narasardula!	O best of men! Wake up!
Kartavyam daivam ahnikam . . .	The divine rituals have to be performed . . .

He got out of bed and started getting ready for the day while the devotional song continued to play in the background. He drank two glasses of warm water mixed with a teaspoon of honey and a squeeze of lemon, as prescribed by Ayurveda, the ancient Indian science of life, for good bowel movement and a healthy body. While he brushed his teeth with a bitter neem-infused toothpaste, he thought about what he had to do. Today was Monday, which meant that the municipal and state elections were now less than a month away. After the HUT morning training, he had a meeting with the candidates he was supporting.

When he turned, his wife, a thin, shrinking woman who looked perpetually ill at ease, was hovering at the door of the bathroom. 'Somebody's come for you,' she said.

'Why didn't you tell me straight away, instead of just standing there like a congealed lump of dhal?' He brusquely snatched the towel she offered, wiped his face with it and dropped it on the floor at her feet.

Outside the house stood the two men who had accompanied

him to Srinu and Gita's house the previous evening. He flung open the doors and said, 'Come in! Don't stand out there like strangers.' Not for the first time, he cursed the bad karma he must have accumulated in a previous life to be lumbered with such a nincompoop of a wife in this one. 'Weren't we going to meet at the training ground? Why are you here so early?'

'Sir, look.' One of the men held out the Telugu newspaper in his hand.

CIA WARNS OF PAK PLOT TO DISRUPT ELECTIONS, declared the headline in big letters. A terrorist group based in Pakistan was believed to have smuggled some operatives into India that were thought to be either in Mumbai or Bangalore. There was much speculation in the article, but not many hard facts.

'What's new about this? I suppose it can come in useful during campaigning, but I doubt it. People in smaller towns and villages are just not excited about terrorism. They see it as something remote that happens in faraway places like Mumbai or Delhi.'

'No, sir. Not that article; look down here.'

The man pointed to the bottom of the page. The priest saw an advertisement for underwear by a company called Zapata, with a picture of the torso of a male model wearing briefs. 'Wear Zapata or wear nothing,' said the slogan. The priest frowned. Surely, pictures and slogans like that were inappropriate on the front page of a family newspaper. At least, he thought, the ad was for underwear for men and not for women.

'What—' he began.

The man's finger moved. 'This news, sir.'

'Municipal corporation announces road-widening project.'

Mr Narayana's eyes widened as he read. The main road going past the temple to the highway would be widened from eighty feet to one hundred and twenty feet, all the way from the highway to the culvert by the Muslim graveyard that spanned the storm drain. The corporation was even talking about laying a footpath on either side for pedestrians – which would be a first.

'More appeasement of minorities,' he said. 'Why stop there? Why not take some of the graveyard land too and widen it past the culvert? Otherwise it will just become an even worse choke point for traffic than it is today.'

'Sir, don't you see? The temple will lose half its courtyard. The Hanuman idol will have to be moved back. People won't fit in the yard during auspicious days. It's a disaster for the temple.'

'True.' The priest's mind felt sluggish without his early-morning tea. And his stomach felt heavy – he needed to go to the toilet after drinking that water with the honey and lemon.

'It's the boy, sir. Yesterday, we made the temple his guardian and this morning the news comes out. The boy's uncle and all those people were right, sir. He is a walking bad-luck magnet.'

The priest's stomach churned as he stared at his men, and a chill spread down his spine.

When Mr Narayana reached the temple, Gita and Mr Naidu were waiting for him. He unlocked his office and beckoned them in, as he did so looking around the yard with pride. He had resisted the temptation, common in India, to use up every single square inch of land for the building itself.

A bevy of young girls came into the yard – college students in bright salwar kameez, their gauzy dupattas trailing over their shoulders, fluttering in the breeze like banners. They continued chattering as they took off their footwear and walked into the temple. The yard had been swept clean and decorated with patterned muggu. One corner, in the shade of a mango tree in bloom, held the idol of Hanuman in a small alcove. The fragrance of jasmine and frangipani mingled with perfume from incense sticks. Mr Narayana mentally tried to calculate how much of the land would disappear and what the temple would look like once it had been so diminished. It had taken years of planning and hard graft to bring the temple up to this standard and it was a shock to even imagine that it could just disappear overnight.

His office would be the best place to put the Hanuman idol, he thought. The office was just a tiny shack with four cement walls and a multi-coloured, corrugated-fibreglass roof. It got too hot in the summer, but he could meet people there away from his house and he liked it. It would be a wrench to lose it.

'Have you heard the news, sir?' asked Gita.

'Yes,' said Mr Narayana.

'I told you the boy was born under a malevolent star. Sani, the ill-luck planet Saturn, must have been ascending strongly at his birth. Actually, when I think about it, there was a lunar eclipse about eight months before he was born – he was pre-mature, you know. So maybe he was conceived during the eclipse.'

'Such boys should not be allowed to go around causing mayhem,' said Mr Narayana angrily.

'I don't want to keep him under my roof any longer, sir,' said Gita. 'I am scared. If even the temple can't protect itself, what hope is there for us mere mortals?'

Mr Naidu said, 'Sir, our village Brahmin told me that if certain purification ceremonies had been carried out as soon as the boy was born, these troubles could have been avoided. But his parents were *educated* people living in the town and they didn't even consider getting a horoscope made for him at that time, so the gandam – the ill luck – remained hidden and now it is too late.'

Mr Narayana nodded. In his mind, he could envision the exact prayers in his mind. It would involve a lot of expense and the feeding of many Brahmins, but Mr Naidu was right: the prayers should have been carried out a long time ago.

Mr Naidu leaned forward. 'Sir, leave Vasu with the Muslim family. If there are any difficulties, let them face them. Why do you want to bring calamity on a Hindu family?'

'But the election—'

'Election?' Mr Naidu and Gita echoed each other, sounding puzzled.

Mr Narayana shook his head. What was wrong with him? He was behaving like a village idiot – the boy was fogging even his own, always-clear mind. He considered what Mr Naidu had said. It made sense. He would have to come up with some other issue to help his candidates in the election. This boy was a 440-volt electricity wire that looked innocent as it lay on the ground, but killed anybody who touched it.

He thought for a moment and stroked his beard. 'I thought the boy was an orphan. I didn't know that he had family members like you who had willingly given him up for adoption. In those circumstances, what can I, as an outsider, say? Let the boy go back to that woman.'

Gita and Mr Naidu looked at each other.

Mr Narayana continued, 'But I want the boy to visit the temple regularly and learn about our religion. And he can never forsake Hinduism and convert to another religion.'

Gita nodded. 'I will talk to Pari about it, sir, and convince her. That should not be a problem.'

'See that you do. And now, if you'll excuse me, I need to organise a rally.'

Less than ten minutes later, Gita and Mr Naidu arrived at Pari's flat with Vasu.

'Do I have to go away again?' asked Vasu.

Pari hugged him. 'No,' she said. 'From now on, we'll be together whatever happens.'

'Good!' said Vasu, smiling widely.

'And that means from tomorrow, you are back in school.'

'I want to go to school. I am missing lessons and my friends.'

Gita cracked her knuckles on her temples to draw bad luck away from Vasu and said, 'It's good to see a boy who wants to go to school.'

'Of course,' said Vasu. 'If it wasn't for school, how would I get holidays?' He skipped off to his room. 'My toys . . . '

Pari leaned towards Gita and Mr Naidu and whispered, 'How did it go at the temple?'

'Exactly as planned,' said Gita. 'I thought I was laying it on rather thick, but he fell for it hook, line and sinker. In the end, he couldn't wait to get rid of Vasu.'

'Thank you, thank you,' said Pari. 'I know you went against your beliefs by lying in a temple, but I'll pray that the good karma you have collected by uniting a mother with her son outweighs it and leaves you both in credit.'

Gita shrugged and smiled. 'Anything for friends ... '

Mr Naidu remained unsmiling. 'I followed Rehman's advice,' he said. 'I didn't tell any lies.'

Monday was Aruna's day off, but on Tuesday she came in to work before nine. Mrs Ali answered the door with a drawn face. Aruna said, 'I saw the news about the road, madam. I'm really sorry.'

Mrs Ali took a deep breath and looked ready to cry. 'Life is not a smooth path. These things are sent to try us. What can we do?'

Mrs Ali went back inside and Aruna switched on the computer. Mr Ali came out soon after. 'I heard, sir ... '

'There is no point talking about what cannot be changed. Let's carry on with our work as normal.'

But Aruna couldn't stop thinking about the impending demolition. From what she'd read in the paper, about twenty-five or thirty feet of the Alis' land would be lost. She tried to estimate what that would mean to the house. The yard with the guava tree and curry-leaf plants – how wide was that? Fifteen feet? Probably. She had no clue, really. The well would definitely be gone. She remembered a well closure that she had witnessed as a small girl. Special prayers and offerings had been made to propitiate the goddess of the well and to ask her forgiveness for entombing her. Would Muslims like the Alis do that? A well is not just a hole in the ground – it supplies life-giving water and was surely holy, regardless of the owner's religion.

Most of the verandah would be gone too. If so, would that be the end of the marriage bureau? Would Mr Ali still want to run the bureau when the house he had saved all his life to build was half gone? Just as a well was more than a hole in the ground, a house was more than four walls and a roof. It embodied a family's soul and its memories. This wasn't her house, but the thought of losing the wall on which she had created the collage of wedding cards and photos of successful matches brought a lump to her throat. No wonder Madam was so distraught.

'Are you all right, Aruna?' asked Mr Ali.

Jolted out of her thoughts, Aruna realised that she had been staring at the collage on the wall and had stopped typing. 'Sorry, just thinking . . . '

The sound of the gate opening meant that she didn't have to elaborate. Mr Koteshwar Reddy, the rich man with the bad hip, limped in, supported by a crutch on one side and his nephew on the other. He looked as if his house had been marked for demolition too.

'Namaskaaram,' said Mr Ali, greeting the two men. 'Please sit down. Do you want a glass of water?'

Despite their refusals, which were expected and which he disregarded as a matter of course, Mr Ali went into the house and came back with two glasses of water.

'Why did you go to the trouble, sir? There was no need,' said Bobbili, Mr Koteshwar's nephew and companion. Nevertheless, the two men drank the water with relief. It was very hot out there.

'You called me some time ago to say that one of our members had contacted you and the match seemed very suitable. How is it going?'

'What can we say sir? Our bad luck itself is going badly at the moment,' said Bobbili. 'As usual, it all went well in the beginning. The family visited us and everything was satisfactory from both sides. The boy is quite good-looking and talked well. He has a good job in the city itself and my uncle here obviously liked that. The bridegroom's family kept saying that they were not particularly interested in money, but the fact that Sujatha is the sole heiress of a substantial fortune wasn't exactly a disadvantage.'

Mr Ali laughed. 'Yes, I can see that her being an heiress would not be a problem. So why the long faces?'

'Simple,' said Mr Koteshwar, speaking for the first time. 'This match too has broken down, like all the previous ones. I have spoken to a Vaastu expert and he says that the door to our house facing east and the window facing west are in a straight line with no wall in the way. The expert says that this is causing good fortune to flow straight out of our house with no obstruction. He has recommended that we block the gap between the living room and the hall. It will be inconvenient because it means we have to go round to get to the downstairs bathroom, but if that is the price, then we'll gladly pay it.'

Vaastu is the ancient Indian science of architecture. In Mr Ali's opinion, it had progressed from being a mere science relating to sound construction to an attempted explanation of every ill that might befall a family. Belief in Vaastu was very strong among all the people in that part of India and while it was not sensible to try to argue against it, he had to try.

'I don't particularly believe in Vaastu. Let me make a phone call that might shed further light on your problems.' He turned to Aruna. 'Please take out the Christian Raju's file.'

The phone call was soon made. While they were waiting for Mr Raju to turn up, they were joined by Mr Koteshwar's granddaughter, Sujatha, the almost-but-never-quite bride, his son, Sukumar and Bobbili's son, Venkat. Mr Koteshwar and Bobbili looked just as surprised to see their family members as Mr Ali.

Mr Ali regarded Sukumar with disquiet and, noticing the glance, Mr Koteshwar turned furiously on to his son. 'How dare you come here? Didn't you promise me that you would never set foot in here again? Mr Ali was quite entitled to call the police after the shenanigans of your last visit and it was only due to the goodness of his heart that he refrained. How dare—'

The young man, Venkat, spoke up. 'We knew you were both here, great-uncle. That's why we came.'

'Why did you come?' said Venkat's father, Bobbili.

'Forget this nonsense about a marriage bureau, Thaatha,' said Sujatha to her grandfather. 'I've decided that I don't want to go through any more viewing-shooing even if it means I have to remain unmarried for the rest of my life.'

'Sujatha, what are you saying?' said her grandfather.

'She is saying something sensible,' said Sukumar. 'Learn from your granddaughter. Don't keep chasing after dreams even after waking up. Don't—'

'Stop it!' said Bobbili, standing up. 'It is not a dream to want the daughter of our house to be married. Uncle has never been a quitter, unlike you who've always thrown away—' He stopped abruptly and turned to Mr Koteshwar. 'I am sorry, sir. Please forgive me. I forgot myself and spoke harshly to your son. I shouldn't have done that.' He bent down to touch his master's feet.

Venkat stood up, looking angry, and shouted 'Don't abase yourself like that, Dad.'

None of them noticed the gate opening until a young man walked in. Mr Ali looked up and greeted him. 'Welcome, Raju. Thanks for coming when I called.'

Venkat stared at the newcomer and said, 'This is the man who changed his mind. What's he doing here? I have to go . . . need to meet a friend . . .'

Sujatha turned away, the shock on her face evident at coming face to face with the suitor who had rejected her.

'No, no. Please sit down. This won't take long,' said Mr Ali. He turned to Raju. 'Is it true that you changed your mind about marrying Mr Koteshwar's granddaughter?'

'I did not so much change my mind as have it changed for me,' said Raju. 'I met Sujatha and I think she is wonderful.'

Sujatha glanced at him quickly and appeared puzzled.

'Sujatha has a sweet face, a lovely voice and a quick wit. I realise that she has been disappointed a few times and is understandably wary, but she is so friendly that one just feels at ease in her presence.'

'If you thought I was such a good match, then why did you reject me?' asked Sujatha.

'I am sorry if I hurt you. Even in my dreams, I did not assume that I could get somebody so wonderful as you, but my opinion was changed for me.'

'I don't understand.'

'After we had met a couple of times and talks were progressing between the families, my parents were approached by somebody from your family and told that you were not suitable marriage material. Apparently, you are already in love with somebody else.'

'What? That's rubbish. I am not in love with anybody. Who said that?'

Mr Koteshwar turned to his son. 'It was you, wasn't it? How low into the gutter can you sink, you wretch? Spoiling your own daughter's chances of a good marriage, how—' He started hitting his son with his walking stick.

Sukumar writhed, trying to get away from his father's blows. 'I didn't approach anybody,' he protested, his eyes wide, and he turned to Raju. 'Don't tell lies. If you don't want to marry my daughter, that's your privilege, but at least have the courage to say it outright, like a man. Don't wuss out behind stories.'

'Yes,' chipped in Venkat. 'It's ridiculous sitting here talking to a man who's insulted our family. Let's go.' He stood up. 'Come on, Suji.'

Sujatha looked confused, her eyes flicking from Venkat to Raju.

Raju said, 'The man who met my parents and said that you didn't want to marry me was Venkat.'

'This is crazy. I am not staying here to listen to this.' Venkat made to leave.

He had reached the door when Sujatha said softly, 'Is it true, Venkat? Did you meet Raju's parents and tell them that I was not marriage material?'

Venkat hesitated, one foot in the air, about to step over the threshold. For a moment, he seemed on the point of ignoring her question and walking away, but then he turned back. 'Suji. . . ' His voice was bleak.

'Did you break up the earlier matches too?'

'How could I let somebody else marry you? I love you, Suji. And you love me. We are made for each other.'

Sujatha shrank back into the sofa. 'I love you, yes, but like a brother. I've never thought of you in terms of marriage. And to go behind my back and wreck so many matches over the years, causing me and everybody else so much misery . . . How could you, Venky? How could you be so heartless?'

'I did it for you, Suji. I did it for us.'

'You don't hurt people you love, Venky. You did it out of selfishness.'

'Suji—'

'Go,' shouted Sujatha. 'I don't want to see your face again.'

But Venkat did not leave. He turned towards his father. 'It's entirely your fault, Naanna,' he cried. 'You've shown no self-respect, behaving like a servant, licking the old man's shoes. How can anybody treat us with respect if you behave like that? Am I any less than any of the men who've come for Suji's hand? Who has more of a right to the family fortune than us? It wasn't Sukumar-Uncle who earned the money. It was you, with your hard work and ideas, that kept this family rich. And what will you have to show for it? In a few years, they'll pat you on your back and turn you out on to the streets like a bullock that can't pull the plough any more.'

Venkat's father, Bobbili, remained mute, his mouth open

with horror. 'What kind of serpent have I been raising close to my bosom?' he said finally.

'You've never understood me,' screamed Venkat and rushed out.

When Bobbili rose as if to follow him, Mr Ali spoke. 'Excuse me for interfering in your family matters, but let Venkat go. He is full of passion at the moment and words will be said that will be difficult to unsay later on. Once he's cooled down, it'll be easier to talk to him.'

Bobbili turned to Mr Ali. 'You saw how he talked. What else is there to say? He has committed a great crime against Sujatha and insulted my uncle. I am ashamed.'

Mr Ali said, 'Nevertheless, discussing matters while emotions are running high will never resolve anything.'

Mr Koteshwar sighed and his age seemed to settle even more heavily on his shoulders. 'We have been fools – blind fools who could not see what was happening in our own house. Venkat might have been a good choice if we had only looked more closely, though it is too late now. But don't worry, we'll bring him back on the right path, set him up in a good business and find the perfect girl for him. Then this youthful indiscretion will be forgotten.'

Bobbili stared for a moment into Mr Koteshwar's face, then took the older man's hands in his own, raised them to his lips and started kissing them. Tears rolled down his face. 'You are a great man, Uncle. My son does not deserve such forgiveness.'

Mr Koteshwar said, 'Shh ... Venkat was right to some extent. The fact that I did not consider him a match for Sujatha shows that at some level I did not regard him as an equal. I too owe both of you an apology.'

Sujatha's eyes were magnified behind the thick teardrops that welled up in them. Raju inclined his head towards her in acknowledgement and, with a silent signal to Mr Ali, he left. The others remained seated.

CHAPTER SIXTEEN

Just then, to Mr Ali's annoyance, a particularly tenacious client turned up. He seemed to spend every other evening at the marriage bureau, looking through the files for a match for his son. Mr Ali had tried to tell him in the past that it was unlikely that his son would get married unless he was prepared to compromise: on the matches' height, complexion, education, familial wealth, absence of siblings, good looks or willingness to move to America. Two, three or even four of these attributes could be found, but not all in the same girl, especially when the boy was an overweight engineer from a third-class university with an unfortunate tendency towards early baldness.

As soon as he saw the other client arrive, Mr Ali left Mr Koteshwar and his family on the verandah, came out into the yard and, telling the man that he was busy, asked him to return another time. The client reluctantly walked back with Mr Ali towards the outer gate. Seeing an expensive Japanese car with a driver standing next to it, he asked, 'Is that their car?' and nodded towards the house.

'Yes,' said Mr Ali.

'The girl looks quite pretty and they are rich as well. Why didn't you show me matches like that for my son? That's not good service. Let me go back in, introduce myself and tell them about my son.'

'No, no,' said Mr Ali. This man's son was definitely not suitable for Sujatha.

'Why not?'

Thinking quickly, Mr Ali leaned forward and spoke softly. 'This is highly confidential, so you must promise me not to repeat it anywhere.' Mr Ali looked around as if expecting spies to be eavesdropping on them.

'All right,' the man said.

'That girl is not suitable for your wonderful boy. She has fallen in love with a classmate in college and her family have just found out about it. That's why she is crying.'

The man looked back, but they were too far away to make anyone out on the verandah.

'They look like such a good family. Do you think she was actually, you know, having an affair?'

Mr Ali shrugged. 'Your guess is as good as mine. But you are a man of the world . . . '

'Wow! Thank you for steering me clear of such dangerous people.'

Mr Ali stood by the gate to make sure the man really had left before returning. When he sat down again, Mr Koteshwar asked him, 'How did you know that young Venkat was spoiling all the matches?'

'Well, I didn't know who was causing the break-ups. So I told Raju to keep an eye out on all of you.'

'Thank you very much for your help in getting to the bottom of the matter,' said Mr Koteshwar. 'But we are back at the beginning again. Can you show us the details of some more bridegrooms? If you have any photos, Sujatha can take a look while she is here.'

'Aruna and I can show you many more matches, but you've already got one with whom you were perfectly happy. I mean Raju. Now that he knows that Sujatha is not in love with somebody else, why not talk to him again?'

Sujatha's eyes widened and she looked up with sudden interest.

'That sounds like a good— Hang on, didn't you say that Raju was a Christian when you asked for his papers earlier?'

'Did I?' said Mr Ali.

Aruna nodded.

'He is your caste. Although his grandfather converted to Christianity, his grandmother never did. But you are right, he is a Christian.'

'How can you suggest a man like that, sir?' said Bobbili. 'We are a respected family. What will people say if we marry our daughter to a Christian?'

'There is nothing wrong with being Christian.'

'Of course not. But just as foxes should marry foxes and it's not a good idea for a cat to marry a dog, Christians should marry Christians and Hindus should marry Hindus.'

Mr Ali said, 'In the National Gallery of London, there was apparently a painting by a great master. It was very expensive, worth millions, and everybody, public and critics alike, thought it lovely and attractive. It took pride of place in the gallery. But then scientific tests showed that it had first been drawn with a pencil painted over with modern pigments, so it was a fake. The painting has been banished to a storeroom and nobody can see it any more.'

Aruna saw that the Koteshwar family looked puzzled.

Mr Ali continued, 'The painting was the same as it was before when people praised it and respected it. Now, suddenly, it's hidden away and it's not worth more than a few thousand. Do you see what I am saying? The painting is no different today than it was the previous day – it's our perception of it that has changed. So it is with Raju. If you thought yesterday he was a good man and that his family was suitable, then why change your mind regarding him today?'

'I see what you are saying but it's not so simple . . . ' said Mr Koteshwar.

Sujatha spoke up. 'Of all the men that I have seen, I liked Ajay the best. But, thinking back now, he was just a Britannia-biscuit boy, a milksop, under the thumb of his mother. Compared to him, Raju feels like a real man.' She blushed when everybody looked at her. 'I think I want to know him better.'

'What are you saying, Sujatha? How can you even think like that? Today has been very emotional and you are not thinking straight. Let us go home.'

Sujatha agreed meekly, but as they left Aruna caught her eye, which gleamed with a determination that showed that, in the girl's mind, an invisible Lakshman Rekha, an unseen Rubicon, had been crossed.

'We must stop seeing each other like this!' said Rehman, smiling.

'On the contrary, I think we should meet even more frequently,' said Usha.

They were on Kailasa Giri, a mountain just to the north of the town that had been named after the abode of Lord Siva and his consort, Parvati. Unsurprisingly, large white statues of the god and goddess were seated side by side, dominating the summit behind Rehman and Usha.

'Is your research for the HUT article finished?' asked Rehman.

'Almost,' said Usha. 'Thanks for helping out. I know you took enormous risks for me.' She reached out and touched the back of his hand.

The feel of her soft fingers on his skin discomfited Rehman and he fixed his eyes on the sweep of the miles-long beach far below. The water was steel-grey except for the white surf of the waves. Several fishing boats powered by sail dotted the ocean and, further out, almost on the horizon, a line of larger merchant ships waited their turn into the port.

He finally looked at her and shrugged. 'I am always glad to help.'

A sad smile stole over Usha's face. 'I know, Rehman. But not many people would do what you did. I often think I made a mistake by breaking off our engagement.'

Rehman looked away again. He had been terribly hurt at the time. And now? What did he feel? Her touch still made him uncomfortable. He had risked his life, or at least serious injury, just because she had asked him to.

'Since then no other man has remotely interested me,' said Usha.

'You should go out more,' said Rehman, finally finding a rejoinder.

'I could search the length and breadth of India and not find another like you,' she replied.

'You don't have to do that,' said Rehman. 'Just join my father's marriage bureau!'

Usha laughed. 'I've had it up to here with marriage bureaus,' she said, putting a hand to her neck. 'Don't talk to me about them. That's all I hear from my parents.'

'What are you going to do after you finish the article?' asked Rehman.

'There are always stories,' she said. 'If you come across anything interesting, let me know.'

The breeze on the mountain was strong, blowing a lock of her hair across her cheek. He almost reached out to push it away but turned his face in the opposite direction.

'Don't stop yourself, Rehman,' she said softly. 'I like it when you do that. It reminds me of the time when we were so close.'

He looked at her and found himself drowning in the liquid pools of her eyes. The errant hair danced across her fair cheeks. His mouth felt dry. Was he really over her as he regularly told himself? He would have to ask Pari, he thought, and suddenly felt able to move again. He brushed her hair away from her face with a steady hand and stood up.

'Let's go,' he said.

It was five in the evening and Mrs Ali, as usual, was in the front yard, drawing water from the well and watering the plants. The day had been hot and muggy, and the water soaked rapidly into the cracked red soil. She heard the rattle of the gate and glanced up; her eyes widened with surprise when she saw who it was and she dropped the half-empty mug back into the bucket.

'Salaam A'laikum, Aapa,' said Azhar. As he was her younger brother, it would have been rude of him to call her by name and she was pleased that, despite what was happening at the mosque, he still called her aapa – elder sister.

'Wa'laikum Assalaam,' she said, wiping her hands with the edge of her sari.

'I read about the road widening,' he said. 'I can't believe that all this will disappear.'

Mrs Ali shrugged. As one of the two or three people who knew her best in the world, he didn't need to ask her why she was watering a garden that would be tarred over in a few weeks. He stood, looking ill at ease, by the gate until she said, 'Come in. Why are you standing there like a stranger?'

They went through the verandah and into the living room.

'He has gone for a walk,' she said.

Azhar nodded, which gave her the feeling that it wasn't a surprise to him that her husband wasn't at home, which, of course, didn't make sense. How could he have known that her husband had left a few minutes ago for a walk with his friends?

'Do you want tea?' she asked.

'No, I just drank a cup at home.' After a moment's silence, he continued, 'Have you heard anything more about when the road will be widened?'

She shook her head. 'Some of the neighbours have formed a group to fight against the proposal but nobody's saying anything.'

'I am not sure that anything can be done,' he said. 'An engineer friend with the municipality was saying that the highway upgrade was financed by the World Bank and it is part of their mandatory standards that all major roads connecting to the highway must be at least a hundred and twenty feet wide. The local engineers don't have any say in it.'

'World Bank? That's just … So some unknown officials make decisions in America and Delhi, and people start tramping up and down my garden and verandah?' said Mrs Ali.

'That's how life works, unfortunately,' said Azhar. He stared at the ceiling for a moment and then turned to her. 'This whole fight over Pari's son is so unnecessary. When Bhai-jaan was turned away from the mosque, I felt very bad.'

'You didn't stop anybody from doing it, though. How do you think I felt when I heard that my brother and my husband were on the opposite sides of a fight?'

Azhar leaned towards her. 'The new imam is a good man. He just wants to raise the religious consciousness of our congregation. If you think about it, what he is asking for is not that unreasonable. He is just saying that if the boy grows up in our family, then he should raised in our deen, our religion. Pari is being totally emotional in rejecting the imam's suggestion and Bhai-jaan's support is making her even more obstinate.'

'What do you want me to do?'

'Talk to Bhai-jaan. We all know that, in this house, you always have the last word. Do you remember how he didn't want to go to the mosque on the day of the imam's first sermon? But when you said that he had to go, he came with me. Bhai-jaan can bluster all he wants but in the end he'll

bend to your will. Tell him not to support Pari. Tell him that
Vasu's religion should be changed and both of them can then
fully join our community.'

Mrs Ali nodded and asked softly, 'Once the boy becomes a
Muslim, the name Vasu doesn't really fit, does it? After all, it's
a Hindu name. Do you think we should change that too?'

'Yes,' said Azhar. 'When he is given the shahada, the oath
of religious allegiance, we can select a new Muslim name for
him.'

'What happens if my husband doesn't listen to me?'

'He will, Aapa. There is no doubt about it. I would lay a
bet that he will bow to your will.'

Mrs Ali said, 'I thought you knew me but you don't; not
at all.' She shook her head and when she spoke again, her
voice trembled with fury. 'What you are asking me to do is
terrible. You are asking me to manipulate my husband to go
against his cherished beliefs. This is not about convincing
him to see a movie instead of going to the beach for an
evening. This is about manoeuvring him so that he rejects
his deeply held principles, so that you can become friendlier
with the imam. What will happen if I convince him and
later he resents me for it? And what will happen if I talk to
him and he doesn't listen to me? Some things in a marriage
should not be tested. To do otherwise is a short route to
marital unhappiness.'

'I—'

Mrs Ali stood up and pointed to the door. 'Out,' she said
firmly. 'Get out of my house.'

Azhar looked startled. 'You are making a mistake, Aapa,' he
said.

'Don't call me sister. Just ... go!'

As soon as her brother was out of the door, Mrs Ali collapsed onto the settee, her face crumpled in misery.

The girl was ten years old and the boy eight. School had broken up for summer a week earlier and this was agni karti – the season of fire, the hottest part of the year. That afternoon the children were lying on either side of their grandmother. The old lady waved a palm-leaf fan, moving the scalding air in a desultory fashion.

'Naani, tell us another story of Amir Hamza.'

Amir Hamza was the uncle of the Prophet Mohammed, the fiancé of the beauteous Mihr-Negar, and hero of fabulous adventures in which he fought strange animals and wicked warriors, while escaping the clutches of beautiful but scheming women.

'No,' said the girl. 'I don't want to hear another fighting story about Hamza and Aasmaan Pari.'

The sky fairy made frequent appearances in the story and the girl was never sure whether the fairy was heroine or villainess.

'What about an Amar Ayyar story?' said the boy.

Ayyar was a rogue, a thief, a trickster and the most faithful companion of Amir Hamza. He sometimes rescued his friends from danger using his tricks when Hamza's more straightforward heroics were no help. Ayyar's subversive antics were more to the girl's taste, but she didn't want to change her mind. 'No,' she said.

'All right,' said their grandmother, laughing. 'Let me think of something else.'

The girl snuggled closer to her grandmother's soft body, with its distinctive smell of ghee and Ponds powder.

'About four hundred years ago, Chittor in Rajasthan was ruled by Rani Karnawati.'

'Why was it ruled by a queen?' asked the boy. 'What happened to the king?'

'The king had died and the prince was too young. Now be quiet and listen ... At that time Gujarat and a lot of western India was ruled by Bahadur Shah and he attacked Chittor. The rani and her soldiers defended their kingdom bravely, but Bahadur Shah was too powerful. When the queen realised that she couldn't defend Chittor, she sent a secret message to the Mughal emperor, Humayun, asking for his help. Along with the message, she also included a rakhi.'

'What's a rakhi?' asked the boy.

'It's a thread that sisters tie on their brothers' hands, silly,' said the girl. 'You don't know anything.'

'Why do they tie the thread?' persisted the boy.

The girl was about to say something, but the grandmother shushed her. 'The Hindus in North India have a festival called Raksha Bandhan. On that day, sisters tie a thread on their brothers' wrists. In return the brothers give their sisters money, and promise to look after them and protect them from any danger.'

'But wasn't emperor Humayun a Muslim?' said the boy.

'Yes, he was. But he took the rakhi that the rani sent very seriously. Saying that he now considered the rani as his sister, he immediately set off for Chittor. But unfortunately, at that time, he was on a campaign in Bengal, on the opposite side of the country, and it took him a while to bring his huge army to Chittor. By the time they arrived there, they found signs of a great battle but no armies. Chittor had already fallen and was now just a smouldering ruin – it had become a ghost town because all the men, women and children were dead.'

'Had Bahadur Shah killed them all?'

The grandmother shook her head. The fan in her hand never stopped moving. 'No. When the people of Chittor realised that they were about to be defeated, they set up huge pyres and all the women and children, including the queen, jumped into the fire so that they would not be captured and dishonoured. The men then went out of the fort and fought to the death.'

The children's eyes were round with concern. 'What happened then?'

'Humayun was devastated to learn that he had not been able to come in time to help his rakhi-sister. Vowing to avenge her, he followed Bahadur Shah back to Gujarat and eventually conquered it.'

'What happened to Bahadur Shah?'

'He escaped and struck a deal with the Portuguese, giving them some islands off the coast of India – Goa, Daman, Diu and Bombay – in return for their help in getting back his kingdom.'

'Did the Portuguese help him?'

'Of course not. Once they got control of the islands, they killed Bahadur Shah when he was on one of their ships and dumped his body in the Arabian Sea. That's what happens when you involve foreigners in your battles.'

The children were silent for a moment. The grandmother's eyelids drooped but even in her sleep her fan continued its desultory movement. The boy spoke to his sister over the old woman's sleeping form. 'Will you tie a rakhi to me?'

'Don't be silly,' she said. 'You don't have any money and *I* will protect you, not the other way round.'

'Shh . . .' said the grandmother drowsily. The children fell silent and soon a silence enveloped them that was as weighty as the baking air.

A bus went screeching past on the road outside, snapping Mrs Ali out of her reverie. That sultry afternoon had been almost half a century ago, but her brother had learned nothing from the story about not involving outsiders. I still have to protect him, she thought. I am not going to let that imam drive a wedge between me and my brother.

She sat on the sofa for almost an hour, thinking fiercely. What could she do? The mosque was the men's arena – women didn't go there, nor did they participate in any of its activities. Even when food was sent to the mosque for festivals and for breaking the fast during the month of Ramzaan, the men took it with them and brought back the empty dishes. Mrs Ali did not pray regularly, except during Ramzaan, but when she did it was always at home, by herself or with other women. She had heard that, in other countries, women went to the mosque too, where they prayed in a separate women's section, away from the men, but such a practice was not followed in Vizag. How then could she fight to get her brother back into the family fold?

'Oh, Amma. I didn't realise you were sitting there in the dark!'

Mrs Ali raised her head to see Leela, the servant maid,

standing in the kitchen and looking straight through the house to her. Mrs Ali realised that the light levels inside the house had indeed dwindled away to nothing. She stood up, switched on the lights and went into the kitchen.

'What are you doing here at this hour?' she asked Leela.

'I brought the ironed clothes back from the washerwoman,' Leela said, pointing to a neat pile of clothes on a stool in the dining room. 'I told her I was coming this way anyway, so she gave them to me.'

'Thank you, Leela,' said Mrs Ali.

'No problem, Amma,' Leela said with her usual toothy smile and turned to go.

She genuinely wants to help, thought Mrs Ali, and called her back. 'I have some left-over fish curry from the afternoon. Do you want to take it home?'

Leela nodded eagerly. Fish, especially the kind of large chanduva or vanjaram that Mrs Ali bought, was far too expensive for the maid. Mrs Ali took out an aluminium pan from the fridge, put it in a thin blue polythene bag and handed it to her.

'Don't forget to bring the pan back tomorrow,' she said.

Mrs Ali had cooked too much because she had been expecting Rehman, Vasu and Pari to come over for the meal, but they had cancelled. I gave the curry to her because Leela was so helpful, she thought, not just because it was left over. Mrs Ali went to the phone to call Piya, the wife of Nasrullah, the old imam's nephew. A smile flitted over Mrs Ali's lips as she heard the phone ring at the other end. She realised that she knew exactly how to solve a problem like Azhar.

★

Mrs Ali pushed forward the platter of samosas and doodh–pedas. 'Eat one more samosa to take away the sweetness of the peda,' she said.

Piya shook her head. 'If I do that, you'll tell me to eat the sweet to counteract the spices in the samosa.'

Mrs Ali laughed. 'What's wrong with that?'

'These doodh–pedas are lovely, melting in the mouth, but I can't.' She pinched the roll of fat round her midriff. 'See how overweight I've become.'

'Nonsense. Don't become one of those modern women who think they have to be skinny to be beautiful. Anyway, how's your mother?' asked Mrs Ali. The two ladies had known each other for years, but Mrs Ali had known Piya's mother even longer.

'How has your husband taken to not becoming the next imam at the mosque?' Mrs Ali asked.

Piya made a face. 'You know how he is – nothing is ever a problem. I was angry but he wouldn't hear anything against the new imam. I finally told him that according to him everybody in the world was good except for me. Everybody always acts for the best and I am the only one who keeps looking for ulterior motives in people's actions.'

Mrs Ali nodded sympathetically. Her husband was exactly the same. How could men be so easygoing? Shouldn't they be the ones who became angry and lost their tempers? Maybe that was just another myth.

'Your husband's uncle was the old imam and all of us wanted your husband to take over. Who selected this stranger?'

'I don't know. My husband and his uncle were obviously

kept out of the loop. But Azhar-Uncle seems to be close to the mosque committee. Have you asked him?'

'You must have heard of the trouble with Pari's son. I am not exactly on the best of terms with my brother at the moment.'

'Tauba, tauba,' said Piya, touching her cheeks with her hands. 'What a time! Families growing apart because of the mosque. What kind of Islam is that?'

Mrs Ali leaned forward. 'Trust me, it will get worse if it is not nipped in the bud.'

'What can we do?'

'Get your husband to ask for an election at the mosque. Who chose this young man to lead our congregation when he hasn't even started growing his moustache properly? It's silly – people of other mosques are laughing at us. Your husband is a local man; he knows us all and can guide us properly. He too knows the Qur'an and, more importantly, he is a good man. Not that I am saying that the new imam is a bad man, but we just don't know, do we?'

'There's never before been an election at our mosque for the post of imam.'

'How do you know? Haji Saab was the imam for so many years that none of us knows what happened before. If the selection process had been open and transparent, we could accept the result, but that's not the case here.'

'I don't think my husband will agree. He would feel that the unity of the congregation was more important than his becoming the imam.'

'That just shows how suitable he is to take up the post. I've always thought that even in politics, those who stood in elections to get power should be automatically disqualified.'

Piya laughed. 'You are probably right,' she said. 'But still—'

'You should tell your husband that Vizag is a very relaxed, peaceful town and we've never suffered any of the riots or troubles that have afflicted other parts of India. A lot of that is because the Hindus around us are tolerant, but it's also because we Muslims are easygoing too. We are not head-strong fanatics who insist on excessive shows of piety or vast processions for the festival of Muharram that deliberately take us past Hindu temples. Tolerance is a two-way street and somebody like your husband is the right man to lead our mosque, especially in times like this when everywhere there is news of bigotry and chauvinism. I have my issues with the new imam because of the trouble over Pari but that's not why I am saying this. The more I think it through, the more I am convinced that we are headed down the wrong path and need to change direction.'

'How?'

'Force an election. Let the jamaat – the congregation – decide. I am sure that right and reason will win.'

CHAPTER SEVENTEEN

'Vote for me.' The candidate's supporters, on motorcycles, spilled all around the front gate of Mr and Mrs Ali's house. The election must be tight: this was the second time they had come canvassing.

'We have elections coming out of our ears at the moment,' said Mrs Ali to Pari and turned to the candidate. 'Why should I vote for you?'

'You voted for me last time, madam. Why break a great tradition?'

'I *told* you I voted for you. How do you know which button I pressed in the booth?'

The candidate grinned. 'I know you are not the sort to lie, madam. Our party is secular and we don't discriminate against Muslims. Why would you want to vote for anybody else?' He glanced at Pari. 'And who is this lovely lady? Is she on the voting register too?'

'Yes, the young woman lives in that building,' said Mrs Ali, pointing. 'But forget this secular–vecular nonsense. I voted for you last time and you have decided to knock down half my house. I can tell you that after that news not only will I not vote for your party, but neither will anyone else in the street.'

The candidate's face fell and his supporters were momentarily silenced. 'Our hands are tied, madam. Even if the opposition party was in power, the same thing would have happened. It's a central government and World Bank rule, and we are just implementing it.'

'Do people in Delhi and America know the conditions in our street? And what can we do when we're up against those faceless bureaucrats? Your party was in power when this news was announced, so you will make a good target. I think you can forget about all the voters on this road, not just for this election but for a long time in the future. Candidates for parliament and the state assembly won't care about a single street, but you are standing as a corporator of this ward and this road is half your constituency.'

'I know, madam. My aunt lives just a few doors down, in that yellow house with the fluted columns by the side of the market, and she keeps shouting at me too. She says that she is now unable to tell anyone that her nephew is the corporator because she is afraid that people will throw stones through her windows.'

As the candidate and his entourage moved on to the next house, Pari said to Mrs Ali, 'What is the point of telling him? He's probably listened to the same complaint at every door.'

Mrs Ali shrugged. 'If a baby doesn't cry, even its own mother won't feed it.'

'The whole city has been gripped by election fever, but the—'

A passing lorry's air-horn overpowered the woman's voice.

The sound engineer-cum-cameraman gave a small shake of his head and drew his hand across his neck in the universal 'kill' signal.

Usha stopped speaking and waited for the relative silence of normal traffic. After a few seconds, she started again.

'The whole city has been gripped by election fever, but the Muslim community of this area has caught a double dose of it. The congregation of the main road mosque – you can see it behind us – are also holding an election to decide their next imam. The incumbent imam is Bilal, a young outsider, a graduate of a Deobandi madrassah, a seminary in North India; standing against him is a local man, who has had a conventional education in Visakha Valley School. Both candidates are Hafiz, men who know the Qur'an by heart. Neither man was willing to speak to us on camera, but we have an important member, the former imam of the mosque, here to talk to us.'

The camera panned slightly and Rehman, who was watching a small-screen monitor, noticed that Haji-saab had now appeared in the camera frame. Mrs Ali and Pari were standing next to Rehman but their attention was directly on Usha and Haji Saab themselves, rather than on their image on the screen.

Usha smiled at the distinguished-looking gentleman wearing a cream-coloured sherwani and a dark-maroon fez. 'I was told that you were eighty-two years old, sir, but I don't believe it. If I look as good when I am half your age, I'll consider myself twice as lucky.'

'Is this a maths quiz?' said the old man, in a surprisingly strong voice, honed by years of calling the faithful to prayer and giving sermons long before the regular use of electronic aids such as microphones and amplifiers.

'I believe you've lived all your life within the precincts of this mosque. Is that true?'

'Yes. In fact, except for the pilgrimage to Mecca, I've never left this town,' said Haji Saab. 'Even my father and grandfather have lived in this area all their life. My great-grandfather and my great-grandmother were a newly married couple when they moved here from Bhopal. This part of town was then a wooded area, far from the centre of Vizag, which at that time was concentrated around the Qila, the fort area, near the harbour.'

'So you know a lot of the history of this mosque. Has there ever been an election for the post of imam here?'

Haji Saab shook his head. 'No. Our problem in the past has been finding even one man willing to be the leader of our mosque – not fending off people who want to become imams.'

Usha barely suppressed her laughter, her white, even teeth just visible. A sudden spark of feminine intuition made Pari glance at Rehman. His gaze, directed at his ex-fiancée, seemed avaricious in its intensity, making Pari flush. How could she compete against such feeling? She must be a fool to think that she had any chance at all of winning Rehman's affections.

Meanwhile, Haji Saab continued to speak. 'We have two candidates and both are very suitable. One is a student of a famous seminary in North India and the current imam. The other candidate is my own nephew – a local man who has lived in this area all his life. I am sure that, whoever wins, our mosque will be led by an able man.'

★

Rehman accompanied his father to the mosque to vote for the imam's election. His protests that he wasn't interested in religious affairs had been given short shrift by both his parents and Pari, who had pointed out that Vasu's future with Pari was at stake and that every vote counted. There had been considerable discussion about the timing of the ballot and other procedures associated with it.

Azhar had, in his career as a civil servant, been the presiding officer at polling stations in various districts during state and central government elections. In those days, before the introduction of electronic voting machines, he had also been part of the vast army of people across the country who had participated in counting the millions of slips of paper, each with pencil marks against the candidates' symbols: the palm of the hand, the cycle, the lotus, the hammer and sickle and so on. His experience now came in useful and he was given the responsibility of organising the mosque election.

Mr Ali had to admit that, overall, Azhar had done a good job. He had insisted on a secret ballot, overriding those on the committee who said that a simple show of hands would suffice. Divisions had already grown in the mosque since the campaigning had started. Mr Ali had heard that Razzaq's sister had snubbed her brother's wife at a wedding because her brother and his son had been asking for votes on behalf of the new imam while her husband supported Nasrullah.

Mr Ali and Rehman walked under the arch at the entrance of the mosque, passing several beggars who had gathered outside. One of them, a wiry, toothless man with bony arms and legs, addressed Mr Ali. 'I didn't think there was a Muslim festival today, sir. So why is there such a crowd today?'

'There is an election,' replied Mr Ali.

'A votes festival? In a mosque?' The beggar scratched his head, clearly puzzled. He rattled the bowl in his other hand, jangling the few coins already in it.

As usual, when going to the mosque, Mrs Ali had made Mr Ali and Rehman wear their best clothes and their worst shoes. An old uncle, a long time ago, had lost his footwear at the mosque, and ever since Mrs Ali always insisted that they wear their ancient, tattered leather slippers. Mr Ali had protested, 'I've never lost any footwear at the mosque.'

'That's because I always make you wear your old slippers and nobody wants to take *those*,' Mrs Ali replied. There could, of course, be no reply to that argument.

The mosque was more crowded than on a normal Friday. The timing of the election had been a matter of some controversy. Supporters of Nasrullah, the challenger candidate, did not want it to be held after the Friday prayers. The imam's sermon would lend him an air of incumbency and authority, and Nasrullah's supporters feared that many wavering votes would be lost. But really, Friday was the logical time to hold the vote as the turnout at any other time would be much lower. The young imam was, however, made to promise that he would not appeal for votes during the sermon.

Groups of men stood around, canvassing for their candidate. Mr Ali's and Rehman's antipathy to the new imam was well known and none of his supporters made a pitch to either of them. Mr Ali noticed that Azhar and two other members of the mosque governing committee stood aloof by the water tank that was used for wazu, the ritual ablutions that were required before the prayers.

'Do you require the wazu?' Nasrullah's cousin asked Mr Ali.

Mr Ali shook his head. 'I've done the wazu at home and come straight here,' he said.

They made their way into the covered area of the mosque where the marble floor was cool under their feet. The air in the mosque, by contrast, was like a warm blanket despite the mosque's open sides and the fans whirring away overhead.

The imam's sermon was on the perfectly innocuous topic of the importance of charity to anybody who called themselves a Muslim. Mr Ali thought the sermon had finished and prepared to stand up for the ritual namaaz, but the imam continued, 'For those of you who have buried their heads in the sand over the previous couple of weeks, or simply for those who simply do not attend the mosque as regularly as they should, I want to say that there is an election today for the post of imam. It will only take a few extra minutes, so don't rush off like scalded cats as soon as the prayers are finished. I do not ask you to vote for me and I do not say that you should not vote for me. You have seen my performance over the last few weeks and you can judge whether I am capable of being your imam. The Qur'an says: The believers are but a single brotherhood. Make peace and reconciliation between your two contending brothers and fear Allah so that you may receive mercy. So, regardless of how the vote goes today, there should be no division tomorrow among our congregation. We are one and in our unity is our strength. After today, I do not want to hear any more talk of division or disarray. Is that clear?'

The young imam paused and scanned every corner of the

assembly, meeting several eyes. Rehman leaned over and whispered, 'He is good.'

Mr Ali nodded. 'Yes, there is no doubt about that.'

The imam sat down for a few seconds for a quick prayer, then stood up for the second part of the sermon. The preceding talk had been in Urdu, but the imam now spoke the standard prescribed phrases in Arabic.

'O servants of Allah! May He be merciful to you. Verily, Allah commands you to act with justice . . . do good to others as one does to one's kindred . . . (Allah) prohibits revolts against a lawful authority . . . '

It was a good thing, thought Mr Ali, who had spent too many Sunday afternoons as a boy learning the Qur'an and Arabic, that most of the congregation did not understand Arabic and these phrases were just a wash of familiar sounds.

'. . . Allah! . . . Rahim . . . Allah . . .blah blah . . . '

After the obligatory prayers, a few men rushed out but most sat back at ease on the floor, some even continuing to murmur additional recommended prayers. Azhar commandeered a couple of teenagers, who carried in from the office a wooden table, setting it directly under a fan and covering it with a parrot-green satin cloth embroidered in sequins with the words 'Allahu akbar' – God is great. Azhar brought in a hinged metal box with a rectangular slot cut in the top. However, the congregation's eyes were not on the box but on the men walking behind Azhar – a police officer and two constables. A mild murmur ran through the crowd about non-Muslims entering the mosque while some men were still praying the recommended rakaats, but it was quickly silenced as the officer and Azhar took their seats.

The constables remained standing behind them. Mr Ali noticed that the policemen had removed their shoes and were wearing socks, and that the heftier, burlier constable had a hole in his right sock that he was trying to hide by curling his big toe.

Once everybody had finished their extra prayers, Azhar clipped a small mike to the top buttonhole on his shirt and said, 'Testing, testing, one … two.' The sound boomed through the hall and he hurriedly lowered his voice as he added, 'Three.'

Looking around at the seated crowd, he said, 'I have invited Inspector Bhimadolu to preside over the election.' He turned to the policeman. 'Thank you, sir, for taking the time to help us.'

'It's my duty,' said the officer, picking up the service baton that he had laid on the table in front of him when he sat down, and then putting it back again. 'In my career as a policeman, I have seen many disputes – brother killing brother over a small inheritance; a wife feeding her husband rat poison because he was being friendly with her sister; priests mired in court cases because they could not decide whether to apply the sacred vermilion mark horizontally or vertically on the temple elephant. So I am glad that you have decided to settle your disagreement by ballot. It is my honour to be present here and help you in this important task.'

The officer looked over his shoulder and signalled with his head. One of the constables stepped around and opened the box, so that its top fell right back on its hinges, like the maw of a hippopotamus. The constable must have been instructed what to do beforehand because, without a word from Azhar or his superior, he showed the innards of the ballot box to all corners of the mosque, rattling his bamboo lathi against its tin walls to emphasise its emptiness. It was then closed and put back on the table.

Azhar addressed the congregation. 'Please step forward one at a time and write your name on the sheet here. You will be given a voting slip with the names of both the candidates. Make a tick against your preferred candidate and fold the paper in half, like this.' Azhar stood up and demonstrated. 'Put the folded paper in the box and leave this area.'

The voting started under the watchful eyes of the police. Slowly the area emptied and the crowd in the unpaved area outside grew. Having cast his vote, Rehman said he had to meet a hydrologist regarding his work and left, adding, 'Call me on the mobile as soon as the results are declared.' Mr Ali nodded.

Once the voting finished, the men filed in again and sank back to the floor in groups. The atmosphere was like that of a picnic, except that there was no food or drink. With the mouth of the ballot box open wide, Azhar and two committee members started unfolding the papers. They held the slip face up so the inspector could see the vote and placed it on one of two piles. When the papers in a pile reached ten, they moved it aside and started a new pile. When they were finished, the table was dotted with these stacks, which looked like white jasmine flowers against the green cloth. The last two piles had less than ten votes each. The men then went into a huddle with the police inspector, whispering. Azhar began to sift through the piles of votes again.

'Were you just as careful when you counted how many layers of clothes your bride wore on your nuptial bed?' shouted someone at the back.

'He started to count, but got distracted when he got to two, so he had to start again,' replied another wag.

'By the time he finished, his bride was bored and had started snoring,' shouted the first man.

The crowd tittered, followed by a shush from some of the elderly men.

The counting finally finished. Azhar signed the sheet of paper he was holding, then got the others at the table to sign too. He stood up, switched on his mike and cleared his throat. The murmuring in the crowd stopped and an expectant hush fell.

Azhar said, 'Two hundred and thirteen people voted. Two votes have been declared invalid.' He held the two out for all to see. One had ticks against both candidates and the other had no ticks at all.

'Don't worry about them,' came the voice from the back. 'Those were men who didn't recognise their brides.'

Azhar ignored the comment, laid the papers down and picked up a longer sheet of paper. 'For those of you whose mathematical skills are as good as your sense of humour, you will realise that there are thus two hundred and eleven valid votes.' He looked up at the audience and then buried his nose in the paper again.

Mr Ali's chest tightened with tension. He wondered how the candidates were feeling.

'Nasrullah, one hundred and five votes.'

Mr Ali desperately tried to calculate whether that meant a

majority or not, but his mind seemed to have slowed and the numbers kept slipping away.

'Our imam, one hundred and *six*.' Azhar inclined his head towards the imam. 'Victory Mubarak to you – greetings on your victory.'

Half the audience raised a whoop. Some men rushed over to the young imam and lifted him onto their shoulders. The rest of the congregation sat glumly staring at the floor, Mr Ali among them, his despair greater than most. What would happen to Pari and Vasu now? Would he too be excommunicated from the mosque? The imam would feel strengthened with the vote in his favour.

'No!' cried a loud voice behind Mr Ali. Someone with heavy steps rushed past him. Mr Ali watched in horror as a young man picked up the ballot box and lifted it high above his head. Before he could dash it to the ground, the police constables tackled him. The young man twisted this way and that, but the constables brought him down in short order. One of them took away the box and the second raised his lathi to strike.

'Stop!' Nasrullah cried out. 'Let him go.'

The constable held on to the young man's collar, his eyes on his officer. Only when the officer gave an almost imperceptible nod did the constable let go of the protestor, who crawled away across the marble floor, like a centipede.

Nasrullah's voice was as soft as just-melted ghee but it carried to all corners of the mosque.

'The vote was fair and held in a transparent manner. Our imam won – it doesn't matter whether by one vote or a hundred. Remember the verse in Qur'an that says: Ya ayyuha allatheena amanooatee ... O ye who believe! Obey Allah and obey the Messenger and those charged with authority among you. And if you disagree over anything, refer it to Allah and His Messenger, if you believe in Allah and the Last Day. That is the best way, and the best in result.'

He looked around, his eyes jumping from one supporter's face to the next, compelling them, by force of will, into submission. Nasrullah's voice now turned steely.

'Our country is a democracy, not because the winner takes power but because the loser gives it up.'

He went to the victorious candidate and hugged him three times – once on the right shoulder, then on the left and again on the right. 'Congrats on your election, imam. I look forward to praying again behind you at the evening prayers.'

'What do I do, Dee?' said Pari into the phone, her voice low. She didn't want Vasu to hear, even though he was in the other room, sleeping, with the fan on full blast.

'First tell me what happened,' came the voice of her ex-fiancé from the other side of the country.

'A shahmat, a disaster, has fallen on me, Dee. I am scared. They'll ask Vasu to convert to Islam, Chaacha will say no, and he and Chaachi will be excommunicated, then the Hindu priest will hear of it and will take Vasu away and put him in a horrible orphanage where he'll be lucky to get one square meal a day and he will end up as a beggar on the roads and I will become crazy and start roaming the roads, asking everybody whether they've seen my son.'

'Shh ... relax, Pari. Tell me what happened.'

It was several minutes before Pari finally told Dilawar about the election result at the mosque. 'The imam will be even more powerful now. Nobody can stop him.'

'I've always thought that you were a brave girl, Pari. I didn't expect you to fall to bits like this,' said Dilawar.

'If it was just me, I couldn't have cared a mustard seed's worth for the imam and his demands,' said Pari. 'But the issue is bigger than me. Rehman and his parents are involved and, more importantly, Vasu's life is at stake. I am his mother, and that unnerves me, I admit.'

'What is the Ghalib's line about love making a man undone?'

Pari almost screamed, 'Ghalib, at a time like this?'

Ghalib was the most famous Urdu poet, renowned especially for his couplets. He quoted: 'Pyar hame nikamma . . .' Love has undone me, O Ghalib; otherwise, I too was a man of substance.'

'Your mother-love has made you weak. Otherwise, the Pari I know wouldn't be talking like this. Be brave.'

'It's easy for you to say be brave,' she snapped. 'You are sitting a thousand miles away. I am *here*!'

Dilawar went quiet for several moments. Finally, Pari broke the silence. 'Sorry,' she said. 'I shouldn't have shouted at you.'

'No, that's fine,' said Dilawar. 'Don't worry about it. What you said gave me an idea. Vasu and you should move to Mumbai.'

'To Mumbai? Are you crazy? I have some money set aside, but not enough to live on in a big city. Where would I live? On the footpath? I've heard that it is very difficult to find accommodation in Mumbai. Also, Vasu has just settled down at his school and it will be a big upheaval for him – not to mention his having to learn a new language.'

'Whoa, stop!' said Dilawar. 'Don't race off like the Rajdhani Express. I am not saying that everything will be easy. You and Vasu will have massive adjustments to make, but I am sure you can do it. And you don't have to live under a flyover like a refugee from some village in the interior. Both of you can stay with me until you find a job and we get Vasu settled into a good school. After that, I know a couple of reliable real-estate agents who'll help sort out a flat.'

'I don't know, Dee. It's awfully kind of you to offer but I can't just move in and stay with you! What will people say? What will your neighbours think?'

Dilawar laughed. 'In Mumbai, you'll be anonymous. Nobody cares about where you live and who you live with. As for my neighbours, my reputation might even improve!'

Pari shook her head. Dilawar's neighbours had once objected to his boyfriend visiting him every day. Her presence would sort out that problem, at least. She realised that Dilawar could not see her and spoke. 'I am not sure . . .'

'I am sure,' said Dilawar. 'This will solve all your problems. You'll leave behind the imam and the priest and all the other difficulties. Now, listen. I am getting a call from Shaan on the other line. Think about what I said. I'll catch up with you tomorrow.'

Pari could only nod mutely as the phone went silent.

CHAPTER EIGHTEEN

Rehman took the stairs two at a time, his leather sandals making a flapping sound on the cement floor. He knocked on the door and Vasu let him in. The flat was in a shambles – with things on the floor, old newspapers and pieces of string everywhere, the sofa strewn with photoframes and books, so that there was no place to sit.

'Who is it?' Pari called out.

'Just me,' said Rehman.

'Hello, Just Me. I'll be out in a moment,' said Pari.

Her sense of humour is still holding out, thought Rehman.

Vasu tugged at his hand. 'Come to my room,' he said.

Rehman allowed himself to be led deeper into the flat. Vasu's room had cheerful yellow walls, one of which was dominated by a large poster of a film hero with a chisel-cut jaw and flinty eyes, standing in front of a building in flames, while a car hurtled through the air behind him. By the window on the other wall, a wooden desk held a computer and a pile of textbooks.

'Hasn't your mother packed your books yet?' asked Rehman.

'No,' said Vasu. 'She wants me to study until the last possible moment. But look at this. What do you think?'

He handed Rehman an A5-sized booklet formed by stapling several sheets together. Big block letters spelled out 'The Adventures of the Three Musketeers', and below it, 'Author: Vasu'. In three corners were pictures of three stick figures holding swords. The fourth corner showed a taller, darker figure.

'That's the villain,' said Vasu, pointing. 'The heroes are me and my two best friends. One for all, all for one, that's our motto.'

'That was the motto in the French original too.'

'French? *The Three Musketeers* is not French. It's English. I saw it in the school library.'

Rehman smiled and shook his head.

'I wouldn't have been able to read it if it was French,' said Vasu, with impeccable logic.

Rehman laughed. 'It's called a translation. Somebody who knows both languages reads the book and rewrites it in the second language. Maybe, when you grow up, you could translate *The Three Musketeers* into Telugu. But that's for later. Tell me about your friends. Are they boys or girls?'

'Boys, of course. How can I be best friends with a girl? Ravi and Abdul are really cool. Do you know that Ravi has a playhouse in the branches of a tree in his garden?'

'Wow! A tree house? I've never seen one of those,' said Rehman.

'I have. We pretend it is our castle and play in it, defending it from enemies.' Vasu jumped on the bed and bounced on it. 'I've made three copies of the comic. I'll keep one and give the others to Ravi and Abdul. I hope that, with the comic, they won't forget me when I leave town.'

'I see,' said Rehman, tonelessly.

'Why do I have to go anyway? You convinced the priest at the temple to let me go. Can't you do the same with the man in the mosque too?'

Rehman sat down on the edge of the low bed, with his long legs tucked under him. 'We tried, Vasu. We tried very hard.'

Rehman remembered the houses his parents had visited before the election at the mosque, talking to people, calling in old favours, emphasising the importance of tolerance and of a leader they had known for years. However, their opponent had the power of incumbency, of formal qualifications from one of the renowned places of learning in the Islamic world, of having no enemies in the local community and a strong fire-and-brimstone line in sermons. They had come so close.

Rehman sighed. 'We tried hard, Vasu, but it didn't work.'

'But I don't want to go away. I want to stay here with you and my friends and my school and everybody else. I don't care which religion I grow up in. I'll become a Muslim if that's what it takes to live in Vizag.'

'It's not so easy. We are caught between a well and a deep hole. If we try to convert you, the priest in the temple will start jumping again. This is the best way, trust me,' said Rehman.

'You are not old enough to understand all this now, Vasu,' said Pari, who had just come in.

'I *am* old enough,' Vasu said and kicked the pillow off the bed. It crashed into an alarm clock on the bedside cabinet, which then fell to the hard floor, its glass face smashing to bits and scattering all over the room.

'Vasu! Stop it this instant!'

'That's what you always say,' shouted Vasu. 'I am too young, I am a baby, I can't decide . . . ' He gave a flying leap and landed near the door.

'Stop – glass,' said Pari.

'It'll be good if I cut myself and bleed to death,' shouted Vasu and rushed out, slamming the door hard behind him.

'What do I do?' said Pari, looking miserable.

Rehman took her by the elbows and made her sit on the bed. He sat down opposite her, about to make some remark about boys, but the look on her face stilled his tongue. He took her hands in his and held them, unmoving. She must have been hard at work packing, because beads of moisture lined her forehead, and strands of hair that had escaped from their confining band were fluttering in the breeze from the fan. The edge of her sari, the pallu, had slipped down and exposed her cleavage – the creamy, fair skin contrasting vividly against the dark blouse. Rehman's eyes were drawn to the sight for a moment, before they snapped back to her face. His eyes met hers and he could see that she knew where they had been, but she made no move to pull up her pallu and hide her modesty. His face flushed and his ears burned, but she looked steadily at him. To his surprise, there was no reproach in her eyes and, slowly, his ears became cool once more. She reached up with her right hand and caressed his cheek. Her skin felt soft and smooth against his two-day-old stubble and he suddenly wished that he had shaved.

'Pari . . . ' he said, his voice hoarse.

'Shh . . .' she whispered and moved her hand to place one finger vertically against his lips.

He shut his eyes, but that only made his sense of touch stronger. It was as if he could feel each molecule of air around him and was aware of the brush of his clothes against his skin, even the tickle of threads against his neck where his collar had frayed. But overpowering all these myriad sensations was the feel of her steady finger against his quivering lips.

He loved Pari! Although he had been in love with Usha, he now understood that his relationship with his ex had never been one of equality – he had always been in awe of her, putting her on a pedestal. Pari, however, was different. He admired her for her strength of mind and her cheerfulness despite the many problems that she had faced over the last few years, but he also felt comfortable with her in a way that he had never felt with Usha.

Stop, he commanded himself. Don't think about the past now. This was a new beginning. It was ironic, and so stupidly sad, that he should have realised his true feelings now, just when it was all coming to an end. Best to hide it, he thought, rather than to cause trouble for Pari. But . . . he would try one last time.

He opened his eyes and smiled at her. 'Do you have to leave Vizag?'

Her hand dropped back into her lap. 'I love you,' she said, and his heart leaped. 'I love you all.'

The silly surge of emotion abated somewhat. Oh, all . . .

'But for me Vasu comes first. He has to, don't you see? And for his sake, I'm going to Mumbai.'

He sighed, then stood up briskly. 'Of course you must go.

Mumbai is not that far away – only thirty hours on the train. We can keep visiting each other.'

She seemed disappointed somehow, which he couldn't understand. 'It is far away,' she said slowly. 'Yes, we'll visit, but it'll never quite be the same again.'

He was struck dumb by her honesty. Could he move to Mumbai himself? His practical, engineer's mind asserted itself – he had committed himself to work on the water project for two years. The work was important and many farmers would benefit from the project. Besides, she was going to stay with Dilawar until she managed to find a place for herself and Vasu. Where would he go?

'We can always hope,' he said. 'I like you and I don't want to lose touch with Vasu. He's my friend's son.'

'He's *my* son,' she said.

'You are my friend too.'

She smiled at that and gave him a quick hug. 'You are my best friend,' she said, and released him.

They moved to the living room. 'Have you got in touch with the removal company?' she asked.

Rehman nodded. 'All arranged. They'll be here tomorrow.' He unconsciously looked at his watch, as if checking the time. 'Around noon.'

He wondered how he could sit there calmly talking about her leaving the town for ever when all he wanted was to stop her by any means.

When Vasu came into the room, Rehman called him over, hugged him and sat him on his lap. 'It's OK to be angry,' he said. 'You are moving to a big city and you have to learn a new language, go to a new school and make new friends. It's a scary prospect, but for a brave and intelligent boy like you, it'll be pipsqueak.'

Vasu threw his thin arms around Rehman's neck and sobbed, 'I don't want to leave you.'

Rehman's voice was hoarse as he said, 'We'll be meeting up frequently. I'll keep coming there and you'll visit us here.' Over the boy's shoulder, he met Pari's eyes. She looked miserable too.

'Today has been a day of dramatic developments.'

Usha was on television, holding a microphone and standing in front of a municipal building. She was wearing a pale blue salwar kameez that looked very fetching on her. Pari shot a glance at Rehman, who was looking at the screen intently, wondering what he was thinking. 'She's pretty, isn't she?' Pari murmured.

Rehman shrugged. 'She's always pretty,' he said and turned towards his father. 'The camera's been placed very cleverly. That's the only angle from which you cannot see the construction material dumped on the road there.'

Mr Ali frowned and said, 'You are right. The traffic there has become so horrendous that I've stopped going that way.'

They were all at the Alis' house, where they had just finished their dinner of masala fish-fry, khatti-dhal and rice. Mrs Ali had told Pari to close up her kitchen and eat with them until she left for Mumbai. Now she pointed to the green lawn behind Usha. 'How much water do you think they waste every day on that patch of grass?'

'I am bored,' said Vasu. 'Can I watch a cartoon now?'

'No,' said Pari. 'Go into the bedroom and read a Tinkle comic.'

The comics, with a mix of humour, adventure, history, Indian mythology, Middle Eastern tales and scientific facts, were a favourite of children and parents. She turned her attention to the television again.

Usha had been joined by a tall, broad man with heavy-set jowls. 'Mr Ramana, can you tell us in your own words what happened today in the council meeting?'

'My enemies have ganged up on me,' said Mr Ramana. 'But if they think that by ousting me, they will win the forth-coming elections, they are mistaken. I am highly respected by the average citizens of this town and the dogs who turned on me will see the result of my anger.'

Usha looked very innocent as she asked her next question. 'Was it the opposition that removed you today?'

'Opposition, bah! I spit on the opposition. It is clear that you know nothing about politics.'

Mr Ramana's eyes bulged and his moustache quivered with indignation. He had to take a deep breath to calm himself before speaking again.

'The opposition is merely the opposition. A politician's enemies are always lurking in his own party, waiting to stab him in the back. But don't write me off just yet. I'll be back with a vengeance and then we shall see who has the last laugh.'

The camera tracked the mayor getting into a white car before Usha came back into the frame. 'As you have just heard, the mayor has been removed with a vote of no confidence just weeks before the elections – in the last council meeting before a new one is elected, in fact. What should have been a simple, valedictory meeting turned into a five-hour-long affair, with much shouting and, we are told, chair throwing – even physical violence, before the mayor was ousted.'

A slim man was walking past. Usha strode up and waylaid him. 'Sir, would you like to say some words to our audience?'

'No comment,' said the man, hunching his shoulders like a prisoner being taken to court in the teeth of a mob, and he attempted to walk away.

'Hey, that's Mr Rao, our corporator,' said Mrs Ali, recognising the man who had come canvassing to their house and whom she had harangued.

Usha was far too experienced to let the man off the hook so easily. Whichever way he stepped, she seemed to be in front of him.

'Mr Rao, I've heard that you were one of the main instigators behind the revolt against the mayor. It would be better if you told the public your side of the story before rumours start circulating. After all, the election is so close.'

At the mention of the election, Mr Rao stopped dead and the camera zoomed in on him. The reason for his reluctance to come before the camera was now clear. His hair was messed up, his thin white cotton shirt was missing the top two buttons and was flapping open, showing the top of his hairy chest, and his shirt pocket was torn and hanging loose. He looked like a schoolboy slinking home after a fight in the playground.

'All right,' he said. 'Our party is facing its most dangerous election in years. The days are gone when our party could put up a donkey and people would vote for it just because it belonged to our party.'

'Like Caligula's horse,' said Usha.

'Who?'

'Caligula – the Roman emperor. He got his horse elected as a senator.'

'Interesting ...'

It was clear that Mr Rao had never heard of the Roman empire.

'Anyway, those days are gone. We have to fight on the basis of our policies. Unfortunately, our mayor did not understand that. He is a great man who has done wonders for our city and our party. I have nothing but respect for Mr Ramana, but, in this instance, he is too stuck in his ways. New blood is needed and that's exactly what we decided in the council meeting.'

'But why so close to the election? Surely you could have waited just a few weeks more? Won't it harm your party's prospects if there is such a show of disunity?'

Mr Rao shook his head. 'On the contrary ... The public is not bothered by either unity or disunity, but by policies. After the change in leadership, we are already working to improve the conditions in our town. Starting tomorrow, water will be released for three hours instead of two.'

'That doesn't matter to us,' said Mrs Ali, who was watching with the others. 'We have our own well, thank God, but Chhote Bhaabhi and the others will be very happy.' She glanced at Rehman. 'Don't say a word,' she said.

He shrugged and the others laughed. Part of his work involved getting farmers not to dig more borewells, draining the underground water table.

On the screen, Usha said, 'That will be appreciated by many housewives in town. But what about those in slums who don't have water piped to their homes?'

'Of course we are concerned about everybody in our city.'

'Especially if they have votes,' said Rehman, *sotto voce*.

'It's not like you to be cynical, Rehman,' said Pari.

Rehman grinned at her. 'Just being realistic,' he said.

Mr Rao was still speaking. 'To this end, we have approved an additional budget to supply water in tankers to various colonies around the city. For example, in Fakir Tekka, tankers will supply water every day instead of once in every two days.'

'Isn't that where Leela lives?' said Pari. 'It'll make a big difference to her.'

'Yes,' said Mrs Ali. Both households shared the same maid.

'How is the municipality paying for all these programmes?' asked Usha. 'Are you just bribing the voters with borrowed money and will these facilities be withdrawn as soon as the votes have been counted?'

'This is boring. Can I watch my cartoon now?' said Vasu, who had just come back into the room. Grabbing the remote that was lying next to Mr Ali, he changed the channel.

'Vasooo!' shouted Pari and lunged at the boy. He tried to hide the remote behind his back, but she managed to retrieve it and told him sternly, 'Leave the room now and don't come back until I call you.'

He stormed out, stamping his bare feet loudly on the granite floor.

'If the boy wants to watch TV, let him. It's all right,' said Mr Ali.

'No, Chaacha. He has to learn to behave. You can't be so easygoing.' She changed the channel back to the local one on which Usha had been presenting.

Mr Rao was still in full flow. ' . . . simple matter of

relocating resources to meet the needs of our people ... This is what our mayor did not understand. The programmes are all being paid for by cuts in other activities and we hope to keep these programmes going permanently. For example, funds had been earmarked for widening various roads that connect to the highway, but these roads are already at least eighty feet wide. Those funds will instead be used for activities that will directly help our citizens.'

Mrs Ali leaned forward. Mr Ali, who had been watching the TV lying down on the bed in the living room, sat up. Rehman and Pari exchanged glances.

'Aren't those programmes mandated by the central government? Don't you have to carry them out?' asked Usha.

'Yes, the instructions did come from Delhi,' said Mr Rao. 'So we are not cancelling the projects. We will write to the Centre and ask for more clarification, but before we can do that, many things have to happen. The assistant engineer has to look at the file, the executive engineer has to make his comments, the financial officer has to work out the impact on the budget, the town planning commissioner's views have to be taken on board. All this will take time. You know how bureaucratic our governments are ...' Mr Rao looked straight into the camera. 'All our residents who are worried about losing their homes to the road-widening projects can sleep more easily now. While we are in power, we will carry out only those activities that help our people – not those that harm them.'

'Alhamad'ullilah,' said Mrs Ali, almost breathing the Arabic phrase. Praise be to God. 'I know who I am going to vote for in this election.'

Pari went up to Mrs Ali and hugged her. 'Congratulations, Chaachi. That's brilliant news.'

Suddenly, tears were flowing down Mrs Ali's cheeks. The others were too overcome by the sudden reprieve to say anything.

The phone started ringing. It was Azhar's daughter, Faiz. The news had reached even her village.

'They've only put it off for now. They haven't cancelled it,' said Mrs Ali, trying not to get ahead of herself.

'You know how the government works, Naani. Once they postpone the project, it'll go into a big pile of files and gather dust.'

Faiz was merely the first of many to call, congratulating them on deliverance from bad news.

It was only late that night, as Mrs Ali was falling asleep, that she realised that her brother Azhar hadn't been one of the callers.

After lunch the next day, Mr Ali went into the backyard and sat on a low wooden stool by the tap. He washed his hands to his elbows, then started washing his face, running his wet fingers all over his skin, including behind his ears. He was about to run his hands over his hair when Mrs Ali walked into the kitchen.

'Who's left the door open? A cat could come in and drink the milk,' she said and peeked out into the yard. 'Oh, you are there! What are you doing?'

'I am doing wazu, of course. Can't you see?'

'But why?' she asked, frowning.

'Because I want to visit a female friend. Why does anybody do wazu?'

'But ...' Mrs Ali was flummoxed. This was totally uncharacteristic behaviour from her husband.

'It's Friday and I'm going the mosque for the weekly prayers. Now let me get on with the wazu. I am sure that some bearded mullah somewhere in the world has issued a fatwa against a man talking to his wife while getting ready for prayers.'

Mrs Ali stared at him for a moment and then turned on her heel, saying, 'Don't forget to close the door behind you.'

Her husband had never gone to the mosque except for festivals and funerals, so this was certainly a turnaround. She was aware that it wasn't so much piety as pride that was driving him, but did it really matter why a man went to the mosque? Wasn't it enough that he prayed? After all, if God couldn't change even the mind of a man who was worshipping, He would be a pretty poor kind of God, wouldn't He?

Mr Ali walked back into the house, shaking the water from his hands. Mrs Ali handed him a towel and said, 'How's it going with the removal firm next door? They were late, weren't they?'

'Yes, they'd just arrived when I had to leave. They were supposed to send two people but only the driver turned up. Apparently, the other man's mother-in-law was unwell or something. Anyway, Rehman is helping to move Pari's boxes downstairs.'

Mrs Ali wanted to lie down for a little while. After the news last night of the reprieve from the demolition of the house, she had been too keyed up to sleep properly. And this morning, she had, in a frenzy of energy, swept up all the fallen leaves under the guava tree with a coconut-leaf broom, washed the path and, with the help of Leela, cleaned all the crevices and curves of the iron grille of the verandah. That activity had taken a toll on her back and knees. Now she just wanted to flop on the bed and stretch out, but she thought she had better go to Pari's flat and see what was happening.

She couldn't believe that in just a few more hours, Pari and Vasu would leave Vizag for ever. They would come back for the occasional visit, of course, but that was never the same. She would miss Pari – and Vasu. It had been a long time since there had been a child in her home, and Vasu had filled a void in her life that she hadn't even known was there. And it was good to have Pari around. She loved Rehman dearly, but talking to a man, even one's own son, was rarely as satisfactory as chatting with another woman. A bit like moonlight, which, however beautiful, was still only a pale reflection of sunlight.

CHAPTER NINETEEN

The white van was a quarter full. Vasu was sitting on the watchman's wooden stool in the shade of the building's portico, while the watchman was standing in the sun, by the van, keeping an eye on the goods inside.

Mrs Ali nodded to him. 'How is it going?' she asked.

'Namaskaaram, Amma. It's going a bit slowly, but should be finished in the next hour or so.'

Mrs Ali walked in through the wide-open gates of the building, patting Vasu on the head on her way past. 'Don't go off anywhere,' she said.

'I am staying here,' he said. 'I have to keep an eye on all the things going into the van.'

'That's right,' she said. 'You have a very important role as a guard.'

Her voice caught towards the end of the sentence and she hurried towards the stairs. Stairs troubled her knees, so she took a deep breath before taking the first step. She had gone up only three steps when she saw Rehman and the van driver above her, coming down with a dressing table – the sinews of their arms straining and their faces pinched with effort. She hurried back down, wincing as she reached the bottom.

Setting down the dressing table on the ground near the foot of the staircase, the men stood up and wiped their foreheads. Rehman smiled at her. 'This is the last big item,' he said. 'The rest will be down quickly.'

'Be careful,' she said and went up to the flat. She found Pari standing by the window of the now-empty living room.

Pari said, 'Why did you come up, Chaachi? There is nowhere to sit here. I'll be down soon anyway.'

'That's all right,' said Mrs Ali. 'I wanted to see the place for one last time.'

She looked around the flat – bare of wall and floor. Some indefinable essence of Pari and Vasu had leached away from this space and it already looked alien and soulless. A home, Mrs Ali thought, was just like the human body. A physical shell indubitably belonged to a man or a woman for seventy, eighty years, through childhood and maturity, health and sickness, love and hate, but then, within hours of that person passing away, it became nothing more than decaying flesh that had to be disposed of. A home too was animated by the family who lived in it, their sounds, their memories, their affections and fights and petty jealousies. Without the family, a house is just four walls and a roof.

Rehman walked in and, after one glance at his damp brow, Pari handed him a small, frilly handkerchief. Rehman used it to pat his forehead dry, then tried to return it, but Pari shook her head. He put it in his pocket. She remembered old tales of chivalry in which knights embarking on some adventure took with them as a token a glove or scarf of the woman they loved. The world has changed since those days – she was the one going off into the world, leaving a token behind with the man she loved.

'Back to work,' said Rehman, turning to go.

'Stay,' Pari said. 'All the big items have gone down. The man from the moving company can manage the rest.' She turned to Mrs Ali. 'Your son is in such a hurry to get rid of me. He booked the removal people and the tickets. Now he wants to make sure I don't miss the flight.'

'I don't—' began Rehman.

Pari stopped him by laughing. 'Don't be so serious, Rehman. I was joking.'

Rehman smiled weakly. 'Don't joke about this,' he said. 'I'd much rather you and Vasu didn't go away.'

'Me? Or Vasu?' said Pari, looking suddenly intense.

Mrs Ali stirred. 'I'll go down and keep an eye on Vasu. We don't want him wandering off at the last minute.'

Rehman stared in surprise as his mother disappeared down the stairs.

'Are you wondering why Chaachi left us alone?' said Pari.

Rehman nodded. A neighbour had accused Pari and Rehman of illicit behaviour. Since then, there had been a tacit understanding among them all to give other people no opportunity to raise a finger against them.

'The door is wide open, the removal man is coming in and out of the flat and there is no furniture, let alone a bed,' said Pari.

Rehman stared at Pari's face, his face flushing, as he took in the full import of Pari's words.

'Your mother's mind is like a computer. She processed all

those pieces of information, and the fact that I am leaving town, before she took a single step out of the room.'

Rehman remained silent.

'So, tell me — is it Vasu that you don't want to go away or me?'

He had never noticed before how gracefully her eyes curved or that their whites were so clear or how vividly they contrasted with her black irises. 'What kind of silly question is that?' he said, laughing nervously.

'Vasu or me?' she said. Her lips seemed to him as soft and rich as a cake in the Hot Breads bakery.

He glanced away but his gaze was dragged magnetically back to drown in the limpid pools of her eyes. He bit his lip with indecision then, finally, took a deep breath and said, 'You.' His voice was husky and all the air seemed to have been sucked out of his lungs, as if he had stepped off a cliff.

She closed her eyes and when she opened them again, they were glistening with unshed tears. 'I love you,' she said. 'On my husband's soul, forgive me for this sin, but I cannot leave town without telling you.'

Under normal circumstances, Pari would not have declared her feelings so openly, but she was leaving and her heart felt as if it were breaking. Once she was out of the way, how long would it be before Rehman got back with Usha? Would she ever be able to visit Vizag and see the two of them together? Could she bear it?

He took her hands in his. 'If I'd only known . . .'

'What would have been different if you had known?' she said, interrupting. 'You were in love with Usha, and I am a widow and a single mother, and I dare not disappoint your parents who have been like a steadfast rock in my support.'

'What have my parents got to do with it?' said Rehman.

'You are a buddhoo . . . That's why I love you. Why would any parents want their only son married to a widow? Especially a son who is as highly qualified as you?'

He kissed her hands and said, 'If we are going to advertise our negative points, then I am an unemployed man who cannot hold down a job for more than a few months. I have a failed engagement behind me and I have no savings or property. I don't like T-shirts, I don't like pop music and—'

'Stop!' said Pari and laughed. 'I love you just the way you are. *In thy face I see the map of honour, truth and loyalty.*'

'That sounds like a quote,' he said.

'It is – Shakespeare, *Henry VI.*' She stepped closer to him and gave him a peck on the cheek.

Rehman gripped her arms above the elbow. 'I—'

A male voice came from the door. 'Excuse me, sir, madam. All the boxes are down.'

Pari grimaced silently and stepped back. 'Yes, we are coming,' she said over her shoulder. 'Go away.'

The sound of rubber flip-flops could be heard going down the steps.

Pari closed her eyes, wanting to say something, but the spell had been broken. 'Too bloody late,' she said in English. Her work in the call centre had taught her slang that she hadn't picked up from Shakespeare. She moved away and said, 'We are both useless fools. What's the point of declaring our feelings now when we are parting?' She glanced at her watch. 'Let's go. I don't want to miss the first flight that I've ever taken in my life.'

Rehman nodded glumly. Would it have been better not to declare his love?

'No,' he said fiercely, as if in answer to his own question. 'I am glad that I told you how I feel. And now that I know that you love me too, I am confident that we will not stay apart for ever. In a couple of years, my work with the water committee will end and nobody here will remember all this nonsense about Vasu. Then we can be together again.'

Pari smiled silently as if agreeing with him. But her experiences of loss and migration over the last few years had given her a maturity that Rehman, for all his intelligence and idealism, did not have. She knew that the most difficult part of moving to another place was the first few months; once those were past, would she want to return to Vizag? She knew that she would never again go back to her father's village and, compared to what Mumbai had to offer, Vizag was a small place. Would her love for Rehman bring her back, once she had found a career and Vasu had settled into a school and made friends? The thought of leaving Rehman, at the very point in time that they had declared their love for each other, made her want to cry, but she knew, better than most, that tears dried faster than anything – except, perhaps, the springs of gratitude.

They went down the stairs. At the front door the van driver held out a clipboard. 'Sign here, madam,' he said.

Pari scrawled her signature and the van pulled away. The taxi, a middle-aged Ambassador, drove up and parked where the van had been. Pari bent down and touched Mrs Ali's feet in respect. Mrs Ali raised her and enfolded her in an embrace. 'Call as soon as you land,' she said, her voice hoarse and her eyes wet.

The watchman hurried to put the suitcase and a smaller bag into the boot. Rehman, who would see them off at the airport, got into the taxi. Vasu bounced in after him. 'Come on,' he shouted to his mother, who seemed unwilling to let go of Mrs Ali. His excitement about the novelty of his maiden flight had apparently eclipsed any misgivings about leaving Vizag and the others.

Mr Ali rode his scooter down the road, dressed in a white cotton kurta–pyjama that felt comfortable, despite its having been ironed stiff as a freshly dried poppadum. The sun was high in the sky but the breeze kept him cool. His lace cap was in his pocket and a helmet hung from a small hook in the footwell of the scooter. The police were on a drive to enforce traffic laws and, while their zeal was bound to be short-lived, it paid to be cautious until they found more profitable ways to busy themselves. As usual when going to the mosque, he was wearing his oldest footwear.

The mosque wasn't far away and within minutes he was parking the scooter at the end of an untidy line of similarly pious steeds. The azaa'n could be heard calling the faithful to prayer and several men were making their way in – shop-keepers, both small and prominent; college students; a couple of gravediggers; retired civil servants; the odd marriage bureau owner – all equal as brothers before Allah.

Mr Ali recognised a friend and hailed him loudly. 'Razzaq, Salaam A'laikum.'

Razzaq, the owner of a Rexine seat-cover shop, turned with a casual smile on his face and said automatically, 'Wa'laikum ... Hey, what are you doing here?' Razzaq frowned and peered at Mr Ali closely, as if he were an old-fashioned schoolmaster.

'What are you looking at? Has the power of your glasses changed?' said Mr Ali.

'There's nothing wrong with my eyesight, but there's something lacking in your sense of direction,' said Razzaq. 'It's Friday afternoon and time for your siesta, not prayers.'

'My reputation has preceded me, it seems,' said Mr Ali.

'Seriously, after the trouble at the mosque last time, why come now, just after the imam's election?'

'It's my mosque, even if I visit it only twice a year,' said Mr Ali.

'Of course, of course,' said Razzaq, holding his hands up in a placatory manner. 'We've been through that before. I was just saying that maybe you should let a little time pass and allow the emotions to settle.'

Mr Ali shrugged.

'You were always a strong man,' said Razzaq.

'My wife uses the word stubborn,' Mr Ali said.

The two friends, whose relationship had been strained for a few weeks but which had recovered after the imam's election, walked together under the arch of the mosque and into the shaded front yard, with its wazu tank to the right and the covered prayer area to the left.

'I've come straight from the shop. I need to clean myself,' said Razzaq and made for the tank.

Mr Ali walked to a corner to take off his frayed leather

sandals. A young man in his early twenties, with a neatly trimmed beard and long sideburns, stopped him. 'Granddad, why did you come here again?' he asked.

Mr Ali said, 'Is this a cinema hall that I need a ticket to go inside?'

'Don't be funny, old man. You were not welcome before the election and you are definitely not welcome now. Go away.'

'Are you my father to tell me where I can go and where I can't?' said Mr Ali.

Men were streaming into the mosque. The corner where Mr Ali wanted to leave his chappals was now occupied by somebody else's footwear.

'What's happening here?' said a voice behind Mr Ali and he turned.

The imam, looking no older than Mr Ali's challenger, was striding towards them, his spindly legs sticking out below the knee from his Arab robe. 'Well?' the imam said to the young man, who had fallen silent.

'I was just telling this gentleman that he is not welcome here,' muttered the young man, looking away.

'Can I help—' said another voice, familiar to Mr Ali.

'Salaam, Azhar,' said Mr Ali, smiling.

The past few weeks of not talking to the man who was not just his brother-in-law, but also a very good friend, had been a sore trial to Mr Ali. He also knew how much his wife had been affected by his tussle with her brother.

'Have you got into another fight?' said Azhar, then nodded to the imam before walking away, into the mosque.

Mr Ali's smile faltered. He opened his mouth to say that it

was not his fault, but he closed it again. His shoulders slumped and the lines on his face deepened. If he had been looking in a mirror, he would have seen himself age about five years in as many seconds. The imam stared at Mr Ali, then towards Azhar's receding back. He nodded, looking pleased, and Mr Ali's anger flared. How dare—

The imam turned to the young man. 'This is a house of God,' he said. 'Let this gentleman through.'

Razzaq came out of the tank room, pulling his sleeves down over his wet hands. He had covered his hair with a handkerchief, knotted at the back. 'Why haven't you gone inside yet?' he asked Mr Ali.

'I was delayed,' said Mr Ali, shrugging. He felt better for having some friends left. 'Come on, let's go in.'

The sermon started soon after. The unity of the Muslim community, the ummah, had been on the Prophet's mind during his final years, the imam said, as Islam went from being a tiny persecuted community to the major religion of the Arabian peninsula. He quoted one of the Prophet's most famous sayings. 'Just as the whole body suffers from a high temperature if one part of it is injured, so does the ummah.'

He looked over the microphone at the congregation. Mr Ali thought the sermon was pitched just right – there was no triumphalism from the imam after winning the vote. He was recommending unity, which was exactly what was needed. If only he was a little less literal in his reading of the Qur'an – but Mr Ali had to acknowledge that it was what quite a few people wanted. They acted in all manner of un-Islamic ways out in the world, but here, in the mosque, they wanted the imam to be strict: to denounce any deviance. This was not something peculiar to Vizagites or even Indians. Mr Ali had read an article in a magazine the other day which had, with statistics, shown that churches in the West that were liberal and admitted women priests had declining congregations, while strict, born-again churches, breathing fire and brimstone, were increasing in size and number. It's the exact opposite of what he—

There was a stir in the crowd and somebody in the front row moaned. Mr Ali snapped out of his reverie and turned to Razzaq. 'What happened?' he whispered.

'Shh . . . The imam, the imam, oh—'

What had got into his friend? Whatever it was, it had affected the wider crowd, too. Mr Ali saw that Azhar, who was several rows ahead of him, had stood up, against all convention, and said, 'No, you cannot do that.'

The imam remained silent for several seconds, then signalled to someone in the front row. The mosque committee member, an energetic man in his forties, jumped up and spoke very loudly straight into the microphone at close range, so that his voice boomed out. 'Sit down, all of you. Silence during the imam's sermon.'

He glared from one side of the room to the other until the crowd quietened down. Azhar, and a couple of others who had stood up, sank back to the ground.

The imam half raised his hands. The cream-coloured sleeves of his robe slipped down, revealing his thin but surprisingly strong-looking arms to his elbows.

'I haven't made this decision in a hurry. I've deliberated long and hard, and thought the matter through carefully. It was hubris that made me think that I could take on a big city mosque as my first posting. A man of God needs to be humble and so I've decided to leave this mosque and go to a mosque in a small village. Allah is the greatest planner, and His plans are the best, as the Qur'an assures us, and I received fresh evidence – if any were needed – of the truth of that saying.'

The imam pointed to Azhar, who sat up, self-conscious at being the centre of attention, then continued his sermon.

'No sooner had the thought of leaving entered my mind before I heard from brother Azhar that his granddaughter's village needed an imam. Some might call it a coincidence, but I prefer to think of it as God's will. I have spoken to the elders of the village and with our own man, Nasrullah, and everything has been arranged. This will be my last Friday sermon at this mosque. Next week, insha' Allah, God willing, I will officiate at the mosque in the village and Nasrullah Saab will lead the prayers here.'

Mr Ali's mouth hung open – it was one of the rare times that he was at a loss for words. Others in the congregation were less inhibited and there was an uproar. The imam and the mosque committee members only added to the din by shouting and asking everyone to quieten down. It was a while before the imam was able to assert control again for the second part of the sermon. He raced through it, before announcing, 'Stand up for the prayers.'

Mr Ali stood up with the others, then suddenly broke ranks and started pushing his way to the back.

'Hey,' one man said. 'The prayers are starting. Where are you going?'

Mr Ali silently elbowed his way through the lines and

reached the exit. He heard somebody, who sounded like the young man who had waylaid him, say, 'First he fights to get into the mosque and now he is fighting to get out just as the namaaz is starting. Paagal budah.'

Mr Ali didn't care about being called a crazy old man. It was as if a djinn – a spirit – had taken hold of him. Out in the yard he searched for his footwear. Unable to find his chappals immediately, he just left them behind and ran barefoot out on to the road. A couple of beggars standing by the exit looked surprised to see somebody leaving so soon. One of them even raised his leprosy-gnawed palm for alms, but Mr Ali didn't pause. He smacked his right fist hard into his left with frustration when he found that his scooter had been hemmed in from all sides by other vehicles. He pulled out one bicycle but its stand came off and fell against its neighbour, which then fell against *its* neighbour. Mr Ali almost wrenched his arms, trying to stop them all crashing down like a line of dominos. He gave up trying to retrieve his scooter. Until the prayers finished and everybody started moving their vehicles, his was stuck. It teaches me to come early for prayers, he thought.

That particular road was usually infested with auto-rickshaws, weaving in and out of traffic with abandon on their three wheels and stopping suddenly in the middle, or making U-turns with just one tiny wave of the wrist to signal their intention. Now, when he needed one, it was not a surprise that no such vehicle turned up.

'Allah hu Akbar,' came the imam's voice from the mosque over the speakers. God is great and he had given Mr Ali two legs. He started running. He had covered less than a hundred yards when sweat began to pour down his face and chest. The stiff starched cotton wilted like blanched spinach and stuck to his body. His bare feet felt every pebble, but the stones were actually a relief from the burning tar of the road. Mr Ali continued to run. His chest wheezed like a blacksmith's bellows. As he passed a plastics shop, he zigged to get past an old woman carrying a lurid green bucket and realised that he should have zagged. His collided with the plastic utensil, knocking it out of the woman's hand and into his path. Stumbling over the bucket, he landed heavily on his knees, skinning them. The woman started to shout, but when she saw his grey hair and wiry old man's frame, she was so surprised that she fell silent. It wouldn't have made any difference because Mr Ali's blood was pumping so loudly in his ears that he was deaf to everything else as he pulled himself to his feet and started running again.

Mrs Ali drew her head back through the car window and mussed Vasu's hair one last time.

'Khuda Hafiz, Pari,' she said. God keep you safe.

The taxi moved forward with a jerk just as Mr Ali came running up, shouting something unintelligible. Mrs Ali was alarmed to see her husband's state: his trousers torn, his cotton top sticking to his sweaty body, his hair wild and his eyes even wilder, looking like the crazed Majnoun in the desert after his lover Laila had been married off to another by her family.

'What happened?' she asked, moving towards him.

Mr Ali's legs suddenly collapsed as Mrs Ali reached him. It took her all her strength just to let him down without a big bump.

'Where is your scooter? Why are you running like a madman?'

Mr Ali just shook his head as tears surged down his cheeks. 'Too late,' he said.

Mrs Ali tried to lift him up but she didn't have the strength. Then four more hands scooped up and cradled Mr Ali, carrying him like a child, so that he didn't have to walk. Mrs Ali looked up to see Rehman and Pari, with their taxi, its engine still running, just behind.

As they made for the Alis' house, Mr Ali patted Pari's hand. 'You don't have to go,' he said, smiling dreamily. 'There is no danger to Vasu now.'

Pari smiled back at him. 'The flight is booked and the luggage has been sent ahead. It's OK, Chaacha. I'm touched that you care so much but I'll be fine.'

'You don't understand,' said Mr Ali, as Rehman carried him to the bed, the way Mr Ali used to carry Rehman many years ago. 'Cancel the flight, get the removal people back, let the landlord know that you are keeping the flat.'

Mrs Ali went ahead and switched on the fan. 'The sun has gotten to him,' she said.

Pari wiped his brow. Mr Ali wanted to explain that it wasn't the sun but instead, he fainted.

EPILOGUE

The early-morning rain had damped down the dust and the lingering cloud cover made the day pleasant. Aruna, who found the heat increasingly difficult to bear as her pregnancy progressed, appreciated the cooler weather more than most. Mrs Ali was sitting opposite her, reading the newspaper. Mr Ali came onto the verandah from inside the house. It was now Tuesday and he seemed fully recovered from his mad dash on Friday.

Mrs Ali looked up at her husband as she said, 'The paper says that there will be a ten-kilometre fun run along the beach road. Do you want to go? After all, you have a lot of experience.'

Aruna stifled a grin. Madam wasn't letting Sir forget what had happened that day. And rightly too, thought Aruna. Anything could have happened. He could have been hit by a vehicle; he could have suffered a heart attack. Her husband, Ramanujam, had visited the Alis' the next day and he had been worried about tetanus.

There was a rattle at the gate and Azhar walked in. A round of salaams followed.

'Did you hear about the fun run on the beach?' Azhar asked his brother-in-law.

Mr Ali groaned. 'Not you too.'

Azhar laughed and sat down on the chair next to his sister. On that Friday, he had come straight from the mosque, not that far behind Mr Ali, and had, with his customary efficiency, taken charge of the crisis, called a doctor and made Mr Ali comfortable. It was as if there had never been a rift in the family – almost.

After a few minutes of banter, Azhar stood up. 'Right, I am off to the bank.'

Gopal, the postman, delivered the post to Aruna and turned to Mr Ali. 'The postmaster said that he saw you running down the road the other day when he stepped out for lunch. Is this a new hobby, sir? He said he hailed you but you did not respond.'

'Isn't your postmaster close to retirement now?' asked Mr Ali.

Gopal nodded.

'Tell him that his eyesight needs testing, otherwise he'll be embarrassed one day when he greets some woman on the road thinking she's his wife and she turns out to be a complete stranger.'

Pari came in carrying a bag of vegetables, greeted them all and then said to Mrs Ali, 'Onions were really cheap today in the farmers' market. I got a couple of extra kilos. Do you want them?'

'Yes, please,' said Mrs Ali, delighted by the news. Her curries used up a lot of onions. 'How come you are not at the office?'

'The van is coming today with the luggage, so I've got to wait for it. I should thank Azhar-Maama for his help.'

The removal people had wanted the full amount to be paid and had refused to return Pari's goods, even though they had travelled only two of the eight hundred miles from Vizag to Mumbai. It had taken a phone call from Azhar to his policeman-friend before they had accepted twenty per cent of the fee to return the goods.

'You just missed him,' said Mrs Ali. 'By the way, did you see this article?'

Pari glanced at the paper. 'Chaachi! I can't believe that you are still teasing Chaacha about Friday's dash.' She turned to Mr Ali. 'Ignore what everybody says, Chaacha. I know you did it for me and I am grateful.'

'Thank you, dear,' said Mr Ali.

'Nobody is questioning why you did it,' said Mrs Ali to her husband. 'But we are not in the dark ages, you know. We now have these things called mobile phones. All you had to do was take it out of your pocket and make one call.'

'I—' said Mr Ali. It was clear from his thunderstruck expression that the thought had never entered his mind.

'Oh, look at this card,' said Aruna, waving a turmeric-bordered wedding card that had just arrived in the post.

The change of topic was successful; Mr and Mrs Ali looked at her with interest as she read out: 'Shri Koteshwar Reddy graciously invites family and friends on the auspicious occasion of the wedding of his granddaughter Sujatha to Shri Raju Sekhar. The wedding is at Prahlada Marriage Hall at three in the morning on 13 August (at dawn it will be Saturday).' Hindu weddings are often held in the early hours because the time is decided by star charts and not according to the convenience of the guests. For early-hour times, the cards always made it clear which night it was so guests didn't turn up at the wrong time.

Mrs Ali frowned. 'Sujatha? Isn't that the daughter of the man who caused trouble here?'

Aruna nodded.

Mr Ali said, 'Raju, that's the man I sent to investigate, the Christian man!'

Aruna replied, 'Yes, sir. And Mr Koteshwar Reddy rejected the match because of the groom's religion, but I got the feeling that Sujatha liked Raju. She has obviously prevailed over her family.'

'You are right.' Mr Ali shook his head. 'I only sent Raju to their house to flush out the secret spoiler of the girl's matches. I never thought it would actually lead to a wedding.'

Aruna smiled. 'All that happens is for the good, sir. Let's chalk up another success for the Marriage Bureau for Rich People.'

'Wah, wah!' said Pari, clapping.

Mr Ali took a bow. Even Mrs Ali seemed mollified. 'Humph!' she said, but looked proud.

Rehman's voice came from inside the house. 'Ammi, is there more curry?'

Mrs Ali said, 'He is twenty years older than Vasu, but he hasn't grown up one tiny bit. I wonder where he gets *that* from.' She gave her husband a sharp glance and made a move to get up.

Pari touched her on the hand. 'Stay here, chaachi. I'll take care of Rehman.'

'You are a godsend,' said Mrs Ali relaxing back into her chair.

Pari jumped up, twirling the end of her plaited hair, like a cowboy twirling a lariat. Only Aruna seemed to notice the spring in Pari's step as she stepped inside.

Farahad Zama moved to London in 1990 from Vizag in India, where his novels are set. He is a father of two, and he works for an investment bank.